MS. TAKEN
IDENTITY

MS. TAKEN
IDENTITY

Dan Begley

5 SPOT

NEW YORK   BOSTON

Copyright © 2009 by Dan Begley

5 Spot
Hachette Book Group
237 Park Avenue
New York, NY 10017

Visit our Web site at www.5-spot.com.

5 Spot is an imprint of Grand Central Publishing.
The 5 Spot name and logo are trademarks of Hachette Book Group, Inc.

Printed in the United States of America

First Edition: June 2009
10 9 8 7 6 5 4 3 2 1

Library of Congress Cataloging-in-Publication Data

Begley, Dan.
    Ms. Taken Identity / Dan Begley. — 1st ed.
        p. cm.
    Summary: "A struggling male literary novelist decides to write a fun commercial novel—but he has to pose as a woman to do so"—Provided by publisher.
    ISBN 978-0-446-50618-2
    1. Authorship—Fiction. 2. Chick lit—Authorship—Fiction. 3. Mistaken identity—Fiction. I. Title. II. Title: Mistaken identity.
    PS3602.E3746M74 2009
    813'.6—dc22

                                                                2008016197

For Robin, always

ACKNOWLEDGMENTS

Ms. *Taken Identity* exists because of the inspiration, wisdom, and love of many people, from a week ago, from twenty years ago. Thank you: Mom and Dad; Tim and Megan; Mama; Lori; Sister Marian Niemann C.S.J.; Mike Lord; Fr. Rick Stoltz; Professor Charles Larson; David Carkeet; Mary Troy; Dennis Bohnenkamp; the University of Missouri — St. Louis MFA faculty; the faculty, staff, and students of Cor Jesu Academy; Tex Tourais; David Nowak.

Dan Lazar, for turning me in the right direction.

Colleen Williamson, for your brilliant comments.

Melanie Murray, for saying yes.

Tooraj Kavoussi, for spreading the word.

Special thanks to my agent, Laura Langlie. Wow. You're simply wonderful.

To my editor, Emily Griffin: what a pleasure this has been. Thanks for your expertise and enthusiasm.

* * *

Thanks to Tareth Mitch, Claire Brown, and everyone else at 5 Spot/Grand Central Publishing.

I overheard the following conversation recently at the gym:

GUY 1: How you doing today?
GUY 2: Just another day in paradise.

And so it is.

MS. TAKEN
IDENTITY

CHAPTER ONE

Here's what I'm doing around six o'clock when the apartment door flies open behind me: poring over *Who's Who in Greek Mythology*, jotting down story ideas, nursing a frosty Guinness. Here's what my girlfriend Hannah is doing: stumbling through the door with her luggage. Here's why it means big trouble: I forgot to pick her up at the airport.

She heaves her purse and her carry-on inside, then starts wrestling a lumberjack-sized suitcase over the threshold. The bag gets stuck, but she promptly unsticks it with one of those vicious, shoulder-socket-ripping yanks, and rubber wheels slam down on the hardwood floor with a heavy *ka-junk*. I can't see her face, but I can see her hair, which is darker blond than it should be and plastered to her skull, and the back of her blouse is sheer in spots and sticking to her skin. I didn't even know rain was in the forecast.

"Here, let me help you," I say, starting toward her.

She whips around to face me so fiercely that drops of water from her hair splatter my T-shirt and boxers.

"*No*," she says—spits, really—and instantly I catch her drift: Back off. Shut up. Drop dead. Two of the three which I immediately do.

It's quite an accomplishment, schlepping all that luggage from airport to cab to apartment, up a flight of stairs—in a downpour—and you'd think now would be a good time for her to catch her breath, say hi, maybe toss me out a window. Instead, she hitches her purse high on her shoulder, balances the carry-on against her hip, and drags the bulging suitcase behind her, clomping her way toward the bedroom, not even bothering to look back when she knocks into a table and sends a vase crashing to the floor. She rounds the corner and is gone, and I'm left in the living room, thoughts and busted ceramic all to myself.

In hindsight, it seems like such an easy thing to have done, keep track of the time. After all, I've been doing it for the better part of twenty years now, usually with expert success. So what happened this time? *Something* in the apartment should have reminded me of her, and that she was gone, and that I needed to pick her up. The TV. The sofa. The coaster I was using. The vase that's no longer a vase. Her stuff is everywhere, as it should be, I suppose: it *is* her apartment. How did I manage to make such a mess of things?

But the soul-searching must wait for later. She storms out of the bedroom like a tornado looking to touch down, and my gut tells me I'm the nearest tin-roofed shed. Miraculously—or alarmingly—she swoops by me like I'm not even there and heads straight for the kitchen. When a few moments pass and I don't hear glass breaking, I ease myself that way and lean in the doorway; this seems close enough for the moment. She's changed into sweats, her hair tousled and frizzy, all her makeup wiped away. She's boiling the kettle for tea.

"So everything was fine in Houston?" I ask. She'd taken a trip there to visit her sister and brother-in-law and their new baby, Hannah's first niece.

She pulls out a mug from the cabinet. One mug.

"And your flight? Smooth sailing?" *Smooth sailing?* Shit, I'm already mixing my metaphors. That's how rattled I am.

She gets out a lemon. And a knife.

I get the feeling this could go on for hours, days, maybe the rest of our natural lives—me speaking, her ignoring me—so I figure it's up to me to set things right.

"Look, Hannah, I'm sorry. Very, very sorry. I can't say it any other way. I forgot to pick you up and it's totally my fault. But just so you know, I knew you were coming home today. I even made the bed." She has to have noticed *that*. "I just lost track of the time."

She blasts me with an icy stare. "You just lost track of the time?" she snaps, incredulous. "Jesus, Mitch. I talked to you yesterday. I gave you my flight information. We said we'd get Chinese on the way home from the airport and have an early dinner, *in bed*. I haven't seen you for five days. Five. And you lost track of the fucking time?"

When she puts it like that—in other words, in English—I get exactly what she's saying, no argument from me. I'm tempted to save her the trouble and tell myself to go fuck off. Still, the least I can do is try to explain.

"I got caught up in my book, taking notes," I offer. "I had my cell turned off, the answering machine unplugged." I give her a helpless shrug. "You know how I get when I'm writing."

She squeezes the knife handle and stiffens her entire body, making it clear, *yes*, she knows how I get when I'm writing. And doesn't think much of it. But just as quickly her expression changes and something darker takes hold. Her eyes glaze over, her shoulders slump, all the life in her goes splat on the floor.

"Oh, god, Mitch. We need to talk."

She braces herself against the counter with all her weight, as if it's the only thing holding her up. But then, by degrees, she straightens and stands on her own two feet.

"My sister was the one who always dreamed of the fairy-tale ending. Great marriage, house with a picket fence, beautiful children at the dinner table. Now she's got it, and she couldn't be happier. For me, it's never been quite so clear cut. Maybe yes to all of it, maybe I'd pick and choose. But most importantly, let love come first, and we'll see where it goes from there. But you already know that."

Right, sure I do, I nod. But here's what I'm thinking: What the hell is she talking about? She never mentioned anything about marriage or houses or kids or love coming around. Did she?

She gazes plaintively into her mug of tea, as if she's searching for something inside. The clock over the sink ticks off the seconds. Finally, she turns to face me.

"You don't love me, Mitch. Not the way I want to be loved. And I can keep making excuses to stay, tell myself that no relationship is perfect and what I have is good enough and maybe it'll get better over time. Or I can take the blinders off and face the truth. That after eight months of doing everything to be at the top of your list, I'm still stuck behind your writing and Bradley and all the other things so important in your life." She takes a breath to steady herself. "And that's the way it'll always be."

She bites at her lip because she's starting to lose it, so I throw myself on the fire. "Maybe I'm just not capable of such feelings."

She practically leaps at me. "But you *are*. I've seen it, in glimpses. Remember my birthday, when you took me out for sushi, even though you hate sushi? You did it for me, because you knew that's what I wanted. Or when you surprised me with the de Sordi print. I just mentioned the guy's name in passing, and you did all the footwork, tracking it down, special ordering it. Do you know how great that made me feel?"

Yeah, I think I do. Because it made me feel pretty good myself.

She looks like she wants to go on, stay with those happier memories, but she wills herself to push them away.

"I can't keep living this way, Mitch, getting bits and pieces of you. I deserve better. And maybe I don't have it all worked out, but I do know this much: I want someone who makes me a priority. Someone who carves out a place in his heart that's just for *me*, and when I go away for a few days, he notices. Because in some small way, I make his life complete. And I know that's not true for you."

I'd love to tell her that she's got it all wrong, if I could, without lying. "Maybe we should start all over," I offer, to be nice.

She gives me a look like that thousand-pound suitcase of hers just fell on her head. "Oh, Mitch. Is that what you really want?"

I know how it'd go if we did; we'd re-create what we had — for a week — then arrive at exactly this moment again. I drop my gaze.

"Good. Because neither do I. It's been exhausting, it really has been. I don't have the energy anymore. I think it's better if we just call it quits, now, before it gets too...Well, you know what I mean."

I do. Before it gets too *ugly*.

Despite the reasonably amicable end to things, we both agree it's best if I just leave now, get what I need for the night, come back in a day or two to collect the rest of my stuff. So I grab my laptop and story notes and dissertation books, and slip into my September-in-St. Louis uniform: cargo shorts, flip-flops, T-shirt. But by the time I make my way to the bathroom for my toothbrush, water's running inside. Hannah's in there. Through the half-opened door, I can see her sitting on the floor, legs tucked under her in an awkward way, head buried in her hands. She looks like a little girl, or a little girl's doll, all crumpled on herself. And even though the rush of water spilling into the tub is loud and forceful and drowns everything out, from the way her shoulders are heaving, it's not difficult to tell what she's doing: crying. Sobbing, really. I pause.

Maybe I didn't pan out as the greatest boyfriend, but what I'd like to do right now, if I'm being honest, is get this whole ex-boyfriend thing off to a good start. Go in there and wipe her tears away, tell her again how sorry I am that I forgot her, and let me explain how it is I *could* forget her and assure her it has nothing to do with her, it's me, and why don't I just hold her or soothe her or smooth her hair back, which I have no intention of turning into a bout of breakup sex. But I don't, because I don't know if I could do any of those things sincerely or insightfully or unselfishly. So I leave.

Bradley is sitting where he's always sitting at this time on Tuesday evenings: Colchester's. His girlfriend Skyler runs a plant nursery, and this is her late night, which means Bradley grabs dinner at the pub. To see him sitting at the bar, brown hair wavy and brushed back, three-days' growth on his face, you'd think you were on a movie set: Hey isn't that Matthew McConaughey, and shouldn't he be out banging on some bongos with his shirt off? But take another look, see if you can't spot the guy who translated his summa cum laude degree in philosophy into life as a rehabber, transforming rundown Queen Annes and Dutch Colonials into something out of *Architectural Digest*.

"What'll you have?" he asks with a smile as I belly up next to him.

"A pint. Of everything."

"Ah, one of those days," he says, taking a bite of his shepherd's pie. "Let me guess. No love from Chaucer? Lost some breathtakingly lyrical metaphor in your head before you could get it down on paper?"

"Nah, none of that." I shift on my stool. "It's Hannah."

"Oh," he says, obviously surprised. "Now there's a switch. But don't worry, Mitchell Samuel," he drawls with an over-the-top Texas twang, leaning closer. "The doctor is in." We hate Dr. Phil. "Speak to me."

There are lots of ways I could go with this. Tell him I spent her life savings on a Porsche. Tell him she's in love with another man. Tell him *I'm* in love with another man. But I opt for the truth. "We broke up."

He drops the Dr. Phil shtick like a bag of rocks. "What happened?"

I shrug. "I'm not really sure."

But after a pull on my bottle of beer, I go on to demonstrate that, in fact, I am really sure, by telling him how I forgot her at the airport because I was writing, which upset her, so there was arguing and a few tears and a bit of a back and forth, which led to our ultimate decision to go our separate ways. I don't pull any punches, put the blame squarely on me, but I expect at least a little sympathy from him, since he knows how the creative process can tend to sweep you away and cause you to forget things. But more than anything he's on Hannah's side, which is to say that in this case, he thinks I'm a total ass. But still, I'm his best friend, so he's concerned.

"So how're you doing with it?"

"Oh, you know." And he does, because he's been out with me when I've seen another woman and made some comment, not as crude as, "Damn, I'd like a piece of that," but enough that he'd get the idea that despite Hannah's top-drawer pedigree—BA from Northwestern, MFA from Iowa—and the fact we're perfect on paper, I was never completely satisfied with that particular match. (Unlike Bradley, who only has eyes for Skyler.) Besides, he knows I still have my novel.

Having a book that's about to be published has a way of keeping your spirits up, pulling you through the dark spots and rough patches in your life that might otherwise be a source of concern. Such as getting kicked to the curb. Again. I should've written it a long time ago, like when I was five and my little sister Emily died of meningitis, or when I was ten and my father had an affair and hit the road, or even when I was eighteen and found Sharon Manus making out with Colby Nash in the boys' bathroom at the prom. It would've saved me a lot of tears (and in the case of Sharon, a busted set of knuckles from punching a bathroom wall).

"And Hannah?" he asks. "How's she taking it?"

I hem and haw and roll my shoulders. "Okay. I think. I guess. She hated to lose a guy like me."

"Right. So she dumped you, then."

"Pretty much."

He gives his head a little shake. "Mitchell, Mitchell. When are you going to get it together?"

Easy for him to say. He loves Skyler, so he just does what comes naturally. For the rest of us, being with people we care about but don't really love, we have to figure out the right thing to do on an hourly basis, moment by moment, woman by woman. There's a lot of hit-and-miss guesswork in that.

We discuss my moving back into the apartment Bradley and I have shared for the last three years (I had a feeling things might fizzle with Hannah, so I never stopped paying rent: Who looks like the genius now?). It's not a problem, since he spends all his time over at Skyler's now, meaning our place is mostly unoccupied. I suggest we celebrate my homecoming by heading back to the apartment and watching a baseball game on cable, but he tells me that's a no-go: He's helping his sister pick up her new furniture.

"In North Carolina?" I ask.

"What?"

"Doesn't your sister live in North Carolina?"

"No, she lives in Chesterfield."

I point west, toward the highway, a couple counties over, where my father lives. "*That* Chesterfield?"

"That Chesterfield. She moved back in April."

So Bradley's sister has been back in St. Louis for five months, living half an hour away, and this is the first I'm hearing about it. Of course, maybe the fact that she's lived in North Carolina the entire three years I've known Bradley, and I've never met her, and she's a *hairstylist*, and what would we possibly have to talk about (Me: "I prefer the elegiac wistfulness of Tennyson to the Romantic pessimism of Housman; Her: "Like, I totally *love* mousse!"), maybe all that has something to do with it. For starters.

"I thought I told you," he says.

"Nope."

"Hmm. Anyway, she did. And she finally decided to upgrade from the furniture she came with. I told her I'd use my truck, save her the delivery charge."

"Need a hand?" I ask.

"Nah, she's got it covered. Her studio friends are helping."

"Her what?"

"Studio friends." He pauses. "Apparently, she takes dance lessons and these are her ballroom buddies. I just hope someone with a little muscle tone shows up so I don't get a hernia."

Much later, back at our apartment, I lie in bed, alone, worried I won't be able to fall asleep. If something's bothering me, this is when my mind spins and whirls and nags me with thoughts, and I'm wondering if it's going to do that tonight, get fixated on what happened with Hannah, and suddenly I'll get panicky and sweaty and realize I've made the greatest mistake of my life, leaving her crying on the bathroom floor, not begging her to forgive me and take me back, and how could I be so stupid, and will I ever be happy again? But before I actually get to those thoughts, I start thinking about margaritas, because I watched a woman at the bar sip on one, and when was the last time I had a margarita, and have I ever had one without salt, and what's that brand of salt with the girl on the label carrying a container and spilling some, and isn't she also holding an umbrella? And then I fall asleep.

CHAPTER TWO

I teach an Intro to Comp and Lit class at the university. I had my choice of something less basic—American Transcendentalism, The Age of Dryden and Pope—but I passed; I figure it's hypocritical to complain about the planet's general tendency toward bad grammar and foggy thinking and not try to do something about it while these kids are still freshmen. Fortunately, two weeks into the semester, I think it's a solid group; they show up on time (noon, so how hard can it be?), don't crunch their chip bags, do good work. In fact, I see no foreseeable problems with the bunch. Except with Molly.

Molly is a knockout blonde (think Scarlett Johansson), extremely bright, and an excellent writer. In most cases, such a combination of qualities would make her the anti-problem. But for each of those favorable traits, there's an evil twin-sister one that not only cancels the good ones out, it puts her in the red. Deeply. She's pretty, but flaunts it. As in the T-shirts she wears (the very, *very* tight T-shirts she wears), with messages like Yes,

They're Real, Stop Gawking; Bad Girls Suck; Future Trophy Wife. Subtle, eh? She's smart, but likes to rub your nose in it. Sometimes you have to delete your favorite bits of writing because they just don't work, and I told the class this is what Hemingway called "killing your darlings," but Molly blurted out, "It wasn't Hemingway, it was Faulkner," and I said, "You know, you might be right, but let's discuss it later"; so next class, apropos of nothing, not even bothering to raise her hand, she announces to the class that, yes, it was Faulkner, and goes on to read the entire quote, and ask me if I'd like a copy for future reference. She's an excellent writer, but thinks she has nothing to learn from me. She asked me where I'd been published, and I gave her the name of a magazine she'd never heard of, and she shrugged and said, "Is that it?" She's the fly in my ointment, the banana peel on my stage, the pain in my ass.

Case in point: Today we're talking about an Updike story in which a grocery clerk quits on the spot after his manager embarrasses a trio of young girls who came into the store in their swimsuits. I want to focus on the final line: "My stomach kind of fell as I felt how hard the world was going to be to me hereafter." Why does he say this, and how will his world be hard? But Molly has other ideas.

"What's the big deal about wearing a swimsuit into a store?" She cracks her gum. "I don't get it."

Of course not. This from the girl wearing a shirt that says Ball Handler.

"It's against the rules." So says stocky Pete.

"So? The rule is dumb. They just went in there to grab a jar of herring snacks. For her mother."

"Doesn't matter why they're there, or who they're there for. Rules is rules, and they broke them." Pete winks at me to let me know the verb conjugation was no accident.

"Then I guess if there's a rule that black people can't use the same water fountain as whites, we should just accept that. Or if there's a law that says women can't vote, that's okay too. Since, as you say, 'rules is rules.'"

Pete looks at me again, this time not so cocky. Donna piles on. "Yeah, exactly. I mean, men probably made those store rules. They're the ones who decided what everyone should wear. They've brainwashed women to be ashamed of their bodies."

Thomas: "But if guys are making the rules, wouldn't they say swimsuits are okay, since they'd want to see girls in swimsuits?"

Pam: "Not necessarily. Not everyone's a pervert."

Thomas: "So I'm a pervert, just because I like to see a little skin?"

Pam: "No. Just a man."

Molly, shrugging: "The bottom line is, some people just can't handle in-their-face sexuality. Look at the Janet Jackson Nipplegate flap..."

And then we're off, swept away, everyone worked up into a lather about sexism, ageism, the fashion industry, plastic surgery, women as priests, wardrobe malfunctions, Justin Timberlake, and whether Britney would've turned into *Britney* if she'd stayed with him. And I find myself jumping in, *on Molly's side*, not so much about Nipplegate or Justin but more on rules not always being rules, and before I know it, class is over and I dismiss them, but I still have to collect their essays, so I'm scrambling around in the hallway trying to track them down, and forget about a homework assignment or the last line in Updike or my entire lesson plan that's been hijacked. And Molly? Molly's just yakking away on her cell phone, making plans for god knows what.

When I get back to the apartment, I give Brandon Suarez a call. Brandon works for a small literary press in Minnesota, and he's the guy who's going to publish my novel. He's also a former student. I thought I'd have to shoot a tranquilizer dart through the phone when I sent him the manuscript — "You want *me* to publish *your* novel? Really? Are you kidding? Unbelievable! This is great! Yippee! I can fly!" — but once we got past the hyperventilating and down to business, he told me to give him a couple weeks to look things over, which I have. Enough's enough. But I don't get Brandon when I call, I get his machine, so I leave a message, telling him I'd like to get the ball rolling on this, take care of any revisions, if there are any, while the semester's still young.

My novel is called *Henley Farm*. It's a sweeping saga about America that spans several generations of the Henley family and their relationship to the land: think *The Grapes of Wrath* meets *The Good Earth*, with bits of *King Lear* and *A Thousand Acres* sprinkled in. Seven years and seven hundred pages to get it just the way I want it, and I won't lie to you: it hasn't been an easy ride. You may have the impression that writing is all about sitting at Pottery Barn–style desks with scented candles and ocean views and breezes gently rustling the curtains, or it's hobnobbing at charming European cafés where the intelligentsia discuss philosophy and beautiful women gather and you write poetry on the back of a naked lover. It's not. Remember Jack Nicholson in *The Shining*, running around with that ax and whacking through bathroom doors and screaming *"Heeeere's Johnny"* and trying to kill people? *He* was a writer.

But as if writing the novel weren't hard enough, the last six months have been worse. Trying to find an agent or publisher or anyone who's interested, sending out manuscript after manuscript, just to get them thrown right back in my face, sometimes half a dozen before I've even had lunch. It's been rejection on an epic scale, like going into a bar filled with a thousand single women, in my best clothes with a bouquet of flowers, even wearing a splash of expensive cologne, and having them all turn their backs, no peck on the cheek, no smiling hello, not even a second look. Talk about your dating disasters.

Finally, I shipped it off to Brandon. I hated calling in a favor like that, especially from a former student, and I know he doesn't have much of a budget and the first printing won't be very large. But what else could I do? I need to believe the last seven years of my life, and all the things I may have ruined in the process (relationships, mainly, with Hannah, as you know, but also with women named Chloe and Laura and Xiang, a cellist, the most beautiful woman I've ever slept with), have all been worth it. Otherwise, I may start looking for an ax of my own.

Thursday afternoon, I go to Hannah's to pick up my stuff. She isn't around, which is good, and I don't have much to pack (which is even better, since I'm riding the bus), and in no time at all, the place looks like I was never there. My presence here, it would seem, as Keats said of himself in his epitaph, was "writ in water."

My brother Scott calls after dinner. Dad's birthday is this weekend, and Leah—my *stepmother* of fourteen years—is having her usual get-together. She let Scott know she'd like me to swing by.

"Have I ever?" I grunt.

"There's always a first. I thought it'd be a nice gesture if you went shopping with Kyle and me and helped him pick out a birthday gift for his grandpa. And I'll spring for lunch, since I know money's tight for you."

Son of a bitch. "I've got a gesture for you right here, Scott."

He sighs. "That's real mature."

This is how it's been for Scott and me the last few years when it comes to my father. Now that Scott's a dad, he wants Kyle to know his grandfather and have a relationship with him. So he's made his peace with the old man, forgiven him for that whole dumping us, buying a golf course, getting remarried, and having more kids thing. Bravo. Wonderful. My hero. But don't expect me to show up for your lovefest.

"So I'll take that as a no," he says.

"Wrong. It's a fuck no."

"It must be tough holding all that anger inside. How long do you plan to keep it?"

"You tell me, lawyer man. What's the sentence for what he did?"

"I seem to have gotten over it."

I'd hit him if I could. "Don't compare us. It's different and you know it."

Another heavy sigh on his part. What kind of lawyer does that, sighs all the time? An annoying one, I'll tell you.

"All right, brother, if you change your mind, give me a call," he says.

"Don't hold your breath."

Here's the thing about my brother: he's a good guy, I like him, and on most days — any other day — we get along fine. But what he always seems to forget is that when he was fourteen, he couldn't stand our dad and was glad to see him go. Not me, not by a long shot. When I was a kid, he played baseball with me, took me to games, even drove me up to church to serve Mass (my Jewish father waiting an hour for his Catholic son out in the parking lot, in winter, at six AM — imagine that). In fact, not that I'd ever tell Scott or my mom or anyone else, but the first person who broke my heart wasn't the first girl I kissed, or slept with, or Sharon Manus, or any type of female at all. It was him. My old man. So go ahead, take a moment, think about the first person who broke your heart. Get a good image of that person, remember the happy days. Now, be honest: are you over it yet? *Completely?* I didn't think so.

CHAPTER THREE

I finish grading the essays Friday morning (topic: critique some aspect of American culture that you find absurd). Later, in class, I read excerpts from the best ones aloud, then start handing all of them back, calling out the various names: Napoleon Dynamite, Beyoncé, Joe the Plumber...(No, really, those *are* the names on them: I make everyone use an alias so I won't let my impression of a student color my reading of an essay, especially if said student has, oh, I don't know, a habit of wearing obnoxious T-shirts; plus, when they have a mask to hide behind, they're not so inhibited and self-conscious.) As each Borat and Kelly Kapowski comes forward to claim a paper, I finally get to see who wrote what and write the grade in my book, next to the student's real name.

When I call out Dr. Ruth, there's snickering — everyone got a kick out of that one, the best of the bunch by far, a wicked, sly, edgy piece about sex, the rules of attraction, and the American diet. But when Dr. Ruth steps forth to claim her paper, there's no snickering from me, not even a chuckle or cracked smile or grin, because what to my wondering eyes should appear but a girl in a tight black T-shirt that says Remove in Case of Party. Molly. She stands there with her hand out, waiting, staring at me, almost daring me to say something, and I don't want to give it to her because I don't want it to be hers, but in the end I do, because I have to, hopefully without creating too much of a scene. But it already is. She takes it with a smirk and saunters back to her seat, and I'm in danger of squeezing all the ink from my pen as I mark her grade in my book: A.

"Oh, by the way. I e-mailed it to *Cosmo*. They want to publish it." She tilts her head, gives me a smile. "Guess I'm in the club now, too."

Jesus. Is it too late to cancel my membership?

I'm writing about *The Canterbury Tales* for my dissertation—or more precisely, "The semantics of ecclesiastical iconography as it relates to Chaucer's portrait of medieval England's moral landscape"—and most days when I'm researching it, there's something about monks or merchants or madames, or a recently discovered letter by Chaucer, or maybe just the poetry itself, that jumps off the page and grabs me by the scruff of the neck and gives me a lift. Not today. It's all an effort and chore, every inch of slogging a cartload of bricks, up a hill, in the mud, and by six o'clock, I'm pedaling my way home from the library. It hasn't been a banner week: I've been dumped by Hannah, guilt-tripped by Scott, and Molly and I now share the same number of publishing credits. What I need is a hot shower, a Cardinals win on the tube, maybe some QT with a pretty young lady at the pub who'll let me buy her a drink. Three out of three would be great, but I'll settle for one, which should be a lock, since how hard can it be to turn a knob in the shower?

Then I open the vestibule door.

*   *   *

When Scott and I were kids, every Christmas morning we tore out to the tree before dawn and pawed and shook everything, to guess what was what. (Emily never got the chance; she died when she was two.) But one package I never had to poke or prod or lay a finger on, no matter the wrapping paper or size of the bow, was the length of a shoebox and half as wide, but not so tall: the entire set of Topps baseball cards, pristine, glossy, mine.

There's another package whose size and shape and heft I've come to know with as much certainty, but for all the wrong reasons. Because each time I see it—the 10 x 13 tear-/water-proof manila envelope, stuffed with seven hundred double-spaced manuscript pages, weighing fifty-seven ounces—it means I've been rejected. I've seen it a lot these past few months lying on the vestibule steps, along with the other mail too big for our slots. That's why I mailed it to Brandon in Minnesota and his independent press, so I'd never have to see it on those fucking steps again.

It's on those fucking steps again.

I lean my bike against the wall and my ears start to ring. Maybe there's been a mistake; maybe it's not from Minnesota at all; maybe there's another of my manuscripts out there, one I lost track of, and it's just now coming back. I check the postmark: Minnesota. Now the ring is a buzz. But maybe it's not *my* manuscript. Maybe the wrong one got stuffed in an envelope addressed to me, and won't we all have a good laugh when it turns out I got the rejected pages of a romance novel meant for someone in Des Moines. But it's mine, *Henley Farm*, all seven hundred pages. The buzz becomes a throb. But Brandon must have a different system: he sends the manuscript back, even when it *has* been accepted. I race through the cover letter: "Dear writer: Thank you for the chance to read your work. Unfortunately, we are not enthusiastic enough about it to publish it at this time...." A fucking form letter. Now I can't hear at all.

I've been rejected. By Brandon. I've. Been. Rejected. By. Brandon. *I've been rejected by fucking Brandon!*

I breathe.

I breathe.

I breathe.

Then I rip and tear and shred and twist and throw and stomp and kick, and I do it not only to the pages of my manuscript but also to the cover letter and envelope it came in, and not only to those items belonging to me but to the other mail lying on the stoop—a *People*, a *Vogue*—which are certainly not mine, but have the misfortune of being in my reach, so their pages, too, are ripped and torn and shredded and twisted and thrown and stomped and kicked, with venom and gusto and rage, so that by the time I'm finished, the entire floor is wallpapered, after a fashion, and I'm panting and wheezing and hoarse (was I cursing? grunting? *screaming?*). And that's where I find myself, standing atop the tickertape remnants of my tantrum, when the front door opens.

It's our neighbor from across the hall—Rhonda or Rhoda or Randi. She sees me and the mess, and probably the sweat on my face, and utters an embarrassed, "Oh, pardon me," like she's intruding and shouldn't be here, and starts to back away. But then you see her mind catch: Hey, I live here. But then you see her mind catch again: But this guy's crazy. You can tell she's weighing this against that, and she decides to take her chances. She drops her gaze and steps inside, moving briskly.

"I got some bad news," I try to explain.

"Sorry to hear it."

She keeps her gaze low and far from mine and scoots over the mess in her heels and prim little business suit and laptop carry case, and almost makes it to the steps free and clear. But her eyes flick at something on the pile and register surprise, displeasure, then she flashes a look at me to see if I saw her, which I did, which makes her gasp, as if now that she's seen what's there, I'll be forced to do the same to her.

"Are they yours?" I say.

"Are what mine?" she says too quickly, her back to me.

"Those magazines."

"What magazines?"

"*People, Vogue.*"

"Oh, were they there?"

Her little act is starting to tick me off. "Don't play games. I know you saw them. Just admit it."

"Hmm, well, if that's what they were, don't worry about them."

"Who said I was worried about them?" I snap. "I'm not worried about them. You shouldn't be reading them anyway. They're garbage. I did you a favor."

It's clear now all she really wants to do is put space between us. Her shoes make a clickety-click as she goes up the steps, and there's something about the way it sounds so grown-up, so professional, so . . . *successful* that lights my skin on fire.

"Then again," I yell up to her, "maybe you *should* be reading that *Vogue.*"

The clickety-click stops; I've got her attention.

"Goodwill called. They want their outfit back."

She exhales a loud, disgusted breath.

"Asshole!" she screams, and with quite the echo. Then she stomps to her door and slams it.

I do that little head-bob, chin-thrust, pigeon-looking thing you tend to do when you feel cool and cocky and confident, because that's how I feel right now: Yo, check it out, my novel might be confetti, but my trash talkin' ain't lost a beat. And this feeling of bad-boy bravado lasts for approximately eighteen seconds, till I realize what I've managed to do. I took a situation in which I was the wronged party, the victim, the neighbor guy worthy of "Sorry to hear it" condolences, and I've thrown it all away by being a smart-mouthed, ignorant prick. And now what Brandon did to me, and all the self-righteous indignation I'm entitled to, it's all swallowed up—every flippin' ounce of it—by guilt and regret over what I said to Rhonda. Rhoda. Randi. *Fuck*. Which means I know what I have to do.

First, I scoop up the mess, stuff all the manuscript and magazine pages into my backpack. Second, I go upstairs and call coward-ass Brandon and give his answering machine a profane and pissed-off piece of my mind. And finally, I set out for the bookstore to replace the magazines I destroyed, since I won't have the proper peace of mind to wallow in my rejection until I've eased my conscience about being a jerk. And, since the bookstore I go to doesn't carry that type of magazine, my penance is even stiffer: a trip into the bowels of Bookzilla.

Here's how ridiculous the parking lot is at Bookzilla: drivers are actually following departing shoppers to their cars, to get their spots. And it's not Christmas Eve. It's the bloody Friday night after Labor Day. But what do you expect when you squeeze a bookstore in with a Linens-N-Things and Petco and Home Depot and Target?

The inside of Bookzilla is just as bloated as the parking lot. It's women, mostly, and hordes of them, all ages and sizes and hair colors, squealing and heading upstairs. Oprah must've had a writer on her show today, someone who wrote a book about shopping or dieting or sex, or maybe she was talking about something like *Love in the Time of Cholera*, which everyone skipped twenty years ago when it was required reading in high school, but now that Oprah loves it, "Girl, I just gotta have it!" My goal is to get in and out of this place without being trampled or lobotomized.

I find the magazines right away, since, thankfully, Bookzilla gives prominent placement to high-minded publications such as *People* and *Vogue*, and make haste to the checkout line. That's where I'm standing when the night-beat reporter for Channel Five breezes in with a cameraman in tow and, like the panting women, they head upstairs.

"What's all the commotion?" I ask the cashier when my turn comes. I've already broken my vow not to say more than "hi," "cash," and "bye."

The woman actually clutches her chest. "Oh my god, you didn't hear? Katharine Longwell is here! Tonight. *In the store.*"

It's a name even I recognize. "*The* Katharine Longwell?"

"The one and only!"

Jesus. So the high priestess of chick-lit is here, the prima donna who's been on Kimmel and Letterman and the cover of *Entertainment Weekly*, and has had a Showtime series and two movies made from her books, and has forty gazillion copies in ten thousand languages of her books in print and has yet to meet a cliché she wouldn't take to bed. What, and no embossed invitation for me?

"She has a new book out," the cashier gushes. If she were a dog, her tail would've already flown off from wagging too hard. "You should check it out for your wife or girlfriend. It's *so* great!"

Here's what I'd like to tell her: a) I have no wife or girlfriend, thanks. b) If I had a wife or girlfriend who read Katharine Longwell, she wouldn't be my wife or girlfriend. c) Give me my fucking change. But I don't. I just glare.

Unfortunately, Tammy—that's what the nametag says—is oblivious to glares. "There's a display right there," she says, pointing exuberantly over my shoulder.

"Super. Can I have my change?"

"Oh, sure." She titters and gives me my change and slides the bag my way.

My plan is to beat it the hell out of there before they run out of Katharine Longwell books and the riot starts. But my eye catches something in the middle of the store: it's Demi Moore, standing next to a display of books, wearing a clingy white blouse that's opened oh so low and tight jeans, and her hair is windblown, and her mouth is opened in a way that's not quite porn star, but not kindergarten teacher, either. But as I get closer I see it's not Demi Moore in the flesh, only a cardboard cutout, then I see it's not Demi Moore at all, it's...*her*. Katharine Longwell. But she's a blonde, or at least she *was* a blonde, last time I tried to avoid seeing her on some show. Now she's a brunette? And from the way those buttons are busting on her blouse, the hair isn't the only thing she's had worked on.

By this time, I'm close enough to make out the title of her latest masterpiece—*The Cappuccino Club*—and it's like being at the scene of a car wreck: you know you should look away before you see something horrifying that will give you nightmares, but you can't help yourself. I pick up a copy. According to the jacket, Sasha and Gisella and Vanessa are best friends, and each is an American Princess—Jewish, Latina, and Black (or JAP, LAP, and BAP, as they would have you know)—and they've been through it all together—men, engagements, breakups, surgeries, broken heels, bad hairstyles—and discussed it all together, usually—you guessed it—over a cup of cappuccino. But lately things have been worse than usual, their men distant or disloyal, their jobs beating down on their self-worth, so they decide to take matters into their own hands: they'll go into business, open up their own coffee shop. Sisters doing it for themselves. What follows, of course, in this "compelling and beautifully written valentine to dreamers" is a year in their lives filled with more heartbreak and laughter, tears and romance, than any of them ever imagined, as they finally discover the true meaning of friendship, life, and love. In other words, another Pulitzer Prize–winning plot about women who just need a good lay.

It's easy to make fun of her books, and fun to do it, and that's what I'm doing, having a merry old time with myself, until a whole ugly parade of not-so-fun thoughts creeps into my head: 1) I've been rejected by Brandon, and everyone else. I can't get my book into print. 2) Katharine Longwell has her books in print. Dozens of them. Like *The Cappuccino Club*. 3) Katharine Longwell's novels are horseshit. 4) Katharine Longwell has sold millions of copies. 5) Katharine Longwell is a millionaire. 6) I've been rejected by Brandon, and everyone else. I can't get my book into print.

And suddenly I don't feel so much like making fun of Katharine's book anymore. My hand is trembling and my breathing's a little ragged, and I'm going *rejected writer* again, like I did in the vestibule of my apartment building, having wild and desperate thoughts, but these are worse than before, because they're so vivid, so tempting, so *delicious*, as in getting gasoline-soaked rags and a blowtorch and burning down the whole goddamned display, turning it into a blazing inferno, like a scene from *Fahrenheit 451*, only now we're not burning books with dangerous ideas, but books with no ideas at all, and everyone, *Run! Run for your lives!* because I'm not stopping here; I'm going through all the books, incinerating the garbage, and the flames are only going to get hotter and hungrier and higher, and you could be next, so *Run! Run for your lives!*

But I don't do any of that. Instead, I dump the book in my bag and leave without paying.

*   *   *

I lay the replacement *Vogue* and *People* on my neighbor's doorstep—with "Sorry!" scribbled on the receipt—then across the hall, at my place, the first thing I do is have a drink. It's also the second and third thing. At some point I realize it's been a long time since I've had anything to eat—when *was* lunch, anyway?—and that whiskey from a plastic cup on an empty stomach is not a good combination, but by that time, the info strikes me as more an NBC The More You Know public service spot than something that applies to me, here, now; and anyway, I'm too comfortable on the sofa, which is too far from the fridge, which would require walking to get to, and I've decided I'm not up for any exercise unless the building catches fire, and then, only if I must.

Besides, there's something on the TV, and it's the greatest show, *ever*, of all time, in the history of the world—look at those colors! and how the people move! and talk!—and it's a program on the Trojan War, and there are lots of battle scenes, and *Jesus*, how did they get that footage? and at one point I'm fairly certain that Hector and Achilles actually make an appearance on my living room floor, throwing punches. Then I pass out.

CHAPTER FOUR

I'd like to say I wake in the morning to the realization that everything about the last twenty-four hours was a dream: Dr. Ruth,
the rejected manuscript, the scene with my neighbor, the trip
to Bookzilla, the drinking. After all, Bobby Ewing got rid of an
entire season of *Dallas* just by stepping out of the shower. I don't
need an entire season wiped out, just a day. Unfortunately I'm on
the sofa, in my clothes, my head is throbbing, the whiskey bottle
is on the table, next to a plastic cup, and my backpack is on the
floor, stuffed with crumpled manuscript. I think it all happened.
Unless, of course, my waking up and thinking it all happened is
also part of the dream, which may not turn out so bad, provided
I, too, am married to the eighties version of Victoria Principal.
But I doubt it.

The Bookzilla bag is lying on the chair, *The Cappuccino Club*
wrapped tightly inside. I pull it out to give the ladies some air.
It's a heavy book, which means I have options: I could use it as
a giant coaster, or doorstop, or cockroach squasher. Good ideas

all. But I have something better in mind: I'll read it, or some of it, just to see how wretched it is, which will make me feel loads better about myself and the type of writing I do. But I can't do it here; that'd be blasphemous, like reading *Playboy* in church. I need a place where I won't be seen by anyone I know or respect or care about and I'll fit right in with my Katharine Longwell tucked under my arm. I know exactly the place.

The menu at Starbucks is such that I have difficulty finding a cup of coffee. Not a mocha Valencia, or espresso con panna, or iced caramel macchiato, or double chocolate chip frappucino. Just coffee. And not a tall or venti or grande. Just a cup. Finally, I get it worked out, I think.

I find a table that's right where I want it: out in the open, in plain view, where everyone can see me. I take a long, hearty breath, even puff out my chest a bit, and open my book, proud. I glance around and catch the eye of a woman a few tables over in a velour tracksuit, lots of clunky jewelry, and a turban of frosted hair. She has a twinkle in her eye, admiring, no doubt, my good taste in literature and the double mocha espresso caramel latte alpacino she thinks I'm drinking. Smile on, oh kindred spirit. Thus, ensconced on my throne with my favorite Starbucks beverage, I begin the task at hand.

It's as bad as I thought. Thirty-five pages in, and the characters have already whined, guffawed, chortled, intoned, babbled, mused, and chirped. Apparently, no one is much for "saying" anything. And how about these gems: "Man does not live on bread alone, but a woman can survive on shoes"; "For Vanessa, a piece of double fudge cake and an orgasm differed only in this: one she had and felt naughty, the other she had only when she felt naughty"; "Gisella knew all about men like Gleason McNeil: tall, dark, and handsome, with enough lines to fill a fisherman's boat";

"Sasha was getting to the age where wrinkles were her friends, but the kind who said nasty things behind her back." One thing Kitty can do, though, is plot. Something is always happening to Vanessa and Gisella and Sasha, and the men who are their husbands and lovers (and sons: a couple of them are up there, in terms of age). But it's so easy to see where all this is going, and who's going to wind up with whom, and it's cloying and trite and formulaic, and if I taught an introductory creative writing class instead of comp and lit, I wouldn't accept it. *Rewrite. Try again. You can do better.* Because they could.

My coffee is finished and I'm done with the book (not done, as in reached the end, but done as in, must throw away before brain damaged permanently). That's when I sense the lighting has changed in front of me and I'm not alone. Some vulture has already swooped in to claim my table. I look up.

At first I think the guy's planning to mug me, because it's that sort of outfit: baseball cap, oversized sunglasses, black T-shirt. *Disguise-ish.* But then I see the guy has earrings and breasts, and not just the breasts a man can sometimes have when he's a bit overweight, or has that kind of build; these, if you'll pardon my saying it, are the real deal, though how *real*, C-cup or better, is questionable. My visitor nods at the book.

"What do you think?" she asks.

"Ah, what do I think?" I say, closing the book and laying it facedown on the table. "Let me see..." I'd like to couch it in something clever and literary, if I can swing it — "How do I hate this? Let me count the ways" — though I also see the virtue of just being blunt — "It's a pile of shit." But as I'm weighing my options, really giving it some thought, she removes her glasses, and this unobstructed glimpse of her face mingles with my recollection of a cardboard image last night at Bookzilla and the author photo staring up from the table, and the faces all merge into one until I realize who it is: Katharine Longwell. In the flesh. *And she's asking me what I think of her book!*

"Hmm. Well, what I think…" I repeat, stalling, marveling, *rejoicing,* "is that it's hard for me to put it into words. Ms. Longwell." I flash her my best Gleason McNeil smile, which, if I'm getting it right, is "boyish yet confident," and then add, "Please, won't you have a seat?"

She's pleased I've recognized her, but then grimaces. "I'm on a tight schedule to make it to the airport. I just popped in for a coffee." She looks at her watch, then back at me. "But maybe I have a minute. If you'll call me Katharine."

"Okay, Katharine," I say, helping her into her chair. "I'm Mitch."

No one else in the place seems to realize who just sat down with me. But why should they? On a scale of one to ten, in terms of conspicuousness, she's about a two, and only because of the size of her…glasses. (Got you, eh?) She's just a woman getting a cup of coffee. Two cups, actually. And since I try to be fair in all things, I will say this: even without gobs of makeup, her face is not unattractive. Her eyes are her best feature, wide and brown and darker than Hannah's, though they do have a fleck of something that picks up the light and brightens them. Of course, maybe she's just wearing colored lenses, since I wouldn't put it past her.

"You must really like your coffee," I say. "Two cups?"

"Skim latte for me, café breve for my assistant."

"And she doesn't get the coffee for you?"

Katharine Longwell shrugs. "I wanted to stretch my legs. And she's a he, by the way. Brent. Which is why I came over. Other than Brent, you're not my typical fan, a young man like yourself." Her voice is a little husky, Catherine Zeta-Jonesish in a way. "I'm intrigued."

It comes across like a pickup line. Then, when she makes no

bones about checking out my arms and chest, I'm certain of it: she's flirting. *With me!* For a moment I almost feel bad for her, since she's in her forties if she's a day and she thinks I might actually be digging on her.

"To be honest, Katharine, I wouldn't exactly call myself a fan." I lean a little closer. "I'm reading your book for another reason."

"Oh?" she says, taking the bait, her lips curling into a smile. *I've got her!* I have her wrapped around my little finger. Katharine Longwell is my pinky ring. She thinks something delicious is coming her way. And that's when it happens.

There's a clip of Michael Jordan playing against the Lakers in the early nineties, ready to slam it home, another easy two for His Highness. But as he soars toward the basket, eyes wide, tongue waggling, you see his body instinctively seize upon the moment, recognize something greater, so he windmills the ball, drops it lower and switches hands, then lays it up and off the glass, kissing it in. A slam dunk, impressive in its own right, has become a shot for the ages. That's where I am today. The lane is open, my path is clear, I have only to stuff it home: "Your book is a load of crap." Slam dunk, *in your face!* But it's too easy. So my brain pulls a Jordan, ratchets into a higher gear, realizes something more spectacular is there for the taking. My mouth simply needs to follow.

"Actually, I'm reading it because of my cousin. She's a huge fan."

"Oh, really."

"The biggest. She's read everything you've written." I flip to the "Also by Katharine Longwell" page. "Like *Confessions of a Serial Virgin, You've Got Male, Ms. Opportunity, Dolce & Gabbana & Heather.* Those are the ones she's always talking about. And the new one here, *The Cappuccino Club,* she told me I'd be amazed. And I am."

She tilts her head in a schoolgirl sort of way. "Nice of you to say, Mitch. And your cousin."

But I'm just revving up. "And here's the thing. She's a bit of a writer herself. Not in your league, of course. But she's serious about it. She wants to be just like you. In fact, she dropped out of college to do it. She was studying genetic engineering or something like that, but how could she do that and hold on to her dream? Because you know how it is: when the writing bug bites you, you're a goner."

I've hit her from several angles and she's not sure which piece of information to respond to. She opts for the one I hadn't expected. "Does that mean you write, too?"

"Who, me? No. Are you kidding? My cousin and I just talk a lot, since her fiancé left her after she dropped out of school. And put on the weight. I just read her stuff. Actually, I represent her, too. I'm trying to help her get something published. It's tough out there, you know. Though you probably don't, since, of course, you are who you are."

She nods, serious-faced. "I still remember those days. I wasn't always who I am."

"But you are now." I give her a wink—*a wink!*—and now I realize where all this is leading. "Which reminds me. She'd absolutely kill me if I told her I ran into you and didn't get an autograph." I slide the book over to her. "Would you mind?"

"Of course not. What's your cousin's name?"

"Bradley."

"*Bradley?*"

"That's right. It's short. For Bradjolet."

"'Bradjo-*what*'?"

"Bradj*olet*. It's French. Her father's a chef. Just put 'Bradley,' though. That's what everyone calls her."

You can tell she's trying to untangle the *French* from the *chef*

from the *Bradley,* and it's not really working, but I'm not helping,
so she just smiles politely and writes a note.

"How's that?" she asks, passing the book back.

I read what she's written and nearly choke. "Perfect."

She checks her watch again and this time says she absolutely
needs to go, since Brent is probably out in the car having a heart
attack. We shake hands again.

"I really enjoyed talking with you, Mitch. A *lot.*" She gives me
one of those deep, lingering gazes, and hasn't let go of my hand.
"So let me give you something." She reaches into her purse and
hands me a card. "This is my office in Chicago, and my e-mail.
And here's something else." She scribbles a number on the back.
"My cell phone. If your cousin has something you think I should
read, give me a call." She gives me the once-over again. "Or if
you just want to come to Chicago sometime, on me, I'm sure we
could find something to do…"

I'm not making it up: that's how she ends our conversation!

"Uh, yeah, sure. I'll keep it in mind."

With that, she puts on her shades, picks up her coffees, and
breezes out the door, and I'm left with an autographed copy of
The Cappuccino Club and the cell phone number of the most
popular chick-lit writer in the country. Just my usual Saturday
morning at Starbucks.

I sit back in my chair and take another look at what she's
written: "Bradley, Never give up. Listen to your heart, and write
with it. Katharine Longwell." Are you kidding me? How gull-
ible is this woman? I'll be laughing about this one for weeks. But
my mind's still humming, still kicking around ideas, not ready
to let it go, till…I bolt forward so quickly that the guy next to
me flinches. Suddenly they're with me at the table—Vanessa,
Gisella, Sasha—Sirens all of them, clamoring for my attention,
whispering honeyed temptations into my ear: Do it, do it, do it.

Do what? Do what? Oh my god, you don't mean . . . *that?*

Yes, *that!*

Outrageous. Unthinkable. *Absurd.* And yet . . .

I mean, how hard can it be? Katharine is no Rhodes scholar, yet she does it and makes a fortune. And look at everything I have going for me. I'm a writer. I have an "in" with a famous author who said she'd read it. I have a built-in pseudonym with Cousin Bradley. This is perfect! The only thing I'm missing is a plot, but who cares? Give me two weeks to work on some cocka-mamie scenario about engagement rings and shopping sprees and bridesmaid dresses and impossibly dreamy guys, and *voila!* Hello publication. Not exactly the way I'd dreamed of getting my name (or my cousin's) into print, but like the Stones once sang, you can't always get what you want. So chick-lit it is.

CHAPTER FIVE

Bradley and I shoot baskets on Sunday, and afterwards I show him the book and tell him my plan. He thinks it's funny but not hilarious—he doesn't have an ax to grind with these people like I do—though he does offer a few words of advice: Baby steps before the masterpiece, little grasshopper. We both agree my first step is to research chick-lit, sniff out its essence, capture it in its pure, undiluted form, before I turn it all on its Prada-loving head. So I'm off to Bookzilla.

I grab copies of all the chick-lit books that have sold at least a billion copies. How do I know they've sold a billion copies? Because if *I've* heard of them, they must have. I prefer to be a gentleman about this and not name names (though Katharine I already have, but you know why), but I will provide summaries, from which you might be able to tell which books I'm talking about, since, by some coincidence, you may have a *friend* who's read one of them and spilled the details. One is about a chubby British girl who keeps a diary, listing all the calories she's consumed and cigarettes she's smoked, and she cheers herself when she's good, and scolds herself when she's bad, and pursues a guy at work, who turns out to be an ass, and winds up with a guy who wore a bad sweater the first time they met. Another is about a chubby American girl whose ex-boyfriend writes an article about what it's like to be involved with a larger woman, which pisses her off, but she decides she wants him back, but he's not interested, but his father dies so they sleep together, and she winds up pregnant, but now he's with someone else, and oh, what to do. Another is about a young fashion assistant who dreams of working for *The New Yorker*, but she's stuck working for the boss from hell, who wears a certain style of designer clothing (which is in the title) and treats her like dirt. Those are three of them. There are others.

For the next few hours, I sit at a table in the café and pick these books apart, and it's like I'm back in high school, sophomore year, dissecting a frog, only without the safety goggles or formaldehyde smell. I pull back the skin and expose a network of handbags and bitchy bosses and decadent desserts, observe the way it's all put together, then go deeper, prodding and poking, till at last I get to the vital organs and the heart of what makes this monster tick: hunks. Of course, along the way I see plenty that's not for the faint of heart, appalling and nauseating sights that, if you're not expecting them, can turn your stomach and make you gag. But I stick with it, so that by the time the store is closing, I have a model of the chick-lit heroine and the plot she finds herself in. I've cracked their code and discovered their Magdalene, who turns out to be ten pounds heavier than she'd like to be. And just in case I'm found out by any keepers of the chick-lit grail secrets, and my notes tampered with or destroyed, I've boiled it down to six Fs for easy recall: female fantasy fulfillment = food, fashion, fucking.

I get back to the apartment and decide nothing should begin tonight, though I do clip the author photo of Katharine from the back cover of *The Cappuccino Club* and tape it on the wall for inspiration. I feel good knowing Auntie Katharine will be watching over me.

I've given the class a Hemingway story for today: "Hills Like White Elephants." It's a spare, tightly written piece, and the students do a good job catching the drift of what's going on, but unlike the fiasco we had with Updike, I want them to give intense scrutiny to craft and technique, crawl into Hemingway's skin, figure out why he made the shadow "warm," the hills "white and long," the country "brown and dry." Because they just as easily could have been something else (lots of words in the dictionary, last time I checked).

I'll admit it's heady stuff, so I'm not surprised when I get a knock on my office door a little later. What I am surprised by is who it is. Molly.

"Busy?" she asks.

For you, always. "I've got a minute."

She swaggers in and plops down before I ask her to sit. She's almost wearing a skirt. And a top.

"What's up?" I ask.

She smooths the fabric of her skirt, which quickly turns into tanned leg.

"So where do I stand in this class?" she asks.

"How so?"

"In terms of a grade."

"Ah, it's way too early for that. We're only a couple weeks in."

"But based on everything so far."

"Okay, fine. Based on everything so far ... one paper, which was an A; homework assignments, which you do; and you speak up in class. I guess I'd say your grade is pretty good at this point. But a lot can change between now and the end," I add ominously.

"So it's an A?" she says, ignoring the last part.

I make a face that I hope conveys the fact there could be some doubt on the matter, but I don't think it does.

"Good." She crosses her legs left over right, and Sharon Stone pops into my mind. *Basic Instinct* Sharon Stone. She flashes me a piece of paper. "Can you give me a hand with this?"

It's one of the fliers that's plastered all over campus, announcing the Shakespeare San Diego Program over winter break. Students need to nab a faculty sponsor to write a letter of recommendation, but freshmen have to make a strong impression and move faster than most (though I'd be willing to bet that's Molly's specialty, making an impression and moving fast). Ordinarily, I'd rather not give her the time of day, but this I'll do, since both of us will know for all eternity that she came crawling to me for help. (Smug? Petty? Who, me?)

"So when do you want it?" I ask.

She arches her brows suggestively. "When do I want *what?*" she says coyly, as if we're talking about something else.

"The recommendation letter, Molly. The letter."

That one makes her laugh. "Oh, Mitch, sorry. You've got it all wrong. I already have one from Professor Anderson. He's the one who suggested I apply."

Professor Anderson? The chair of the department? The guy I can barely squeeze five minutes out of to discuss my dissertation?

"When did you talk to Professor Anderson?" I grill her.

"Actually, I *do* talk to him, every Tuesday and Thursday. I have him for Poets of the Harlem Renaissance."

But that's a junior seminar! I start to object, then cut myself short. Because that's exactly the reaction she wants, so she can gloat about the special consent form and dean's signature and whatever the hell else she coaxed out of half the administrators on campus to get into the class.

"Wonderful." *Shoot me.* "So what do you need from me?"

"Just your phone number. They may call to ask you how I'm doing in class. Reference sort of thing."

"Whatever."

She pulls out a little black book and I rattle off the number, then make it clear I'm busy and have plenty of work to do and this conversation has come to an end. She stands and lingers in the doorway.

"You know, your campus number would have been fine. But this is cool, too." She puts a hand on her hip, a little extra arch in her back. "Not accidentally on purpose trying to tell me something, are you, *Mister* Samuel?"

She winks and breezes on her way, and I slam the door till it falls off its hinges. In my mind, anyway.

When I get back to the apartment, I ditch any plans that might require an ounce of brain, like coming up with a lesson plan, or reading for my dissertation, or putting the cap back on the toothpaste. This is all about getting in touch with my inner chick. So I watch *Oprah.*

I'm hoping for something that'll build on yesterday's time at the bookstore, maybe a show called "A Male Writer's Guide to Further Understanding the Ways and Habits of the Chick-lit Heroine." Of course, I'm asking a lot there, so I'll settle for a makeover episode. But what I get is Jay Leno, and Jay talks a lot about comedy and kids doing comedy, because he's written a book about how to be the funniest kid in your class, and he brings out a group of precocious kindergartners who giggle a lot and pick at their clothes and do stand-up bits, which include a couple of haltingly told knock-knock jokes about poo. Cute, but not exactly the show I was looking for, to be honest.

And maybe it's the disappointing *Oprah* that leads to an unproductive evening with the writing. I can't seem to get anything going, since those topics — Jay Leno, kid stand-up comics, poo jokes — weren't high on the list of chick-lit plot devices I gleaned yesterday. Even so, when Oprah gives you lemons, you make lemonade, so I sit and wrangle with it, and the best I can come up with is that my very witty heroine is slightly overweight, so she becomes addicted to fashion to help her feel better about herself, which causes her to go into debt, which causes her fiancé to get angry and break up with her, which makes her eat lots of ice cream and run the credit card up even more and sink into despair; but then she gets her scrappy on and decides to go off to comedy camp, where she becomes the world's most famous knock-knock joke teller and meets a Hugh Jackman look-alike who loves a size-twelve woman who can make him laugh, and they have lots of sex and live happily ever after. I think I have everything I need in there, but the plot strikes me as a bit ridiculous, even by chick-lit standards. (I think.) Which means my evening is a total waste.

I go to bed that night feeling not quite so rosy as I did yesterday at this time. I thought I'd have a few chapters done, or at least a draft. But no need to panic yet. I've only been at it one evening, and I figure even the real chick-lit aficionados like Katharine Longwell need at least a week or two to crank out one of these things. I fluff my pillow, get comfortable, and cheer myself with the thought that tomorrow is another day. Yes, things will be better in the morning.

But they aren't.

Nor are they any better in the afternoon, or evening, or night, nor on Wednesday or Thursday or Friday, despite the fact that

I've revised my methods, expanded my field of research, become more inclusive, so that instead of just watching *Oprah*, now I'm watching *Dr. Phil* and *Rachael Ray* and *Ellen* and the Oxygen and Lifetime and Hallmark networks, and everything on Bravo, and shows like *Grey's Anatomy* and *Ugly Betty* and *America's Next Top Model*, and any movie with Meg Ryan, all the while eating my Chunky Monkey and M&Ms; and I'm paging through *Glamour* and *Allure* and *Marie Claire* and *Town & Country* and *W* and *Cosmo* (no Molly article, yet) and reading articles called "Put the *Oh!* in Your Orgasm" and "Blow His Mind with These Down Under Tricks" and "Seven Saucy Secrets to Spice Up Your Booty Call," and I've been into mall stores and boutiques called White House/Black Market and bebe and Bronx-Diba Shoes and Claudia Milan and Ylang Ylang and Aeropostale and Harari and Lucky Brand Dungarees and Satine and Anthropologie and BCBG Max Azria, where I've seen metallic sweater dresses and floral halters and linen flounce skirts and lace dot camisoles and raw-edged capris and fringed denim shorts and halter jumpsuits and silk charmeuse shirts and bra top dresses (with hidden bralette shaping) and paisley tunics, and shoes, lots of shoes, such as slingbacks, sandals, stilettos, platforms, pumps, slides, wedges, and boots — ankle and mid-calf and knee high — and I've seen purses and clutches and totes and pochettes and slouchy hobos and saddlebags and satchels and baguettes, and I've smelled perfumes and held diamond rings, all the while thanking the clerks for their patience, since I'm only a stupid guy taking notes, trying to find the perfect gift for my girlfriend, but all of it to no avail, so that by Saturday night, as I lay on the couch with my empty ice cream cartons and candy wrappers and new love handles, I don't have a single useable page of the novel. And I am a total wreck.

So what's the problem here? Oh, sure, my characters look the part, in their Balenciaga minis and Jimmy Choo shoes, with their

Lancôme brush-on lip shine plumper stashed in their Louis Vuitton purses. But get up close, stand next to them, and poke them with your finger, and you'll notice something odd: they don't flinch, they don't poke back. They're mannequins. They're like those Indians in the old westerns who speak slowly and drop all the articles and use bad grammar: "I tell white man he have nothing fear from buffalo rider." Wooden, stilted, one-dimensional.

And the reason I can't make them breathe or move or talk is that I don't understand the real people they're supposed to be like. Women who take surveys to find out if they're more like Jen or Angelina, or know that wrap dresses tend to slim a curvy figure, or that skirts in twill or gabardine give shape to a saggy butt, or that bows are in but sparkly brooches are out, or how to apply Enjoue Beaute Skin Glow in Pearly Pink or Giorgio Armani Luminous Silk Foundation in No. 5 to get Eva Longoria's smoky eyes or Kirsten Dunst's flushed cheeks. Who are these people? They may as well be from another planet, and if you're saying, "Actually, men are from Mars and women from Venus," then you're precisely the type of woman I just don't understand.

Women like Hannah, or Skyler, or any of the women I've ever dated, or hung around, or liked, they don't say things like that, or care much about wrap dresses or lip plumper or bows or sparkly brooches or Jen or Angelina or skin glow or Eva's smoky eyes. And I guess I've always known such women exist—one hears rumors—but I haven't exactly made the effort to get to know them and their habits and mannerisms. It seemed like a good and honorable thing, to have missed out on all their frippery. But now I'm paying the price.

CHAPTER SIX

Bradley and I are watching football Sunday afternoon, and even though the Rams have won and the Chiefs are winning, and big, I'm not enjoying any of it. Bradley notices and asks me what's wrong, so I tell him.

"Don't sweat it, man," he says, like we're talking about a hangnail. "You just need to spend some time with my sister and her dancer friends."

At first I think it's code for something else, and I expect him to repeat it and make finger quotes around "sister" and "dancer friends," or at least one of them, and then explain the true meaning. But he doesn't. He just goes back to watching the game. Then I remember: he actually *does* have a sister and she *does* have dancer friends. Still...

"What the hell are you talking about?"

"That day I helped her with her furniture, some woman was eating a candy bar, and she said, I swear to God, 'I may as well be gluing this chocolate to my ass.' Then two of them get into a discussion about which is better, Godiva or Ghirardelli or some other crap, then somebody else jumps in about the style of jeans the ass-gluer's wearing, and how that's a good fit for her, since she's short-waisted. Whatever that means." He stuffs a few nachos into his mouth. "I suggest you get down to that dance studio and make like SpongeBob and soak it all up."

Oh, *that's* what he's talking about: go to a dance studio. Yeah, I'll do that, right after I jam a screwdriver through my ear. "News flash: I don't know how to dance."

"No kidding. That's why they give these things called lessons, so people like you can learn. It's the perfect cover: a public place, lots of chatter. You'll fit right in."

I picture the studio, and me at the studio, and other people with me at the studio, and little beads of sweat begin to form on my upper lip. But if it would help ... "What's the name of the place?"

"Dance something or other."

"Oh, I love that place. I'll head right over."

"Just get me the phone book. I'll know it when I see it."

I fetch the yellow pages and he thumbs to the dance section. "Aha! Here it is," he says, "Dancing Daze."

Jesus. A place that likes to pun. I despise it already. "So what kind of dancing does she do?"

"Hmm. That part never came up."

"Okay. What nights does she go?"

He shakes his head. "That part either."

"What *did* come up?"

"The half-off shoe sale at Macy's, chocolate, jeans for short-waisted people. Oh, and the instructor's name. That came up a lot."

I wait for him to give it to me, but he doesn't. Instead, he conspicuously turns away and takes a swig of his beer and holds the bottle up to his mouth for quite some time, like maybe if he does this long enough, I'll forget what we're talking about, and my own name, too, and we'll move on to something else. But I wait, patiently.

"Well?"

He sets his jaw, serious-like. "Let me ask you a question, Mitch. How important is it for you to pull off this stunt?"

"Give me her name."

He clears his throat. "Uh, his."

"Fine, *his*."

He chews at his lip. "It's ... Adonis."

No fucking way!

"Mitch, he's a dancer. He's Greek. What'd you expect? *Jim*? And anyway, remember what the Bard said: 'What's in a name?'"

A hell of a lot, I'm guessing, when you're a dance instructor by the name of Adonis. How tight are this guy's pants?

"Look, if it'll help any, I'll call my sister, explain the situation, tell her to be on the lookout for you."

I almost toss the remote at his head. "Oh, that's brilliant. 'Hey, Sis, I have a writer friend who's working on a book about shallow, superficial characters and he wants to research the project by eavesdropping on you and all your friends. Be especially trite and vacuous with your comments, because that would help a lot.'" I give him a look.

"I'm just trying to help."

"Yeah, well that doesn't help. That's idiotic. 'I'll call my sister, explain the situation,'" I mimic in a lunkheaded voice, to let him know how I really feel, in case he doesn't already. "In fact, with help like that..." I start, but I can't think of a way to complete it, not that gets it right, lets him know this whole thing is driving me nuts, that nobody told me there'd be days like this. But maybe that's just the point. I *can't* think right now. And that's my goddamned problem.

He shrugs. "Your call, Baryshnikov." Then he starts yelling at the referee on TV.

There's a scene in the first *Indiana Jones* movie when Indy's about to lower himself into the chamber where the Ark is buried, and he sees all those snakes, and he rolls back on his side, repulsed and disgusted and horrified, and says, "Snakes. Why'd it have to be *snakes?*" That's how I'm feeling later, tossing and turning in bed, only I'm saying, "Dancing? Why'd it have to be *dancing?*" Because I hate dancing. I am repulsed and disgusted by dancing. And not because it's unmanly or unhip, or in any way snake-like, because, brother, it ain't; I'd trade places in a heartbeat with Gene Kelly in *Singin' in the Rain* if it meant having any part of my body near Cyd Charisse's. The problem isn't even the dancing per se. The problem is that I'm *no good.* And I don't do a thing if I'm no good at it, because I can't stand looking ridiculous and foolish and klutzy, or being reminded of my deficiencies and inadequacies and shortcomings, even if it's only for the electric slide, and I *never* do those things in public, where there is gawking and guffawing and pointing, and where I could be the butt of a joke ("Hey, look what that guy does with his arms. It's chicken-man!"). And maybe I'm overly self-conscious about all this—or thin-skinned, or kakorrhaphiophobic, or whatever a shrink might say—and maybe I should just get over it. But fuck that, really.

So...

As I see it I have three options: chuck the whole project and live with the knowledge that Katharine does this better than me; keep plugging away as I am and go insane; head off to dance class with Adonis and Co. and make a total ass of myself. Not the most soothing plotlines for a bedtime story and, as a result, I sleep terribly and dream awful dreams, and this is how desperate

I am when I wake: I'm prepared to cloak myself in tips gathered from *Cosmo*'s "Now and Zen" article. I shall be calm and still, a pool of tranquil water, and listen to the universe for answers.

I give the writing another try and it gets me nowhere. *I breathe deeply from the diaphragm.*

I go to the bookstore to check out the new *Glamour, Harper's Bazaar,* and *Vanity Fair,* and they yield nothing. *I delight in my oneness with consciousness.*

I consider talking to Molly, even if it means she'll know for all eternity I came crawling to her for help, but she's wearing a T-shirt that says Taster's Choice and the same skirt she wore to my office the other day, and I'm guessing it might be hard to talk with her about plunge bras and v-strings and Italian lace tangas and keep my mind—and eyes—where they need to be. I take a cold shower (which, strictly speaking, was not mentioned in the article, but seems like the thing to do).

I give Oprah another shot, and she has a show on transgendered people—women trapped in men's bodies and vice versa—and while any one of them could easily write the book I'm trying to write, since they seem to have a finger in both pies, so to speak, this is no help to me. The universe, I conclude, has spoken by not speaking, which is very Zen of it: it must want me to dance.

I call the studio and a pleasant female voice tells me that, yes, there is an instructor named Adonis, and he teaches recreational ballroom on Mondays and Thursdays, championship tango on Tuesdays and Fridays, and gives private lessons on the weekend. Since Bradley mentioned nothing about his sister being a dancing savant, I'll assume the recreational class is her speed. Which means there's a lesson tonight. A *dancing* lesson. I take a moment to find the center of my being, so I'll know where to plunge the knife, if need be.

The annals of literature are filled with individuals who went to extreme and dangerous lengths to capture the story. Ernest Hemingway drove an ambulance in World War I, got injured, and we have *A Farewell to Arms* and *The Sun Also Rises* for his pains; Jon Krakauer climbed Mount Everest for *Into Thin Air*; George Plimpton played quarterback for the Detroit Lions to get *Paper Lion*. These men endured artillery fire and subzero windchills and 250-pound brutes in cleats, all for the sake of their art; Mitch Samuel has only to dance. So I slip into my jeans. I put on a button-down shirt. I lace up my sneakers. I stare into the mirror and give my hair a little brush back, channel Travolta in *Saturday Night Fever*. I'm Tony Manero. I'm cool. I'm confident. I can do this.

A half hour later, on the bus, I realize I'm not cool, I'm not confident, I can't do this. Bring on the bullets and blizzards and blitzing linebackers. *Please*. I ring the bell; let me off at the next stop. As for the book, well, I can mail Katharine a letter and tell her what I was up to, let her know I made her look like a fool—you autographed a book for Bradley, my best friend, a guy—and be done with it. Maybe I'll include a picture of Bradley, naked, using the book to cover his privates. Good enough, I suppose.

And this is the plan, or the early stages of it—though I'm already having second thoughts about the naked picture of Bradley, since that seems borderline...*criminal*—when I hear Snoop Dogg. His music is pouring from the old-school headphones of some teen standing next to me, waiting to get off. (How do I know it's Snoop Dogg? Because I've seen my share of MTV.) But Snoop is really Calvin Broadus, which means, of course, that Snoop Dogg is just a stage name, an alias, just like Bono and Sting and Slash and 50 Cent and Eminem; like Mark Twain and O. Henry and George Eliot and Bradley/Bradjolet, for that matter; like Cary Grant and John Wayne and Jon Stewart; like the names I let my students use when they write their papers. And the benefit of hiding behind an alias? It's not you on the stage, or the other side of a camera, or in print. Not really. It's your alter ego, an actor, someone else, and this someone else can take risks and be crazy and let it all hang out, because if he fails, *he* fails, not you. Which means...

Mitch Samuel doesn't like to dance. He hates it. He's self-conscious and awkward and stiff, but more than anything, he's not interested in making a fool of himself in front of others. Fine, Mitch. Go home. Bug off. We don't need you tonight. Because tonight we have a special guest. Jason (my middle name). Jason Gallagher (my mom's maiden name). For Jason, dance is the rhythm of life. It is the soul making love to the body. It is the motion of the heavenly hosts. And Jason has the perfect attitude about taking lessons: he basks in the spotlight of attention, he's willing to take chances, and most importantly, he won't cry or throw chairs or punch anyone if he messes up. Or so he says.

CHAPTER SEVEN

Here's what I expect when I get there: spandex and sequins and strappy heels, feather boas and fake nails and teeny tops. And that's just the guys. But what I get instead is cotton and polyester and denim, and a fair share of leather, but leather where leather belongs: in shoes. A couple dozen people are sitting around on metal chairs, chatting and laughing, waiting as another lesson finishes up, and to my eye, there's nothing to set them apart from a regular crowd of people, except they're sitting in a room with mirrors covering three walls and a bunch of trophies and plaques and photos of dancers on the fourth. Of course, Jason would've been fine with the glitz and glitter, had it been there, but he's not complaining.

I take a chair in the corner, next to a couple about my age. The guy gives me a smile.

"Steve Carlton," he says, extending his hand. "This is my fiancée, Jennifer."

"Nice to meet both of you," I say. "I'm, uh, Jason. Jason Gallagher." There, I've said it: *Jason Gallagher.* And my nose isn't growing.

"First timer?" Jennifer asks. She's one of those strawberry blondes and freckly.

"It is," I say. Then Jason adds, brightly, "I'm looking forward to it." Steve and Jennifer are changing out of sandals into what I can only presume are dance shoes. I am not. "You two must be pros at this."

Steve peers up from his laces. "I wouldn't go that far. I'm just trying to learn a few steps so I don't trip over myself at our wedding." At mention of the wedding, he turns to her, and she to him, and they get goofy smiles, and I swear someone coos.

"How about you?" Jennifer asks. "Wedding coming up, or something like that?"

"Wedding? No, nothing like that. It's for work." *Work?* "I'm in sales. I'm, uh, a pharmaceutical rep actually, and sometimes, um, we have conferences, with dinners and dancing, and I always feel like a klutz. So, for that." *Jesus.* "Anyway, I hear the instructor is good. Adam, Adrian…"

"Adonis," Jennifer says, her face going chandelier bright. "He's great. You'll really like him."

I can tell she doesn't just like him, she worships him — I think Steve should be worried — and I'm tempted to tell her that according to Greek legend, Adonis wasn't actually a god, just a mortal, and he got gored to death by a wild boar. Not much to like about that, now is there? But I let it go.

"And which one is Adonis?" I ask.

Jennifer gives the room a quick scan. "Hmm. I don't see him." Steve gives it a try, coming up empty too. "Maybe he's in the office," he says.

Maybe. Or maybe he's one for theatrical entrances; descending from a disco ball would be good. But enough about him. What I'd really like to ask is, "Which one is Marie?" But it turns out I don't have to, because I've found her all on my own.

She's sitting several chairs down, across from me, in a satiny blouse with fake jewels for buttons. She doesn't really have Bradley's squared-off jaw or deep-set eyes—her face is fuller, rounder, more animated—and maybe she's a bit more big-boned than I would've expected his sister to be, but what gives her away is the hair: highlighted, teased, huge, the telltale sign of someone in Marie's profession. That's one thing I'd like to tell the hairstylists of the world, if they'd care to listen: Whoa, cowgirl. Slow that pony down. Just because you have all the fancy clippers and scissors and products, don't be so itchy with the trigger finger. Subtlety and understatement go a long way. Perhaps I can find a way to mention something to Bradley and he can find a way to suggest she tone it down.

People start migrating toward the floor, as if summoned by a pied piper's song, and I go too, even though I don't hear a thing, since I assume something is about to happen. It does. A guy steps out from the office area. He's lanky and pale and seems to be in need of a good dentist, and he's wearing baggy jeans.

"Who's that?" I ask Jennifer.

"That," she says, doing her best to build up the moment, "is Adonis."

Skinny and balding and pale? Adonis? Now I get the name, and it's actually kind of funny.

Adonis starts by welcoming the group, especially the new faces, and tells us the dance we'll be learning tonight, and for the next few weeks, is salsa. Salsa, he explains, is a four-beat dance, but there's a pause on the four, so it turns out to be more like a quick-quick-slow, quick-quick-slow, where the slow is held for two beats. We step it off, one-two-three-pause, four-five-six-pause, with the men always starting on the left foot, going forward, the ladies on the right going back. That's the basic. Of course, now it's a matter of getting the weight distributed properly, because it's not a march, stiff legged and upright, but something loose and swively, where you send the weight out and snap it back, so we work on that. About the time I feel my body's getting the hang of it, and not so badly, he puts on the music, and now we have to find the beat in the music, *and* step it off, *and* get our weight distributed, which overloads the circuits of a few of us and causes our feet and hips to malfunction. But whereas Mitch would have already stormed off the floor and knocked someone down for looking at him, Jason calmly regroups and eventually gets it; and then we work on posture and arm placement, pretending to dance with someone; and then we work on a turn; and even though there isn't a ton of time left in class, he wants us to put it all together, steps and music and posture and turn, with a partner.

Mine is a woman named Fran. Her hair is gray and permed, and she's a bit on the heavy side, but her slacks have an elastic waistband to accommodate such a shape. She also has a fanny pack strapped to her middle, and I can see the cap of a water bottle poking out. Practical gal, this Fran. But she's a talker, one of those nonstop kind, so while I'm trying to concentrate on the music and my steps and my arms, she's going on and on about her cats, letting me know that her Persian likes to sit on the refrigerator, except in summer, because then she likes to lie in the tub, not with water of course, but on the cool porcelain, which makes sense because she doesn't keep her house all that cool; but her tabby likes to lie on the sofa, year-round, but he's always been more sociable and friendly and likes to be where she is, especially when she's knitting, because he likes to play with her ball of yarn. And just about the time I'm ready to ask her if she has one of those balls of yarn in her fanny pack so I can stuff it in her mouth, Adonis calls out for us to change partners.

What this means, I discover, is that the men stay in place, but the women slide one spot down the line, so that I lose my Fran and gain a brunette in Lucky Brand jeans. It's a whole new set of arms and hands and feet to get used to, a different body type, but we muck through it, do well, in fact, then change partners again, then again, and a few more times, so that just before nine, I look over to my left and Marie is next on my dance card, one slot away. But Adonis stops the music, and I figure that's that, the show's over.

"Last dance," he calls out, and Marie, visibly relieved, swaggers my way with a big flirty smile.

We join hands. "Fresh blood," she purrs. "I've been looking forward to this all evening."

Great. Bradley's sister is hitting on me. "Hope I won't disappoint."

Adonis cues the music and we're off.

She's one of those enthusiastic types who's not necessarily good, but she does it with such gusto and commitment that it makes up for the shaky steps. She throws her weight around—and there's a bit to be throwing around—uses her hips a lot, styles her arms and shoulders in poses, and if the perpetual motion machine of her body weren't enough, she tosses out comments like rice at a wedding. When she messes up a step: "Bad feet! Bad feet!" When she turns: "Look out, handsome, hips coming through!" When she has to spin more than once: "I'm so dizzy. What'd you put in my drink?" And her favorite, when we get something right: "Vavoom!" It's all a bit over the top, like her hair and blouse, and fun, mostly, but I'm beginning to see why Bradley kept her in the closet and out of my sight all these years.

We finish and the lesson is over, and we all give ourselves a round of applause. "New kid on the block, I like you," she says, putting one hand on her hip, the other on my shoulder. "You know how to move."

"Thanks," I say. "You did a good job leading."

She's scandalized. "Who, moi? A lady never leads. I was just helping us get where we needed to be."

"We got there, all right," I say with a grin. "I'm Jason, by the way." My plan is to stick with the faux name for now, sort it out with her and Bradley later.

"And I, my dear, am Rosalyn," she says a bit breathily. "But my friends call me Rosie." She gives me a wink. "I *hope* you'll be calling me Rosie." She turns on her heel and sashays away, glancing back over her shoulder to make sure I'm checking out her backside.

So Marie isn't Marie at all; she's Rosie. I look around at the other women in class. She must be one of these, except for Fran or Jennifer; or maybe she's not even here, since no one else looks even remotely like Bradley. But as I take a seat with the other dancers, I realize it doesn't matter. Steve and Jennifer are chatting with another couple about wedding invitations and her dress. Lucky Brand woman is squealing to another gal that she knows someone who knows someone who *actually has a Derek Lam purse!* And there's a woman in the floral print dress with empire waist and ruffled hem I saw in Anthropologie, and I know she paid $79.00 (unless they're having a sale). I've hit the jackpot. If I can just grit it out, force myself to come back a couple more times, and keep track of everything I see and hear, then flake it up a bit, I'll have everything I need to assemble the perfect cast of characters.

The woman in the chair across from me tugs at the back of her sandal, a Kenneth Cole T-strap, no less—*god, I'm in heaven!*— and smiles at me.

"So did you have fun?" she asks.

It must be obvious I'm the rookie, since everyone else is doing what she's doing—changing into street shoes—and I'm the only one with a free hand to pick my nose, if I wanted. I think of my haul of treasures.

"I did. Though I don't think I have it perfected, so I'll probably have to come again."

"Ah. Slow learner, then." Her hair is cocoa brown and thick and pulled back in a ponytail, and she has eyes that remind me of honey, with that translucent quality. I'm trying to remember if I danced with her; you'd think I'd remember eyes like that.

"I don't know if anyone mentioned this," she goes on, "but there's a bar across the street with a dance floor. A few of us are heading over there for drinks and to work on our moves. Feel free to join us."

I figure she must be joking, because it's such a preposterous notion, more dancing after the dance lesson, like now that you've stabbed yourself in the neck, do you want to chop your hand off? But her face is so open and honest, I can see it's no joke. I think about it: I could go and get more useful information, but if Fran comes along and says another word about her cats, or Rosie does one of her *vavooms!*, I might just strangle one of them, and they'd haul me off to jail, and that would blow my cover.

"Thanks," I say, making it clear I could go either way.

She packs her dance shoes in a gym bag and stands. She's taller than I would've imagined, sitting there. I stand too.

"Well, if you don't make it to the bar, I'll see you next time," she says pleasantly. She offers her hand. "I'm Marie."

I take her hand in mine, and shockingly, it's normal human skin, and we shake, and she stares at me, and I realize the reason she's staring at me is that instead of giving her my name, which Miss Manners would advise you to do in such situations, I've allowed my jaw to drop.

"Oh, sorry," I say. "I'm, uh, Jason."

Thus do I make the acquaintance of Bradley Colson's sister.

The place we go to turns out to be one of those sports bars with a hundred TVs, all tuned in to *Monday Night Football*, but they do have a decent dance floor tucked in the back, and that's where we set up. They're not playing the type of music we heard in class—this is U2 and Donna Summer and something called Fall Out Boy—but word is you can still find the right beat in any of this, if you listen. Thus, "She Works Hard for the Money" and "I Still Haven't Found What I'm Looking For" are salsas. Who knew? Rosie did, and she's more than thrilled to demonstrate, along with cologne-happy Dave and his goatee.

I'm glad Bradley hasn't told me much about Marie, because this gives us a chance to have a real conversation, without my having to play stupid. Yes, I know she's a stylist and that she used to live in North Carolina, but when I find out she and Rosie went to high school together and are best friends, and Rosie is also a stylist, and Marie works in Rosie's shop, it's all news to me. (And gratifying news, since it means my hairstylist radar wasn't completely off-kilter when it blipped at Rosie.) For my part, I recycle the pharmaceutical rep line, since Steve and Jennifer are sitting right next to me and I more or less have to, but I don't embellish, don't give her the drug name, don't tell her I'm the number one salesman in my region or anything like that, since this isn't Katharine Longwell at Starbucks and I'm not interested in making her look like a fool.

We dance and drink and talk about topics such as cooking (Marie loves to cook), desserts (Rosie loves to eat), and weddings (Steve and Jennifer's favorite topic), but we also get around to other things, like our worst first dates (Dave had a girl throw up into the glove box of his Camaro), or if a celebrity has ever had a baby and named it something like John or Helen instead of Suri or Apple or Papaya, or whether it's actually more ballsy to be under thirty and female and *not* have a tattoo, especially in the small of your back (Rosie and "I-used-to-have-a-lisp-but-now-I'm-a-speech-pathologist" Gina have them; Jennifer and Marie, no). I also find out that Fran (who didn't come) is the mother hen of the group and a maven for crafts, so if she likes me, she'll be bringing me a gift one of these days.

It's all fun and entertaining and light, and even Jason manages to get caught up in the spirit and say things that aren't sharp or pointed or condescending, which means Mitch is content to observe, soak in useful information for the novel, and relax. Only once does he jump into the fray, for the sole purpose of soliciting information — in other words, to be a spoilsport — but it leads to the most interesting exchange of the evening.

We're talking about hair, more specifically haircuts, and Mitch perks up.

"Do men come into your salon?" he asks Marie.

"All the time."

"And what about the charge: is it the same for men and women?" I go to one of those chain places where it's the same price for everyone — twelve bucks — but the characters in my book would never set foot in such a place. I need to get my facts straight.

"Usually," she says. "But the price isn't based on gender. It's based on hair length, and the time it takes to cut and style it."

"So if I come in, you'd charge me less than him." I nod to a guy with a ponytail, who, truth be told, probably isn't the sort who'd go to a salon in the first place.

"Right. But if you came in, I probably wouldn't cut yours."

"Oh? Why's that?"

"You don't need it."

I lean on my elbow. "Wait, so you're telling me you'd pass up a sale? Aren't you afraid you'd tick me off?"

She shrugs. "I'd try to be nice about it and tell you your hair's short enough. Maybe we could do a little styling, add some product, but not a cut."

I take the hard line. "Not good enough. I've come for a haircut, I've decided it's got to go. Here's my cash, now cut my hair."

She traces a line of condensation on the side of her glass with her French-manicured nails, which I take for stalling. "Then I guess I'd have to tell you the real reason." She clears her throat. "I'd say, 'Customer Jason, you have a handsome face with very strong features. Short hair makes them jump out a little. With longer hair you get a little movement, and it would make you look even more handsome.'" She goes back to fingering her glass. "That's what I'd say."

"To 'Customer Jason.'"

"To 'Customer Jason.'"

She buries her head in her drink and takes a long sip, but I think she's beginning to blush. As, I think, am I.

We leave around eleven and troop back across the street to the studio parking lot. There's a bit of an awkward moment when I tell them I took the bus, since I don't have a car, then I realize my gaffe—a pharmaceutical rep without a car?—and quickly explain that I don't have a car *tonight* because I don't like to drive when I don't have to, since I drive so much for my job. Get it? They seem to.

At home I make a transcript of the evening, write down what people said and wore and looked like, and when I see it on paper, the whole lot of them—Jason included—seems like a gaggle of idiots. Like the characters I created last week. But it didn't seem so kooky when I was there. I...*enjoyed* it. Which leads me to believe that possibly, *maybe*, my characters and I got off on the wrong foot when they showed up in their Versace and Max Mara and Chloé, and started bragging about their brooches and bubble skirts and booty calls, and I told them all to go to hell (or Barneys). Perhaps I played Mr. Darcy to their Elizabeth Bennet, and we all rushed to hasty judgment. Now, I believe, we all have a better understanding of each other. We may not read the same books or watch the same movies or apply the same brand of age-defying anti-wrinkle serum, but we're still human. We all bleed if you cut us.

Rosie's the ringleader of the group, the engine that makes it go. If the studio and its inhabitants were a half-hour sitcom, it'd be called *RosieTown* and she'd be the star: Rosie learns to surf; Rosie meets the Prez; Rosie wears a puffy shirt. But the one I keep coming back to is Marie. She's quieter, less flashy, cute in an Anne Hathaway-ish sort of way—I can say that about Bradley's sister, right?—but she's no pushover, the kind who'd tell you that you had a piece of spinach caught between your teeth, not to embarrass you or make you feel stupid, but so you wouldn't feel stupid later when you got home and looked in the mirror and realized it had been there all night. I get the feeling if she took a little time and did herself up, she could be the sort who just might catch your eye. That is, if you're the type of gent who doesn't mind having a beauty school graduate hanging on your arm.

And maybe it's this combination of factors—reflecting fondly on my stint in *RosieTown*, thinking about Marie, not being such a bully toward my previously mannequin-like characters—that leads to a breakthrough with the writing. (This, and an excellent *Oprah* episode with Mr. *He's Just Not That into You* himself, Greg Behrendt.) I spend Tuesday and Wednesday and Thursday going at it, and with such fervor that I catch myself glancing at the clock, startled by how much time has passed, and frightened that I've forgotten someone else at the airport. But I haven't. In fact, I have no obligations except for my comp class on Wednesday, which I skate through as fast as I can, and I've begged off doing anything with Bradley, so that by Thursday evening I'm feeling good. I have a plot: a down-and-out second-tier model (pajamas and jeans for Target and K-Mart—the Marie type) gets discovered by a bigwig, then—*poof*—instant makeover, and she's off to Monte Carlo with her wacky group of friends, led by a Rosie-type, where it's fast cars and yachts and all sorts of superhunks and paparazzi chasing after her, and tons of exotic food and sex. I have an outline: sixty pages and counting, complete with beginning, middle, and end, and ideas for dozens of scenes. And I have another date at the studio. And that's where I'm getting ready to go when the phone rings. It's Scott. He's shaken and out of breath.

"Dad had a heart attack."

"*What?* When?"

"This afternoon. He was out at the course and having chest pains and blacking out and they called the ambulance and got him to the hospital. He just got out of surgery. Emergency bypass."

"And…?"

"It went fine, thank god, as far as they can tell. But he's still unconscious and in intensive care. I'm on my way there now."

I don't say anything.

"Mitch, are you there?"

"I'm here."

"Do you want to know what hospital?"

"Uh, sure."

"Jesus. You're not even coming, are you?"

"You said he was in intensive care. He's unconscious. What can I do?"

"You can come out. You can give some support to Leah and the kids. He might even come around tonight." His voice is much louder than it needs to be.

"What, and see my face hovering over his sickbed? You want him to have another heart attack?"

There's sputtering on the other end, just a collection of sounds and half words, and none of it English, till he finds what he wants to say. "You are fucking unbelievable."

My brother doesn't often curse; this one got him.

"You handle it your way, I'll handle it mine," I tell him.

But I do get the name of the hospital, just to humor him.

CHAPTER EIGHT

The crowd at the studio hasn't changed from Monday night, but I have. I'm official now, legit, one of the group. I've been in the trenches with these people, sweating, swiveling my hips, counting it off—quick/quick/s-l-o-w, quick/quick/s-l-o-w—distributing my weight on the syncopated beat, providing a lead that's not too rigid, not too noodly, and minding all the other nuances of chin placement and shoulder squareness and toe pointing, and they see it and appreciate it. Plus, I've harmonized portions of "Come on Eileen" into a beer bottle microphone with them. I'm in.

We review the basics from Monday night, and they all come back with surprising ease, then we move on to more complicated steps and holds and turns. I get these, too, at least the stepping and holding part, but there's a problem with the new turns; they're sharper, quicker, and my rubber-soled tennis shoes keep sticking to the floor when I try to spin or pivot. Not only does this have a tendency to throw my timing off (timing, for all you non-dancers out there, is what dancing's all about: even if you know nothing about dance, you can still look at a guy and say, "This guy's got it," or "What a clown"), but it also creates a high-pitched squealing noise that would be commendable at varsity basketball practice ("Way to hustle, son"), but here gets me looks. I do my best to smile and shrug, but I can tell I'm in danger of earning a nickname like Squeaky or Screech or Chirpy.

After the lesson, when everyone else is sitting on chairs changing their shoes and I'm sitting on a chair not changing my shoes, Marie addresses the problem straight on.

"If you're going to stay with this, you need a pair of these." She holds up her shoes. "You'll spin and turn a whole lot better, plus no racket."

To my eye, they're black leather sneakers. Mine are off-white. "What's so different about them?" I'm not in the business of spending money just to spend it.

She tosses me one. "Turn it over."

I do. The sole is soft and fuzzy, almost like suede.

"That's why we don't wear them into class. They'd get chewed up on the pavement."

Ah, so that little foo-foo habit of changing their shoes that was starting to get on my nerves—*Look, I'm a dancer! I'm changing my shoes!*—actually has a reason.

"Just make sure you get practice shoes, not performance shoes," she cautions. "They'll wear better and last longer. And watch out for the heel. You want flat soles."

"Get the ones that lace up with both Velcro and shoelaces," offers Gina, enunciating her *s* sounds with particular precision. "You can control the tightness better. And they're unisex, so don't be embarrassed about that."

"That's what I have," Steve says brightly, without a hint of embarrassment.

"And buy them to fit you right now," Rosie chips in. "Maybe a half size small. The way you move out there—" and here she tries to give a little bump with her hip, even though she's sitting, so her chair skids a bit, "the leather will always stretch."

Graphic designer Vicky with red-framed glasses speaks up: "Showtime is a good brand. So is Supadance."

Dave: "Just stay away from Aztec. El cheap-os."

I feel like I should write all this down. "Where do I get them?"

Jennifer: "Adonis's catalogue."

Dave: "EBay." He looks around to make sure Adonis isn't listening. "Save yourself a few bucks."

I turn to Marie.

"If it were me," she says, "I'd probably just go to a store. That way you can try them on, make sure they fit the right way, especially for a first pair. There's a place not too far from here called Dance Loft. Do you know where Fratelli's Pizza is?"

"I'm afraid not," I say.

"Crafty Corner?" Fran inquires.

"I'm not so familiar with that either."

"What about Chesterfield Mall?" demands an incredulous Rosie.

Marie picks up on the "man overboard" look that must be plastered to my face. "I'll tell you what," she says. "I could meet you here on Saturday, we could drive over together. That is, if you think you need the help."

"I'd *love* the help."

We swap cell phone numbers and it's settled: I have my first ever shoe-shopping date. At least, Jason does.

I call the hospital when I get home, since I figure I owe my father at least that much. They tell me he isn't taking calls, but he is resting comfortably in intensive care. Do I want to speak to someone in the family? No thanks. I don't bother telling them I *am* family.

The writing goes well again that night, and the next morning and afternoon and night, and I'm beginning to think I've punched a winning ticket with this Cinderella theme. (But of course I have: *Cinderella* is the archetypal chick-lit story — down-and-out girl gets extreme makeover, glitzy gown, fancy shoes, handsome guy. No mention of bedding her Prince Charming, but we all know that comes standard with happily ever after.) My method is to create a scene — at the coffeehouse, jewelry shop, fitting room — and then ask myself what Rosie or Jennifer or Gina or Marie or any of them would do, based on what I've gotten to know about them. And it's not like I'm stealing their lines, since I've yet to hear any of them say, "I wonder if I should get that Brazilian wax job or just a bikini bottom with more coverage"; it's just that getting to know them has allowed me to crawl into their heads and move around and see the world through their eyes, and the view isn't entirely repulsive. In fact, everyone's been so friendly and helpful that I already feel guilty for jerking them around with the whole Jason bit. Can I get a do-over on that, maybe slip the truth in there *discreetly* over drinks ("Speaking of Singapore Slings, my name's really Mitch, not Jason, and I don't rep drugs, I teach, but I like mine with a dash of grenadine")?

I haven't seen much of Bradley, which is a good thing, at least for now, because it means I don't have to explain what I've been up to on Monday and Thursday nights, or why the writing is suddenly going so much better, or do I know some strange guy who's been chatting up his sister at the studio. But in a way I wish he were around, in the sense that I'd like to pinch some information out of him, namely: did he ever think about setting me up with Marie? I think I know the answer: Hell no. That's because she's been living in North Carolina for the last few years and I've been in St. Louis, and even though she's been back for five months, I've been living with Hannah the entire time, except the last week. But even so, I still don't think he'd do it, because he'd just assume she wasn't my type, what with the dancing and hairstyling and Kenneth Cole T-straps. That's the thing about Bradley: he can be so narrow-minded. Though sometimes, I guess, so can I.

CHAPTER NINE

Marie and I meet around noon at the studio parking lot. I was afraid Rosie might show up, not in person, but in the form of Marie wearing big hair and too much makeup and a matching earring and bangle set for the big day out. But she looks the same as always—fresh, natural, with flared jeans and flip-flops and a gauzy white top, maybe even a spritz of Calvin Klein's euphoria and some lip gloss in sheer peach (Bare Escentuals? MAC?). She's driving a convertible VW bug, top down, and since I've shown up again without my car (today's excuse: it's at the shop), she drives.

Dance Loft is one of those mom-and-pop stores, though I'm guessing pop didn't want to have much to do with it since I'm the only guy around. The signs are homemade—"Women's Tops," "Men's Shirts," "Women's Skirts," "Men's Ball Hugging Pants with Lots of Sheen" (at least, that's the sign I would have printed up)—as are the price tags. There are a fair number of sparkly and glittery items, as you might expect, but also a few pieces you could almost wear out in public, for a nice occasion, maybe dinner at Cardwell's. One skirt, a little black one hanging right there on an end cap, catches my eye. Marie sees it too.

"You like that?" she asks.

"Not my size. And my legs are a little too hairy to pull it off. But on the right person, I'm sure it would look great."

She slips it off the rack and holds it up to her waist. Slit and all, it reminds me of something Molly might wear — to class. "Shows a lot of leg, doesn't it?"

"Denim, actually," I say, since that's all I see of her below the hemline.

She glances at herself in the mirror, adjusts the skirt this way and that, and I'm tempted to tell her to try it on, just for fun, since I wouldn't mind seeing just how much non-denim leg it covers, or doesn't. But I don't, since that would be a little self-serving. In the end, she seems embarrassed about the whole thing and puts it back on the rack.

The shoes turn out to be more expensive than I imagined. I've paid this much for basketball shoes, but that was for real shoes. If I were alone, I might just walk out of the store, give it more thought, see if I'm a hundred percent — and a hundred dollars — committed to this whole dancing gig. But I don't want to seem like a cheapskate, and Marie has assured me a dozen times that the right shoes make a huge difference, and the saleslady has promised that if I don't like them or they don't work out, for any reason, I can bring them back, so I pick up a pair of size eleven unisex Urban Trainers in black with crisscross Velcro fasteners.

"How about lunch?" I say, when we get outside. "I'd like to pay you back, for your time."

"Don't worry about it. This was fun." In the sunlight, her top is a little sheer, and without even trying, I catch a glimpse of lace.

"I'm doing this for me, Marie. I'm hungry. Shopping for dance shoes always takes it out of me. How about that pizza place you mentioned?

"Fratelli's?"

"Yeah. Can you take me?"

She gives me a look like I'm trying to con her. "I'll take you. Just don't try to make me eat anything." She tugs at her waistband. "Still working on those last five pounds."

But of course, we get there, and the place smells great, and maybe she's a little hungry after all, so we both take a look at the menu and agree on a large Hawaiian pizza, thin crust, which should be just about right for two, one of whom only plans to nibble. Right. So that's what we order, plus two root beers.

"Do you always have Saturdays off?" I ask.

She shakes her head. "Every other one, usually. Unless it's December or prom season or something like Mother's Day weekend or Valentine's Day. Then the place gets crazy busy. Today, since it's none of those, I'm free. Though I do have an appointment at three."

"On your day off? That's odd."

"It's a bit of a special circumstance. I have a customer who's been through a nasty divorce and she's been trying to date, but she keeps getting guys who drink too much or are too much into their money or cars or themselves. She finally met a guy she likes, and they've talked a couple times on the phone, but they both have kids and getting their schedules to coordinate is tough. Tonight's the first night they're going out, just the two of them. A jazz club, which she told him she likes, so she thinks it's a good sign. She's a little nervous, so I told her to come in and we'd give her a style for the night."

"Wow. And you got all that info just by cutting her hair?"

"People sit in those chairs for a while. They talk."

"And you like hearing all that?"

"I don't like hearing that people have problems. But I like people, so if they trust me enough to talk, I listen."

The waitress brings out our root beers and sets them on the table.

"So does that have anything to do with why you got into hairstyling in the first place?" I ask. "The therapy part?"

She fiddles with her straw wrapper. "Maybe a little. I mean, I used to do all my friends' hair in high school, and we'd talk about our boyfriends or parents or whatever, and I got a kick out of that. But I think the real reason is that I figured out pretty early I wasn't cut out for college, and I'd have to make a living somehow, and if I had to spend the rest of my life getting up in the morning and doing something, it might as well be something I enjoyed. For me, that was cutting hair."

I suppose a bank robber would also say he enjoys getting up and doing his job, so I'm not sure that qualifies as the number one reason to choose a career. But whatever floats your boat, I guess. "Hey, listen, Marie. Can I ask you something that may sound a little rude or insulting, but I don't mean it to?"

"Sure you do, at least a little. Otherwise you wouldn't put it that way." She manages to say it without sounding sour. "But go ahead."

She's right, of course. That's why we use those disclaimers, "I don't mean to sound rude or judgmental or racist or selfish or coldhearted," so we can go ahead and say something rude or judgmental or racist or selfish or coldhearted. Now I feel a little sheepish. "Are you sure?"

She nods. "I'm sure."

"Okay. People spend money on haircuts and mousses and gels and shampoos and blow dryers and flat irons and color treatments, and if you added it all up, worldwide, it has to be in the billions every year. Agree?"

"Agree."

"So here's my question: Isn't it just *hair*?"

She takes a long moment to mull it over, and I can tell she's giving it real thought, the way she keeps narrowing her eyes and playing with her lower lip and looking like she's about to speak, then stopping, then cycling through the whole routine again.

"The quick answer or the philosophical one?" she finally says.

"Quick." Then, to distance myself from her brother, "I hate philosophy."

"Then, yep, it's just hair. An outgrowth of dead cells from follicles in the dermis, composed primarily of keratin, with a certain color, texture, thickness. And that's pretty much all it is."

"Good. Now the philosophical one."

She gives me a mock-stern look. "And you won't laugh?"

"We'll see."

She picks up on my tone immediately. "Fine. Forget it."

"Oh, go on already. I won't even crack a smile." Which, ironically, makes us both smile.

"All right, then," she says, pushing her root beer a little to the side. "Everybody says it's what's on the inside that matters. And it's true. That's where you want to have it together and be kind and patient and have all those good qualities. But we also have these bodies and faces, for better or worse, and these are *us*, too. There's nothing wrong with taking a little pride in the way you present yourself to the world, coming up with the best possible version of you. And hair makes a difference in how we look. Certain lines and curves and colors and styles flatter a certain nose or eye color or mouth or chin. That's what we study in cosmetology school, how to assess an appearance, see what might look better, bring out what's most attractive or appealing or natural. Because the eye knows what it likes when it sees it."

"Sure it does. Just like with the ancient Greeks."

"Huh?"

"I mean, not that I read much, or know much about the ancient Greeks, other than they were Greek and lived in Greece." *Shit.* "But I think I heard they used to build some of their temples based on certain geometric proportions that tended to please the eye. Plus, some of their columns tapered as they got higher, because it made them more aesthetically pleasing from the ground." I fear I'm confusing her. "Uh, *prettier,* like you were saying."

"Yeah, thanks. I got it. And the other thing about hair is that it has this kind of symbolic quality. For instance, say you just got a new job, or lost your boyfriend, or started a diet, and you want something to reflect a goodbye to the old you and hello to the new you. Most people can't just go out and buy a new car or house or have plastic surgery. But what you can do is change your hair. Go shorter or more styled or change a color. And even though it's just hair, something about it taps into a deeper place inside and makes you feel like a whole new person and gives you confidence and a different attitude."

She might be on to something with this last part, hair tapping into a deeper place. There's hair as strength — Samson of Samson and Delilah; hair as beauty — Botticelli's *The Birth of Venus;* hair as a cable to heaven — the dreadlocks of Rastafarians; hair as sign of obedience — the monk's tonsure or the military's crew cut; hair as ladder — Rapunzel. We have movies and plays and TV shows about hair: *Hair, Shampoo, Hairspray, Barbershop, Friends* (isn't that what that show was about?). We even have hair as embodiment of the crudest tendencies of human nature: the mullet.

I look at her sitting there, her own hair back in a loose ponytail draped over her shoulder, sunglasses pushed on top, and I can see the resemblance to Bradley. Not so much in the looks but in the things she says. Or rather, the way she says them. Like she . . . *believes* in them.

"I'm curious, Marie. With all the thought you put into this, your clients must've loved you. Why'd you leave North Carolina?"

She stirs up the ice in her glass. "Because Rosie opened her shop and we made a promise to each other that whoever opened a shop first, the other would come and help out. She beat me to it."

I sit up straighter. "Wait. She opens a shop, so you pack it all up and move?"

"Not the day I got the call. But a few months later."

"And you made this promise when you were how old?"

"Eighteen."

Eighteen? What kind of person makes a teenage promise like that and keeps it almost ten years later? For a class clown, like Rosie. Worse, what kind of person holds her to it?

"I'm surprised she didn't let you out of it."

"She offered. I wouldn't let her."

"But . . . but what if you'd been *married*, or had a kid in school, or had a place you didn't want to leave?"

She shrugs. "I don't know. That wasn't how it was, so I don't give it much thought. But I guess things would've managed to work out okay. They always do."

Oh boy oh boy. *Here* we go. That's the kind of harebrain lamebrain mushbrain nobrain two-bit idiotic worthless-piece-of-crap comment that people always make, and it always drives me crazy. As if the universe has nothing better to do than tend to comets and asteroids and black holes and antimatter and the level of CO_2 in the atmosphere and create a weather pattern or two and keep the planets orbiting the sun, but oh, let's make sure everything comes up roses for Susie Smith in her crappy little life. Things don't just work out; *people* make them work out, with planning and finagling and haggling and sheer grit and effort. And then there's no guarantee. But for whatever reason, today, sitting here with Marie, I can't seem to muster up my usual ten-gallon hat load of moral indignation to give her the tongue-lashing she deserves. Maybe I'm just too hungry.

"Anyway, I don't think it's a big deal," she says. "I'm just another pair of scissors in her shop. It's not like I'm saving lives or anything, like you are."

"Pardon?"

"With the drugs you rep."

"Oh, right. No, of course not. Those drugs certainly help people out. But I really can't take too much of the credit, since, you know, I didn't actually invent them. And speaking of inventions, look what's coming our way. Pizza!"

It's a stroke of masterful timing, and allows me to steer the conversation to pizza, then the studio, then dance, and keep it far away from pharmaceutical drugs and saving lives, and *Jason*, so that in this instance, on this one occasion, for this one time only, I'm willing to acknowledge that maybe every once in a while the universe does manage to turn away from more important matters—management of the Andromeda galaxy, let's say—and toss us measly humans a freebie.

Marie has done a kindness for me—taking me shoe shopping—and when I get back to the apartment, I pay it forward to the characters in my novel. Each time I'm tempted to put a knife in someone's back, have her look silly or stupid or say something half-baked about a Kate Spade purse that makes her sound like a shopaholic ditz, I give her a different line, make her not so foolish, even make her seem sensible and bright. It's the only outlet I have right now for my charity. That, and my mom. I go over there and cut the grass, my usual job, but this time I skim the pool, which is above and beyond.

After I've taken a dip of my own, to cool down, and I'm lounging in back with a beer, she pulls up into the shade of the back drive. She sees me and I give her a small wave, but she just sits there in the car, like she's in no big hurry to see me or anyone else. Maybe I'm wrong, though, and it's just a good song on the radio. Finally she gets out.

"I thought you'd be heading out about now with the Saturday Night Club," I say as she crosses the patio. My mom teaches at a college prep school, and she and a few colleagues usually hit the symphony or a gallery opening or movie at the Tivoli on Saturday nights.

"I canceled," she says, her tone clipped. "I'm not much in the mood." She pulls out the chair across from me, roughly, the metal legs scraping on the concrete.

"You okay?" I ask.

She ignores me. "Scott called this morning. He wanted me to know about your father. That's where I was. At the hospital."

My instinct is to ask, "What happened?" until I realize I know what happened. He had a heart attack. He had surgery. It's the first time I've given him any thought since Thursday night. Of course, that's the last thing I can tell my mom. For years now, I've played this little game with her called "Big Fat Lies": I lie to her that my dad and I are good, we're fine, we're great, heck, sometimes we even go out for drinks, and she believes me. (Why wouldn't she?) She feels guilty enough about the divorce as it is, so this is my way of protecting her from worse.

"And how is he, *today?*" I say it like I've been keeping up.

She looks at me hard, almost a glare. "So you're concerned, are you?"

I don't like this. "Sure. Yeah. Why wouldn't I—"

She angrily waves me off. "Oh, Jesus, Mitch. Cut the act. He asked about you, wanted to know what you've been up to. Since the two of you haven't talked in months. *Months.* Why didn't you tell me things had gotten to this point?"

I shrug. "I figured I'd deal with it. And I knew if I told you, you'd be upset and try to do something."

She rubs at her temples and takes a moment to recollect her thoughts. I wish she'd just drop it. "How long has this been going on?"

"A while. Forever. Look, who cares? We're both done with it. He has his life and I have mine, and that's how it is. It's fine."

"It's not *fine*, Mitch. It's horrible." She's on the verge of tears, she's so worked up. "Your father had a heart attack. He almost died." Her eyes bore into me. "For god's sake, don't you care?"

Christ. "Yes, Mom, I *do* care. Okay? I care. I care because if he lets go, I'll have to go out and buy a new suit for the funeral."

I feel like I've been goaded into saying it, like she got together with Scott and the two of them came up with a plan to push and pile on the guilt and try to get me to do something stupid. Well, it worked. They got me. I snapped. And if she wants to keep staring at me till her face freezes like that—shocked and appalled—let her.

Fuck.

"Look, Mom, I'm sorry. I shouldn't have said that. But he's not exactly my favorite person in the world, for obvious reasons." What is it with these people? Doesn't anyone get this? "Besides, I thought you'd be on my side, especially after what he did to you."

She narrows her eyes. "What he did to me?"

"Yeah, Mom, what he did to you. Oh, come on, if we're spilling our guts here, let's spill them all the way. I'm not ten anymore." But apparently she thinks I am, because her mouth refuses to work. "Fine. Then I'll say it. He was screwing around and you kicked him out. He had an affair. There. See how easy that was?"

The blood instantly drains from her face, till it's as white as her cotton blouse.

"That's what you've thought all these years?"

"What do you think?"

"Oh, god," she whispers. "Then I am to blame for so much." Her eyes dart around like they're searching for the safety of high ground, but there is none.

"Mitch, I don't even know how to say this. Your father didn't have an affair. *I* did."

Remember that scene in *The Matrix* where Keanu Reeves is on the rooftop and the bad guys are blasting away, and the motion gets super slow, and Neo bends his body back at an impossible angle, and the bullets leave liquid tracks as they float harmlessly by? That's me right now. My mother's words are coming at me like those bullets—"Your father didn't have an affair. *I did I did I did I did*"—and I'm doing everything I can to give them the slip, contorting my body as much as I can, but I don't have Neo's training or agility or special effects budget, and they plaster me square in the chest. I can't breathe.

"When?" I eventually manage to get out.

She looks stricken, panicked, pale. "After Emily died. Your father and I were going through a miserable time. We were barely speaking to each other. I found someone I could talk to, someone who cared . . . and it happened."

Jesus. My mom had an affair. "And Dad found out?"

"No." She's nasally now, sniveling. "I told him. I threw it all in his face. I wanted to punish him for not being there in the way I needed. I wanted to give him a reason to be done with me, with us, and go away. But he wouldn't."

No. Not then. Not for five more years. "But I don't understand. Then why did he leave when he did?"

She wipes her tears away with the back of her hand. "I don't know, Mitch. I don't know. He just said he needed to go." And I believe her, that she doesn't know, since she wouldn't hold anything back now, not after the damage misunderstandings and half-truths have caused all of us to this point.

A light breeze stirs through the trees, sending some leaves skittering into the pool, disturbing the surface of the pristine water.

"I'm so sorry, Mitch," she says, and that's the last time either one of us speaks, for a long time.

You've probably seen those newscasts where somebody does something bad and they interview the neighbors and coworkers, and they all say something like, "He seemed like such a nice guy"; "He's the last person I would've expected"; "I never saw it coming." And I always think: You people are morons. You saw him every day. You ate lunch with him. Your kids cut his grass. And you had no idea he had a meth lab in his basement and a hit squad of mafia hookers? Nothing odd about anything he said? Not even a goofy smile or weird sense of humor? *Please.*

That's what I'm playing out in my mind the whole way home. I've known my mother for twenty-eight years. For twenty-three of those, while she was doing all those mom things—reading bedtime stories, checking my homework, putting on my Band-Aids, taking my temperature, cooking my pork chops, picking out my corsages—she's been hiding the secret she had an affair. And I never got a whiff of it. And what about my dad and his part in this, and how it all sailed over my head? *Shit.* My entire universe was swimming with liars and connivers and secret-keepers, and I never had a freaking clue. Who looks like the moron now?

I go to see him Sunday afternoon, after basketball, and it's awkward for all the obvious reasons. I haven't seen him in months. I haven't talked to him since his heart attack. I didn't call before I came over. He's my father.

"How are you feeling?" I ask. I'm sitting in a chair across from his bed.

"Okay," he says in a raspy voice.

My father has a bit of a Martin Scorsese look—the hair, the bushy eyebrows, even the glasses—but right now his skin is puffy and jaundiced, and he has enormous bags under his eyes, so maybe it's the way Scorsese would look if he were on his deathbed.

"How long are they planning to keep you?"

"Another few days. They want me up and out of here as soon as possible. I'll be happy to oblige."

He tries to shift his position but pulls up short, wincing, and Leah, who's standing right by his bed, helps him scoot to the side. She's heavier than the last time I saw her, and maybe a bit more gray, but for the most part looks the same. The kids do not. Nathan has feet nearly the size of mine and that croaky on-the-cusp-of-puberty voice, and Jessica is walking now, and talking, and no longer uses a pacifier, and is nine.

"One of the joys of turning sixty, I guess," he sums it up.

"That's right. Happy belated birthday."

"I'll take it, since I'm still around to hear it."

"And what's the prognosis? You'll be okay?"

He shrugs. "The heart attack did some damage. But they fixed what they could. Now I just have to be careful with my diet and get some exercise." He pats Leah's hand as if it's something they've discussed before and he's finally seen the light and is ready to get with the program.

The kids are watching one of those funniest home video shows on TV, caught up in that world. It's odd to be in the same room as them, knowing they're such strangers to me even though we share the same last name and half our DNA.

"Your mom was here yesterday," he says. "She said you're waiting to hear back on your book."

"I heard. They rejected it." I blurt it all out without thinking. "But if you talk to her anytime soon, don't tell her. She doesn't know."

It's a strange moment for us, my sharing a secret like that with him, both of us knowing I'm keeping it from my mom. But I guess I can trust him, since he's had experience in the keeping big secrets hush-hush department.

There really isn't much more to talk about, since I don't want to ask him if he likes the food, or the color of the walls, or how his par-three golf course is running without him. This is probably enough of a reunion for one day, so I get off my chair.

"I just wanted to come by and say hi." I pick at the belt loop of my shorts. "So I guess I'll talk to you later."

"Thanks for coming, Mitch," he says. "I mean that."

For an instant he gives me a closer look, and I'm certain he can see inside my head and all the questions burning a hole in my brain: Why did you stay? Why did you leave? How did we come to this? But then I realize it's not that he suddenly gets me any better; I just might be starting to see him through different eyes.

My mom calls in the afternoon to apologize again and make sure I'm okay and ask me if there's anything else she can explain. I tell her not to worry about it. I'm fine. I understand. I get it. She doesn't need to keep beating herself up over it. Then my phone rings five minutes later and I think it's her, calling to beat herself up over it again. But it's not; it's Marie.

"Hey there," I say, flushed with panic, afraid I'm on speaker phone and Bradley is standing right next to me. Only my cell doesn't have speakerphone and Bradley is at Skyler's.

"I hope this is okay, just calling you up out of the blue."

"Yeah, absolutely. Call anytime. So what's up?"

"Actually, I was thinking about your dance shoes. I forgot to tell you yesterday that it'd probably be a good idea to break them in before tomorrow night. Take it from a woman, a new pair of shoes can kill."

I'd like to ask her how, exactly, they can kill, especially a pair of Betsey Johnson Aries bronze peep-toe platforms, since that's what my heroine just bought. I refrain. Instead I ask a better question. "What's the best way to break them in?" Duh. How about put them on and wear them around the apartment?

"Well, you may just want to put them on and wear them around your place. Do some light dancing. In fact..." she seems to be thinking on the fly, "if you want to, we could meet up tomorrow before the lesson, go over some moves from last week, get you used to the feel."

"Yeah, I'd like that. What time?"

"Say... seven?"

I run the bus schedule through my head, for the trip that way, and I think I've got enough of a grip on it to know it'll work. "Sounds great."

And then, because Bradley's not around and not going to be, I stroll to my bedroom, lace up my new shoes, and salsa a good part of the afternoon away.

CHAPTER TEN

My comp class on Monday is normal, just like they've all been for the past week. For some reason, I figured after Molly visited my office and got my number, things would get weird. Like she'd sit in class and pull out her black book and thumb through it, pretend to dial a phone, chat with me, mouth all sorts of distracting things. Instead, she wears her T-shirts and speaks her mind and gives me fits and does great work. We're in a bit of a rut, if you want the truth, but it could be worse.

I leave for the studio after dinner and, as it turns out, I do *not* have enough of a grip on the bus schedule running that way: I miss a connector and wind up there at 7:45, forty-five minutes late. But Marie shrugs it off and we still manage to find a corner of the floor not being used by the fox trot crowd. We work on the underarm turn and hammerlock, and I do feel the difference being in dance shoes. I'm more in contact with the floor, and the spins and turns flow more freely, and we have such a good connection during this warm-up time that once the real lesson starts, we stick together and don't change partners, which technically isn't forbidden—Steve and Jennifer do it—but draws the ire of the group in the form of boos and catcalls, especially from Rosie. Even Adonis seems to notice, and when the lesson is over, he calls us over, presumably to have us scrub the floors or write five hundred times on the blackboard, "We will learn to play with others." But that's not the reason at all. Instead, he tells us that he had his eye on us all evening, and we looked great and have a ton of potential, and he wants us to be in the Showcase in November.

"The what?" I ask.

"The Showcase. Basically it's a big dance party for all the students, but before the party starts, we have a few couples demonstrate certain dances. The two of you really have the salsa down, and I thought it'd be a great chance to show off your stuff."

"Wow," I say. "So this would be dancing in front of...people?"

"Just other students from the various classes. It's a friendly crowd. No judges, no rotten tomatoes, no trophies. I promise." He pauses. "Of course, you don't have to decide now."

Good. Because that's what I'll need: time. Which is what I'm sure Marie would like too.

"I'm in," she says.

What *is* it with this woman? No asking questions, no hedging, no wanting to look at things from a hundred different angles. No wonder she just picked up and moved from North Carolina.

I should just say *no*. I don't have the time. I'm teaching. I'm scribbling away at my chick-lit novel every opportunity I get. I haven't cracked a book for my dissertation in two weeks. I'll have to keep up this whole Clark Kent secret identity gig for so much longer. Besides, it's dancing.

"Fine. Yeah. Sure."

Marie is pleased, Adonis more so, and he says he'll do everything he can to help us work on a routine, including putting in extra time before or after lessons, whatever works with our schedules. This is exactly what I'll need, plenty of extra time, but I can see it also means more comings and goings at odd hours, more mishaps trying to figure out the bus schedule, more looking like a bumbling, irresponsible idiot when I show up late. I need a more reliable means of transportation than a fleet of Bi-State buses. In other words, I need a car.

I drove a beat-up Cutlass in high school and it got me where I needed to go: school, a few concerts, dates. I sold it when I went off to Wisconsin for college and did like everyone else in Madison—got a bike. I haven't owned a car since; my legs or bike wheels or the bus or MetroLink or a girlfriend's car or Bradley have always been just fine. But now I inhabit a different world: I'm a Showcase dancer.

I go to the lease lot Tuesday morning and tell the guy I sell pharmaceutical products and need a car for a while and what kind of car does he recommend. He shows me cars that are far too big and expensive, since, of course, he makes the mistake of assuming I actually do sell pharmaceutical products and make that kind of money, as opposed to being a PhD candidate/writer/teacher and making *that* kind of money. I look at the compacts, something that's fuel efficient, but those seem tiny, so I finally settle on one that isn't the kind of car I'd always dreamed about when I dreamed of getting a car, but it has four wheels and it'll do: a sandstone metallic Chevy Malibu.

We talk terms of the lease and I'm a little thrown, since I don't know how long I'll need it. At least till the Showcase, possibly longer, so I settle on a round number: three months. We do the insurance and paperwork, and I sign my name a hundred times and I write a check and he gives me the key, and just like that I'm pulling out of the lot, drumming my fingers on the steering wheel of my brand-new car.

I kick off Wednesday's class with a freewrite, and here's the way it works: a student brings in a prompt—a poem, a quote, a picture, anything to set their minds abuzz—then they all scribble away till I call "time." It's more a stream-of-consciousness sort of thing—no concerns about grammar or spelling or punctuation—and tends to jiggle the wires on the creative side of the brain, which is good for them. This morning, a pimply-faced kid named Patrick uses his iPod and docking station to play the Beatles' "Yesterday." It's a good choice, I think, since who can't come up with something after that melancholy melody and those lyrics? They get busy in their notebooks, then I stop them when three minutes are up.

"I like that song," pint-sized Jan says brightly, like she's found a new friend. "Who sings it?"

Now, I have to remember that these kids have been weaned on the likes of Baby Boy Da Prince and Ludacris and Insane Clown Posse, not acoustic ballads of the sixties by mop-topped Brits. Also, as their instructor, I am a font of equanimity, nonjudgment, and encouragement, and to say anything that casts me otherwise would be a mistake. However, with her peers, she's fair game.

"You gotta be kidding me," snorts Pete, with a blend of disbelief and disgust I find just right. "Ever hear of a freaking band called the Beatles?"

"Sure," pint-sized Jan says, trying to shrug it off. "Just not that song." But you can tell he's gotten under her skin, rattled her a bit, so she does what any female in the class would do backed into a similar corner: sends up a flare to Molly.

Molly heeds the call. "Hey, I agree with him. You probably should know that. Since I'm sure he knows everything about every other classic song from *forty years ago*. Like who did, say, 'The Ghetto.'"

Pete pretends to bite his nails, frightened kindergartener style, then elbows the guy next to him, like *Watch this*. He turns to Molly. "Sorry, didn't quite hear you. Were you talking about '*In* the Ghetto' by Elvis, or 'The Ghetto, Part 1' by Donny Hathaway?"

There's something of a gasp from the class, since this is the first time all semester that anyone, including their instructor, has been able to sting her. Even Molly looks a little dazed. But before she has a chance to gather her wits, get back on her feet, and kick his ass into tomorrow — this is Molly we're talking about: it's only a matter of time — I ask for volunteers to read their freewrite.

Patrick's hand shoots up immediately, which is a bad sign, since it means he brought the song in for the specific purpose of playing it, then talking about why he played it: in other words, he set us up. Unfortunately, he's the only volunteer, so I'm forced to give him the floor, which he uses to gloomily tell us that he's been playing the song nonstop, since yesterday all his troubles *did* seem so far away, but now it looks as though they're here to stay, and of course it's because of a girl: she cut him loose and he can't seem to get over it and at the moment he's stuck. A chorus of sympathetic "*Aws*" rains down from the girls, and I can see, musically speaking, that we're about to leave "Yesterday" behind and move on to the Bee Gees' "How Can You Mend a Broken Heart?" Jangly braceleted Donna is chomping at the bit.

"What's your favorite food?" she asks him.

"Pizza."

"Then eat it whenever you want. With extra cheese. It'll make you feel better."

Pam: "And ice cream. Eat a *ton* of ice cream. Ice cream helps you get over anything."

Estella: "Go shopping."

Tory: "Hang out with friends."

Cassandra: "Get a facial."

The guy Pete elbowed earlier sits up. "What?"

"Don't look at me like that. I read that Denzel gets one once a month. And no one better tell me that Denzel's not fine."

A guy named Lou starts to stir in the back. Lou wears a braided gold chain and sleeveless shirts that show off his muscles, and with his sleazy good looks you get the feeling Lou might know a thing or two about messy breakups, especially causing them.

"Look, Pat, all that eating and shopping and other crap may help you forget her for a while. But she left a hatchet in the back of your head, man, and every time you lie in bed, you're gonna feel it. You need to put yourself in a win-win situation. Get over her or make her want you back."

Lou has the attention of the entire class, and probably the entire universe, if they could hear him.

"How?" Patrick asks.

Lou considers this a long moment, like he's a trained professional with vast experience, and this stunt should not be tried at home. But he proceeds, with his voice lowered. "Go to where your ex hangs out, make sure all her friends are there, bring another girl. Be laughing, happy, but don't overdo it, almost like you're embarrassed she noticed. Then scram, let gravity take over. Her friends will close ranks around her, tell her she was right to dump you, that the girl you were with was nasty. But the more they do it and harsher they are, the more she'll get paranoid that they're just saying those things to try to protect her, since you looked happy, your date looked happy, and everyone knows it. She'll start to question herself, replay the whole relationship, ask herself if you were really that selfish or ugly or thoughtless or whatever the problem was. Maybe your stock goes up. At best, she gets in touch, says she'd like to work things out. At worst, you've saved a little face, proved to yourself life hasn't stopped, gone out with another girl."

"Just be sure she's hotter than your ex," Cal chimes in, who's either aware of the technique or a very quick study. "That'll really make her feel like she lost out."

I'm not sure if the hottie part was crucial to Jedi Master Lou's plan, but he doesn't object, so he must be okay with that.

All the students seem lost in their thoughts, imagining, I suppose, what it would be like to see an ex with another person, and the ex was happy, and the other person was hotter than you, and you and your friends and everyone else in the room knew it. Lou of the gold chain and muscle T-shirts could be on to something.

"So that's what that was all about?" growls Cassandra. "My ex bringing that floozy around, parading her up and down, acting like he's never been happier in his life. He was just trying to mess with my head?"

"Maybe," Lou says, poker-faced. Then he gives her an oily smile. "Or maybe he's never been happier in his life and he thought you might like to know."

Cassandra shows Lou a fist. All the guys try not to laugh.

Glad to see I'm opening up the lines of communication between the sexes.

Fran breezes into Thursday's lesson bearing gifts for me: scarf, hat, and a pair of gloves, all of which she's knitted herself. She wants me to be warm this winter. I let her know how much I appreciate it by putting everything on and dancing a few steps with her and singing "Let It Snow," which makes her laugh but makes everyone else ask what I've been drinking, since it's pushing ninety degrees outside, and the AC's not cranking too well inside, and I'm dancing in wool. Rosie of *RosieTown* seizes on the general theme of the remarks—dancing, warm weather, drinking (but not so much wool)—to suggest a group trip out to a winery in Augusta a week from Saturday night. Most of us say we're in.

After the lesson, Adonis works with Marie and me for an extra forty-five minutes. He's patient with both of us, attentive, and he points out that I have a tendency to round out my shoulders and don't finish my lines with my arms, though my hips move well; and it's just the right touch with the criticism, less about him showing off and being a know-it-all and more about helping me get better. Of course, it helps that Jason's the one who has to hear all this, not Mitch. I imagine it's somewhat like it was for Paul Hewson, when he was just a young lad, and he and his band got together to make some godawful racket in someone's garage, and the guitarist might get pissed off because Paul forgot a lyric and kick over the amplifier and bark out something uncharitable like, "Hey, Bono, you sound like bloody rubbish. Feelin' okay, mate?" and Paul could just smile and say, "I'm okay, Edge, I'm okay," and he *was* okay, because Bono had mucked up, not him.

When we finish for the evening, Marie and I head out to the parking lot together. I make a beeline straight to my car and lean against the trunk.

"I drove," I say.

"Hmm," she mumbles. And that's it. Of course, maybe I'm expecting too much, since as far as she knows, I've had this car long enough to change the oil a few times, have the tires rotated, replace a timing belt or two. Still, it seems flimsy.

"What do you think of this color?" I ask. "I'm thinking about getting it painted."

"Really? It looks nice to me."

"Yeah. You might be right. Sometimes I get a little bored with it, is all."

It's almost ten, but still warm and humid out. Music from the nine-o'clock waltz seeps through the windows.

"Any big plans for the weekend?" she asks.

"Nope. Not really." Cardinals game tomorrow night with your brother. "Birthday party tomorrow night for my aunt. It's a surprise," I add, unnecessarily. "You?"

"I'm off tomorrow night, then work Saturday."

"That's right. Last Saturday you had a free pass for shoe shopping."

"Good memory," she says, then realizes it was only last week, and I was with her, so it's not such a good memory on my part. She laughs a little awkwardly.

"So no plans for Saturday night?" I ask.

"No. Nothing. How about you?"

"Same. Nothing. Not that I know of. Things have a way of popping up, though. You know how it is."

"Yep. Sometimes they just come out of nowhere, don't they?"

"They sure do."

She tucks a piece of hair behind her ear and stares at my shoes. I kick at a clump of pebbles.

"Shoe shopping was fun, wasn't it?" I say.

"Yeah, that was fun. And lunch, too."

"Man, that pizza was great. I loved that pizza. Didn't you?"

"It was good pizza."

"I loved it. Oh, and I hope my question about hair wasn't rude."

"No, it was fine."

"So no hard feelings?"

"No. None. Really."

"Good."

She tucks another piece of hair behind her other ear and stares at my shoes again. I kick at more pebbles on the lot.

"Well, I guess I should be going," she says.

"Yep, me too. Enjoy the weekend."

"You too."

She starts to walk away.

"Hey Marie."

"Yeah?" she says, turning quickly.

"You know, uh...I feel like I keep doing the same thing with my hair. Wash, dry, comb. I was thinking maybe I should do something different, maybe get some gel or something to shake it up a bit. You have that stuff at your shop, right?"

"Tons."

"So maybe if I came in, you could help me pick something out."

She pulls out a card and walks it over. "Here's the address. Come by on Saturday and I'll help you out."

"Great. Thanks. Not that I know for sure I'll be coming, but in case I do, I'll look for you."

"Okay. Then maybe I'll see you there."

We get into our cars about the same time, as you might expect, but I let her back up first. Then, as she's getting ready to pull off the lot, she gives me one of those friendly little toots, and I toot right back, because she started it and it seems like the thing to do.

Bradley and I've been spending squat for quality time lately—rare comings and goings at the apartment, phone tag—so I'm looking forward to the ball game. We have an early dinner at Colchester's, then hop on MetroLink (he has no idea about my car, since I park it three blocks over), but I'm still wrapped up in my thoughts about my mom and dad and the affair, and I guess it shows because on the way down he asks why the look, and am I constipated. I don't want to tell him the truth, since I haven't even told Scott yet, and as much as he drives me crazy sometimes, he deserves to know first (if anyone does). So I just shrug and say, "It's nothing." Bradley, however, interprets "It's nothing" in a different way, more as "I'm lonely and desolate since Hannah dumped me," and assures me that now that I've issued my cry for help, he and Skyler will get right on it. As in find me a date. Fine. It could be a lot worse than having Bradley and Skyler track down my love connection. As for him and Skyler and their love connection, things are going well. Great. In fact...

"One of these days," he says giving me one of those ear-to-ear, not-even-trying-to-play-it-cool grins.

"One of these of these days what?"

But we both know what. Yep. *That.* On bended knee and something with carats.

Women of the world, this is the part where you're supposed to jump up from your sofa and scream at the top of your lungs: "But guys don't commit! They're commitment-phobes!" Right. Now, if you're done with that, I've got news: they can commit. It's easy. They do it all the time. They commit to jobs and insurance plans and IRAs and sports teams and cars and jogging routines and dogs and friends and children. And, yes, they even commit to women. Sure, there may be two guys in your state to whom this doesn't apply—and George Clooney—but the rest of us are like Bradley: when we meet someone we love and she loves us right back, we're in. We're good. We're committed. So if you have a guy, and you've been sexy and smart and funny and loyal and compassionate and honest, and he still won't commit—and he's not George Clooney—it's not because he can't trust his feelings, or he got burned by his last girlfriend, or he just needs space, or his mom wore pearls when he was a baby, or any of the other 101 bullshit reasons you see on TV or in movies or read about in magazines. There's a simple reason for it: he doesn't love you enough. Because if he did, he would. It's brutal, it's harsh, but it's true. So dump the bastard already.

The Cardinals win the game by five, and we leave in good spirits with forty-five thousand other people, and the only hiccup of the evening occurs as we are getting back on the train, when Bradley asks about my book.

"Which one?"

"The one with chick-lit woman. Katharine what's-her-name."

"Oh, that one. Hmm. Yeah, I guess I've done a little." Only seventy-five pages in two weeks. And a complete outline of all the scenes. And all the character sketches. "I'm still working it out." Which is true.

"Did you wind up going to those dance classes?"

Suddenly English is my second language. "Uh, dance classes?"

"Yeah, Mitch, dance classes. My sister, Adonis, you screaming at me when I brought it up..."

"Ah, those dance classes." Just tell him. Just get it all out there — the shoes, the Showcase, Jason — have a good laugh, come clean, *finally* — maybe ease some of that guilty conscience about stringing along everyone at the studio — "Jason" this, "Jason" that — not to mention keeping your best friend in the dark, even though he and Marie don't run in the same social circles and you could probably keep this up for the next two years, scot-free.

"Yep," I say. "I sure did."

He just stares at me. Kinda like I've smacked him. "And you didn't fucking tell me?"

Idiot. What are you doing? He could get pissed that you didn't tell him sooner, or that you're duping Marie now, and he might tell her, which would ruin everything. Then you'd never get the book done. Or get your money out of those shoes. "Only one time, though. And the wrong night, I guess. There were lots of old people doing the fox trot. Your sister's not seventy, is she?"

Now he looks disappointed. "And here I thought it would help."

"Don't blame yourself." I give him a clap on the back. "Actually, it wasn't a total loss. I did get some things I could use."

And since I'd rather end it on this kernel of truth, and a friendly pat on the back, and a silent promise to fess up *everything* soon...someday...before I die, that's when I zip it and lock it and toss the key to the other side of the tracks.

The address on the card Marie gave me says 42 Wilshire Boulevard, but it may as well say 42 Ickety Bickety Boo. I don't know this area. The salon could be in some strip mall sandwiched between a Dollar General and a Big Lots; it could be in the lobby of a Ritz. When I do finally find it, a little after three, it turns out to be near an open-air farmer's market, in one of those whitewashed stone buildings that shares the same sleepy street with an antique store, a florist, and an Italian bakery. I like it.

The first thing I notice when I step in the place is the smell. Roses. Of course, it's Rosie's in Bloom, so that makes sense. As does the color scheme: hardwood floors, but the walls are painted the shade of pink you'd find on the petals of a China rose, not too garish or flamboyant, but mild, pleasant. There's a fireplace on one wall, chairs—the waiting area, I assume—and trellises are stenciled on both sides of the hearth, with rosebushes creeping up. A little cottage-y for my tastes, but not a deal-breaker. The music is a good touch, though: old Motown. But no sign of Marie or Rosie, just a few other stylists and their customers, which worries me. Panics me, really. Maybe I'm in the wrong shop (who knew there was another Rosie's in Bloom?). Maybe they've left for the day. Maybe I should run.

"May I help you?" the young woman at the front desk asks. She's a petite brunette, and I realize I know her: it's Audrey Hepburn. She could have the most beautiful face I've ever seen not in a magazine or on a movie screen. Seeing Audrey Hepburn in Rosie's doesn't do much for my nerves.

"Uh, yes, please. I'm here to see Marie."

"Great. And you have an appointment with her?"

"Er, no. Actually I don't."

"A walk-in, then."

"Actually, not that either."

She narrows her delicately arched brows. "But she's expecting you."

"I think. Maybe."

Audrey gives me one of those patient smiles like she's going to start this all over. "Marie's in the back right now, and I'll be happy to tell her you're here. Your name, please?"

"My name. Right."

A couple of the stylists and their clients glance over, and I fear what they're seeing makes me look nothing like Mr. Suave, but a lot more like Mr. Creepy Stalker Guy.

"*Jason!*"

It's Rosie, calling out from the back of the salon, with Marie behind her. They've just stepped out from whatever they have back there—bathroom, break room, shopping mall?

Rosie makes an elaborate display of putting her hands on her hips. "Get over here and give me a hug." But apparently what she means is, "I'm coming over there to give you a hug," because she bounds toward me, her breasts bobbling up and down like mighty sea waves, and locks me up in a bear hug.

"Look at you, standing right here in my shop! The best-looking *salsero* in town!" She looks like she wants to pinch my cheeks, excited as she is. "Picture time!" she announces. She pulls a cell phone from her pocket and tosses it to the front counter woman. "Samantha, be a dear and snap us, please. Marie, scoot over here."

Marie joins us and gives me a smile, then the three of us huddle together. Rosie drapes both arms around me like she's giving me a kiss, and after the picture's taken, she plants the real thing on my cheek with a loud smack.

"So, you decided to come after all." She turns to Marie. "See, I told you he would." Marie starts to blush. "But enough with the chitchat. Time's a-wasting." She grabs my hand and starts pulling me back toward a station. "Let's fix you up."

"No, wait, that's not why I'm here."

"I know why you're here, handsome. And don't be afraid. Rosie will be *very* gentle."

I shoot Marie a look. "I thought you said I didn't need a haircut," I say in desperately low voice.

"It's not a haircut," Rosie chides. "We're just going to style you up a bit."

She brings me to one of the chairs, sits me down, and throws a poncho around my neck. Marie stands off to the side.

"First, look at your face. It's long. Not Droopy Dog long, but long. So you don't need any of that pouf on top." She pats my hair. "Makes your face look even longer. Second, we're going to let these sideburns grow out a bit. That'll give a little more definition on the jaw. Got it?"

"Uh, sure."

She mists me down with water, or whatever's in those bottles, and combs it all flat.

"Now, your hair is very thick. I'm going to thin it out, give it some texture, but I won't take off length."

I look at Marie. She nods.

It takes Rosie all of about two minutes to snip off a bit here, a bit there.

"Done. And now we just need a little product." She reaches for a jar on her shelf. "This is pomade. Ever used it?"

"No."

"Then pay attention. Dry your hair about three-quarters, then rub it in. Get it nice and messy, as so. Then use your fingers like a rake, pulling it forward. The product gives it a bit of a sheen, makes your hair sleeker, plus adds a little hold."

"Will it be stiff?" I ask. I have an image of being in a windstorm and the whole thing lifting in one piece, like Trump hair.

"No. Touch it."

I do. It's not hard at all.

She dusts me off with a brush and holds up a mirror so I can see my new look, front and back. "Well...?"

Overall it's not much different. But there's something about it that makes me look sharper, more GQ. I'd give myself a second look, I think. "I like it."

"Fan-tastic!" she says, whipping the poncho off. Then her face gets serious. "Forty-five dollars, you can pay Samantha up front."

I don't say a word.

"Ha! Gotcha!" She slaps my back and roars. "You thought I was serious, didn't you? I tell you, I crack myself up sometimes. No, this one's on the house, so that now you'll come back when you realize you can't live without a Rosie-do."

I get out of the chair and give my foot a shake, to get a clump of hair off my shoe.

"But I do need some of that styling stuff," I say. "The pomade."

"You sure do." She reaches for her container. "Take this one, I've got plenty."

"No, I want to buy it."

She shrugs. "Suit yourself, Moneybags. Samantha will get you a new one."

I reach into my pocket and pull out a five and try to slip it to her. "For a tip, at least."

"Oh, *pu-leeez*," she says, brandishing her scissors, threatening to cut Abe Lincoln in half. "You want to pay me back? Give me some dance time on Monday, instead of letting Marie hog you. That's what you can do for me."

"Deal," I say.

She does a little salsa step and points at me. "I'm holding you to that."

Marie and I go up to the counter, where Samantha rings me up, then Marie walks me to the front door.

"So, how's the day been?" I ask.

"Extremely busy, all morning and most of the afternoon." She's wearing a lace cami in lilac and ivory palazzo pants, her hair flat-ironed and brushing her collarbone. She always looks decent for lessons, but I've never seen her like this, so sophisticated, stylish, feminine. "We just slowed down about twenty minutes ago. So good timing on your part."

"And you get off soon?"

"Less than an hour. I have one more appointment." She tilts her head and fingers one of her hoop earrings. "Actually, Rosie and Samantha and I are planning to head out for a rush-hour movie, then off to dinner. I'm sure they wouldn't mind if you wanted to join us."

Absolutely, I'd love to join them. Spend some time with Audrey Hepburn and Rosie and this version of Marie. But my little outing here has already cost me time I'd planned to spend writing. "You know, as much as I'd like to, I think I'll have to pass..."

She gives me a coaxing look. "You sure?" The way she's standing in the light, her eye shadow brings out the tiniest flecks of green in her eyes.

Of course, maybe I could pick up some good tidbits for the book, in which case it wouldn't be pleasure at all, but work. "Well...maybe just for the movie."

"Great!" she says, her face brightening.

Their plan is to leave at four, so I have about forty-five minutes to kill. I tell her I'm just going to walk around, investigate the neighborhood. I lean into the door with my elbow and push it open.

"Oh, and Jason?" Her gaze doesn't quite meet mine, then she nudges it up a bit. "Rosie did a good job with your hair. You look great."

"As 'Customer Jason'?"

"Nah. Just Jason."

Remember that sensation as a kid, getting a brand-new pair of sneakers with spongy new soles, and lacing them up and tearing through your backyard or up the street, thinking you were faster, lighter, springier, and look out rabbits and squirrels, I just might catch up with you? Didn't you feel quick as the wind? I did. Walking down Wilshire Boulevard, passing other people strolling on the sidewalk and greeting them, that's a bit how I feel right now: changed, *springier*, more confident, ready to take on anything, like I want to make eye contact, see and be seen. I feel...*better* about myself. And it's silly, really, because nothing has changed: a few hairs trimmed, a few others pushed a different way, some goop mixed in, just like nothing had changed all those years ago with the shoes. It's all in my head. But sometimes, I guess, that's really the only place you need it.

I duck into the antique shop first, and they have all the things you might expect—old dishes, lamps, jewelry—but they also have a book in the glass case: a first edition of *The Hound of the Baskervilles*. I loved Sherlock Holmes as a boy, and I'd be tempted to spring for it if the eight on the price tag had only one zero after it, not two. So I head to the bakery. The place smells great, the air swirling with vanilla and cinnamon and butter and cocoa and ground espresso beans. I grab a coffee, then something decadent for the girls for dessert tonight.

After Rosie locks up the salon, we pile into Marie's car, top down. Rosie and Audrey are willing to surrender their claim to shotgun, provided I let them choose the music. Fine. Marie pops in a mix CD that has Gwen Stefani and Coldplay and Shakira, so the entire way over I'm serenaded by The Three Stylists (never to be confused with The Three Tenors), who let me know in all manner of vocal stylings and shrill notes and head bobbing that their hips don't lie and they ain't no hollaback girls. As if I ever doubted it.

At the theater I buy a bag of candy, but I quickly find out that the Sno-Caps I paid good money for are not mine at all; they're community property. Marie instructs me to dump them into the tub of popcorn she bought, along with Rosie's Milk Duds and Audrey's Whoppers. As she mixes it all up, Marie brings me up to speed on the rules for partaking in this buttery/chocolatey confection. No hogging the bucket for more than sixty seconds. No rooting around to find the good stuff. Chew with your mouth closed. Rosie tries to add a special rule, which applies only tonight and only to her: I must make out with her before the lights come back up. I break it to her as gently as possible that I'll probably just stick to the rules about the popcorn and chewing with my mouth closed.

Our movie turns out to be the one with Hugh Grant and Kate Hudson where he plays a washed-up former teen TV heartthrob who's making a comeback, thanks to Kate, the spunky publicist who used to be president of his fan club when she was a chubby twelve-year-old in pigtails and braces. They wind up falling in love. (Surprise.) It's all right, if you like Hugh Grant. Of course, there are the tear-jerking moments, like when Hugh breaks up with Kate because he thinks he'll ruin her life if they got too serious because he knows he's a cad, and she flies away to Greece brokenhearted, then he flies off to win her back, which he does, under the moonlit steps of the Parthenon. Marie and Rosie and Audrey do their share of crying, along with every other female in the theater. At one point, Marie even passes me a Kleenex.

"I'm fine, thanks," I whisper.

"Not for you, for Rosie," she says, unable to pull her tear-stained eyes off the screen.

Sure enough, Rosie has the same glassy-eyed devastated look. I slip it into her hand and she starts using it without even knowing how it got there.

After the movie, we drive back to the salon lot. They ask me once again if I want to join them for dinner, since the restaurant's only just down the street, and it's Thai and delicious. But I tell them I really do need to go. Over at my car, I open the door and the smell of the pastries hits me right away.

"Oh, hey, wait up," I call out. "I forgot something."

I grab the bag and trot over. Marie meets me halfway, the designated envoy. Rosie and Audrey hang back.

"What's up?" she asks.

"I forgot to give you these."

I hand her the bag, and even though it's only one of those plain white, waxy ones, her face instantly lights up.

"Noni's!" she says excitedly. She peeks inside: amoretto truffles and cannolis and dark chocolate tortes and apple fritters.

"Jason, how'd you know?"

"I asked. Noni told me the three of you come in all the time. She said those were your favorites. She also said the calories don't count, since I bought them. So enjoy."

She gives me a quick hug. "That was so sweet. Thanks."

I slow down and give a little wave to the girls as I drive by— Rosie pats her stomach and blows me at least a dozen kisses. It's a pleasant evening, the temperature's perfect, but I keep the windows rolled up; it still smells like Noni's inside and I wouldn't mind savoring the aroma a little longer.

Bradley takes a rain check on our Sunday basketball and day of watching football; he'd forgotten that he and Skyler have plans for brunch and a matinee with another couple. But I don't mind, since the writing went well last night and even better this morning. That's how it's been every time I sit down, flowing through me quickly, with ease, and it's almost like I've taken an enema, which means what's coming out should be...well, you know. But it's not. It's good, great actually. And if it keeps up like this, I could be finished in a couple months.

This pace is outrageous. Writing is like chess for me, a move every hour, or ten, and I've been known to spend an entire day working on a single paragraph, fretting over commas, pulling out *Moby Dick* because I want the sky to be the same gray color as Melville used for the underbelly of the great fish. But this writing is different; it's crisper, quicker, more bang bang: get those characters on stage and get them talking or laughing or kissing or shopping or taking their clothes off. Get them *living*, I guess you'd call it. So it's not like chess at all. It's more like riding a bike: popping wheelies, letting go of the handlebars, freewheeling and having fun, and maybe there's some pedaling on level ground, or an uphill stretch, but mostly it's coasting downhill, the wind in my hair.

Now that I've gotten the hang of it, I've even jazzed up the original plot. Old storyline: Valerie is a second-tier model who gets discovered and leaps to the big time. New storyline: Courtney (like the name?) is a hairstylist (thanks, Rosie and Marie) in her late thirties with an ex-husband who left her for a younger woman (though she still, god help her, pines after the asshole) and a teenybopper daughter; it's the daughter who wants to head to the mall for an open casting call for models, and Courtney takes her, but it's *Courtney* who gets discovered. Hello extreme makeover and unlikely runway star, and handsome young studs who love the idea of bedding an older woman, and lots of exotic trips and food and sex, and a husband who now wants her back, and she takes him, and everything is on track for sorta happily ever after—*but hold on*—because she's getting caught up in a web of glitz and glamour, and losing her daughter and her way and her self-respect, and she realizes all this with the help of her lifelong male friend from college who's always loved her from afar but could never tell her how he truly felt, but eventually he does, and so now she must choose between staying with her ex-husband in this seductive world that's sucking the life out of her or starting a new life with the soulful and quietly handsome man who thinks she's the most beautiful woman in the world, even without makeup or fancy clothes or touched-up photo spreads. Hmm. Who do you think she should choose?

And I've even come up with a title: *Catwalk Mama*. Kinda catchy, if I do say so myself.

CHAPTER ELEVEN

One of my favorite books of all time is a book I can't even read because it's written in Latin. It's called *Les très riches heures du Duc de Berry* and it's an illuminated manuscript, one of those medieval books with fancy first letters and lots of calligraphy and gold leaf pages and illustrations of churches and palaces and angels. (Mine is a reproduction, obviously.) A few years back, I bought a cheap calligraphy kit because I wanted to learn how to do it. But I didn't. In fact, I never opened it. On Monday, I bring the kit and another copy of the book to the studio and give them to Fran.

"I thought you might like these," I tell her. "Since you do such creative things with your hands."

Now it's not like I've gone out and spent a fortune: the kit, as you know, I had lying around the apartment, and the book's under twenty-five bucks. But from Fran's reaction, you'd think I gave her a Cadillac. She starts getting teary eyed and gives me a hug, and I realize I've made a huge mistake because it's all turning into a scene, and the fewer people who know that our resident pharmaceutical rep has literary tastes more along the lines of a certain medievalist PhD candidate named Mitch, the better.

Fortunately, Fran and I are off in the corner and everyone else is out on the dance floor, buzzing about something. I calm her down as quickly as I can, then offer to take her goodies out to her car so she won't have to lug them out after the lesson, and thankfully, she gives me her keys. By the time I come back in, her eyes are dry and she's retired her Kleenex, and it's just like nothing ever happened.

The reason for all the commotion on the dance floor, I discover, is that we have guests. Dancer guests. Shandi and Tony, Latin Champions, Midwest Region 2008, friends of Adonis. They're certainly dressed the part: Shandi, with heels and a shimmery outfit that must be taped on in places to keep it from showing more; Tony, with slicked hair and a satiny shirt. And despite his questionable judgment in leaving so many buttons unbuttoned (though I suppose when you've got a chest like that, you want people to see it), they look great together. They do a demonstration, and it's a little breathtaking the way he whips her around, and she doesn't break, but looks sultry and sexy and makes faces at him that suggest she's having an orgasm.

After their bows, she comes over to work with the men, Tony with the women. I catch myself glancing over to their side every now and again, and it's pretty revolting the way they're fawning over him, laughing for no reason, making googly eyes, though I guess it'd be fair to say we're doing our share of tripping over ourselves on this side. I realize this whole Shandi/Tony thing is a mixed blessing. On the plus side, it lights a new fire under all of us, makes us want to do better, rise to the occasion of dancing with such a partner. But it also sets expectations off kilter. After tonight, we go back to dancing with the likes of Rosie and Vicky and Gina, and worse, they go back to dancing with the likes of Steve and Dave and me.

Afterwards, we go out to the bar and have the type of conversation you'd expect after a lesson like that: given the chance, would you sleep with either of them? Rosie jumps right in.

"*Va-voom!*" she whoops.

Marie gives her a look. "So just like that, you'd do it?"

"Yep. Just like that. And like this, and like this, and like this," she says, making comically vulgar gyrations with her hips. "Did you see him, Marie? Did you see that body and that face?"

She did. We all did.

Marie mulls this over. "Great. So let's say you meet a guy at Wal-Mart, same body, same face, and he asks you if you want to have sex. Then what?"

Rosie is horrified. "*Then what?* I'd smack him upside the head with his tackle box, is what."

"But it's the same guy."

"But he's at Wal-Mart."

"So are you. You love Wal-Mart."

"For my soap and toothpaste and paper towels. Not for my guys." Rosie swirls the ice in her drink. "Come on, Marie. One's a professional dancer. The other guy's just a guy at Wal-Mart."

"So? One guy has a fancy outfit and fancy steps, the other guy just likes to fish. That's why you'd rip your top off for one and knock the other guy upside the head."

"Yeah, more or less. Plus Tony's... *someone*." She shrugs, at a loss. "What can I say?"

We're all at a loss. What *can* you say?

Steve clears his throat. "May I?" he asks. He's been quiet and patient up to this point.

"He roomed for a year with a psychology major in college," Jennifer adds proudly, explaining his expertise.

He leans in to us and lowers his voice. "Is it all right if I get a little graphic?"

By all means, we tell him.

"What it sounds like to me is the star-fuck syndrome. First, take a reasonably attractive person, which itself gets the sexual juices flowing, then give him a position where he's in the spotlight, say rock singer or actor or dancer, where his skill is viewed and admired by a lot of people, so that he becomes *desired* by a lot of people. This gives him power and stature, and he becomes a sort of prize, so that if he chooses to take you to his bed, you're not just sleeping with any person, but a person *everyone* wants, and you're bringing him pleasure or he's pleasuring you, controlling him or being controlled, depending on which fantasy you have. There's a sweetness and luridness about a star-fuck that makes you drop your inhibitions, get swept away, do things you normally wouldn't do."

We all sit in silence.

Rosie begins to fan herself. "Whatever it is, Dr. Freud, I'm getting all hot and bothered just thinking about it. It's still a no to Wal-Mart guy, but I'm in for the dancing man. Who else?" She looks around. "Gina?"

Gina shrugs, waggles her head, can't make up her mind. "Probably," she says weakly. "I think."

Rosie turns to Marie. "Miss Priss, no. Jennifer, I hope not. So not much competition for me, other than Gina. Now, how about you boys, with the tiny dancer girl. David?"

Dave nods and gives a thumbs-up and smiles from ear to ear and starts rocking eagerly on his stool. "Yes, please," he adds, in case there was any mistake. "Dancer *or* Wal-Mart girl."

"Little Steven, no. Which leaves us with Jason. How about it, mystery man?"

"You really know how to put a guy on the spot."

"I can think of another spot I'd like to put you on." She says it with a wink, and even though it makes no sense at all, it still sounds sexual; Rosie has a way of doing that. "Come on, handsome. Shandi girl walks in here in that outfit, shakes her little tail feather in your face, says she'd like a little company tonight. You're single. She's single. Up for it?"

"Honestly?"

"Honestly."

So here's honest. She looked great, fantastic, sexy: Jessica Biel with sparkles and longer legs. What guy wouldn't entertain the thought? But I really don't need another notch, just to say I bedded the star dancer girl (not that I've had thousands and thousands of notches, by the way). And if I just want to have an orgasm, well, I know ways to take care of that. So if I'm going to sleep with her, I'll need to know a few things first; not worthless sappy things like her sign or does she come here often, but just things to let me know she likes to laugh and has a little bit going on upstairs so that the next time I see her, in clothes, I'll like her that way, too. And some people might disagree and say sex is just sex, and if you get stirred up or worked up or hot enough, then by god, just do it, and who cares if you like them or know a name. Which is fine. It's just not me. And since Shandi seemed like the type who wouldn't bother too much with the names, I'm left with this:

"I think I'd want to. But I don't think I would."

Rosie blows up. "You *gotta* be kidding!" Even Dave looks let down, like I've violated some sort of man-law. But that's okay. Let them think what they want, rather than try to explain all that.

I never bring my cell phone to lessons (too dangerous: what if I lapse into Mitch?). It's ringing when I get to the apartment.

"It's eleven o'clock. It's Monday night. Where the hell you been?" Bradley.

"Out. Busy."

"Doing what?"

"What do you think I was doing?" Not having a couple beers with your sister and friends from the dance studio talking about whether we'd do our guest instructors, that's for sure. "Dissertation, remember? So, what's going on?"

What's going on, it turns out, is that he's found me a perfect match.

"The couple Skyler and I went out with yesterday brought a friend. And get this: She went to Johns Hopkins. She's gorgeous. And single. I talked you up, she'd like to meet you. The four of us, this Thursday night."

Thursday night? That's dancing. "Sorry, Bradley. Can't."

"What do you mean you can't?" His tone indicates that wasn't an option.

"What I mean is, I can't. I'm having dinner with my mom." Lately, the lies come as easy as breathing. Scary.

"Fine. Then we'll switch it to Friday. But I'm not taking no for an answer."

But he's got it all wrong: why would I say no? Johns Hopkins. Gorgeous. Single. I'm ready to meet the woman of my dreams.

Tuesday morning I actually do head to the library to work on my dissertation. I haven't cracked a book in a couple weeks, and it's high time I return to the dusty fourteenth-century road to Canterbury Cathedral with Chaucer and his motley crew. It's the perfect day to do this—gray, drizzly, cool. But even though I'm only dealing with Middle English and not Old English, it's no piece of cake and demands concentration, not a mind still bucking to get a latté with *Catwalk Mama* and stroll the glossy aisles of Bergdorf Goodman. I do manage to make some progress on the "Knight's Tale" (two sworn blood-brothers vow to kill each other after they fall in love with the same woman: testament to the incredible power of love, or its destructiveness?), then reward myself by browsing through magazines.

The current issue of *Travel + Leisure* and its cover story about North Carolina catch my eye, so I page through. It's a great spread, with photos of the Biltmore Estate and the Smokies and Chapel Hill, which are nice, but the best ones are along the coast—the Outer Banks and Ocracoke Island and Pamlico Sound, with their ink blue water and streaky-cloud skies and old weathered lighthouses. It's all gorgeous, smell-the-salt, feel-the-wet-sand-squishing-between-your-toes, hear-the-waves-crashing sort of gorgeous, and then I think of Marie, who lived in Raleigh, and even though it might take a couple hours to get there, it's the ocean for chrissakes, and it beats what we have running through town (there's a reason why the Mississippi is called the "Big Muddy"), and this is what she gave up for *Rosie*? It floors me again, as it did in the pizza parlor, and all seems a bit absurd. But then another thought leaps from the bushes and throttles me, one that wasn't there two weeks ago: maybe she *did* get this right. I mean, Rosie may have a big mouth and be overly horny, but she grows on you, I like her, and it's pretty clear she thinks the world of Marie and would do *anything* for her. Which means, if you were inclined to tally it a certain way, Marie traded something she might get to see once a week or month—the ocean—for a best friend she gets to see every day. Some people might even call that . . . *winning.*

I go to my father's house on Wednesday, after class. I've chosen a weekday because I don't want his kids around, and I'd prefer it if Leah weren't around either. But she is of course, since what kind of wife leaves her husband all by his lonesome less than three weeks after he's had his chest cracked open in the OR. I think my father's spoken to her, though, because after she says hello and brings us iced tea and a plate of cookies, she excuses herself with some suspicious-sounding story about needing to go work in the garden, which gives us some time alone.

He's propped up on the sofa, and we talk about his heart, obviously, and the meds he's on, and my teaching and Scott, and how Nathan has cut the grass most of the summer, and boy, we could use some rain, and I guess this is how normal people talk, or at least normal fathers and sons, but we're not that, so I just want to leapfrog all the small talk and ask him why *why* WHY he left when he did. But an hour in, I can see it's not going to happen, not today anyway, because even though his color's better and he's not wincing as much, he still looks like one of those front-porch Halloween scarecrows—unnatural, stiff, *lumpy*—and putting him through the ringer with all my questions wouldn't be too charitable on my part, so it looks like I made the trip out here just to eat a bunch of cookies.

"You want to tell me what's on your mind?" he asks out of nowhere.

"Mmm? My mind?" I wipe some crumbs from my lips. "What do you mean?"

"What I mean is, great as it was to see you in the hospital, it was a surprise. As is this, today, just stopping by to shoot the breeze." His eyes zero in on mine from behind his glasses. "I don't want to sound cynical, Mitch, but that's not us."

What's the use lying to him now, especially when he's giving me one of those "Go on, give it to me straight" looks.

"Okay, Dad, I'm not going to beat around the bush," I declare. Then I go on and beat around the bush, at least a little, in my head, fumbling for a different—and gentler—way of saying it, but I can't come up with anything. "Mom told me about the affair."

For a long time he doesn't speak.

"I wish she hadn't."

"She didn't have a choice. We were talking about how bad the relationship is between you and me, and I said the only thing that would change for me if you died is that I'd have to get a new suit." I feel squeamish saying it now. "I told her one of the reasons I couldn't stand you is that you cheated on her. She wanted to set me straight."

His face remains fixed, expressionless.

I rub my hands on my jeans. "So will you help me understand a few things about that time? How everything…happened?"

He offers a barely perceptible nod.

"Mom told me she was petty and spiteful when she threw the affair in your face. That she wanted to hurt you with the news, give you a reason to go. Why didn't you?"

The muscles along his jawline flare and tighten, as if I'd poked my finger into a nerve. He shifts awkwardly on the sofa, his thoughts obviously taking him to a place he'd rather not go.

"We were a mess after Emily died, Mitch. The whole family was, but especially your mother and me. We could hardly get out of bed in the morning, look at each other, breathe. But we had to get on with living, and we tried, best as we could. Your mother made it clear what she needed. She needed to talk about what'd happened, replay everything we'd done, or hadn't done, be sad and angry and bitter and let whatever was there come out. She cried a lot. But I didn't want to hear it. Not the tears or the second-guessing or the '*Why Emily?*' So I shut her up. I shut her up and shut her out, turned myself into a stone. Because that was the only way I could deal with knowing we'd let our daughter die."

"But you didn't let her die. She had viral meningitis. The doctor said—"

"I don't care what the doctor said," he cuts me off sharply. "She was two. She was counting on us. We were her *parents*. And we let her die." There's anger in his eyes, and pain, but it's almost like you can see right through all of it to the part of his heart that's still a heap of burnt-out ash. Gradually his look grows softer. "Anyway, what your mother needed was comfort and hope, someone to listen to her, and I wouldn't give her any of it. She found it with someone else. How could I blame her for that?"

"So you stayed, out of guilt."

He nods. "And for Emily, because I couldn't stand the thought that her death would be what ripped our family apart. Plus, I still had two sons."

He says it in such an offhanded way, like it's a no-brainer—what father *wouldn't* stay with his two sons under such circumstances?—but then we both fall silent because we're thinking the same thing: he still had two sons five years later, and that didn't keep him from bolting.

I'm starting to feel a little bad for him, now that he's backed himself into a corner and he's already so physically uncomfortable.

"Look, Dad. You don't have to talk about it now. Not if you don't want to."

He musters an awful smile. "No, Mitch, I don't. Because it's beyond the pale, and you'll realize what a small and ugly man I was to you. And I always, *always* thought it'd be better for you to think the worst of your old man, whatever crimes and misdeeds your imagination could conjure up, than know the truth. I'd hoped to take it all to the grave with me, and I nearly managed to pull that one off. But you deserve to know."

My hands are actually sweating, so I stuff them down into the sides of the chair cushion.

"When your mother and I got married, all I wanted was a happy family. That's why I let your mom take the lead in raising you children, bring you up Catholic. Because she was the smart one, the cultured one, and I wanted her fingerprints all over your growing-up years. And those early years were good, Mitch. They were wonderful. You have to believe that. But your sister's death...*changed* things. Your mother and I didn't cope well, we showed our worst colors to each other, and she had the affair, and even though we stayed together and tried to do the right thing, we were dead to each other. She didn't love me anymore. And somewhere along the line, Scott turned against me. He hated me, Mitch, you know that. And just like that, everything I'd loved and cared about was gone. Except you. You were the relationship I could be proud of. My youngest son. And then it was the summer you turned ten, and you and I'd been working on your baseball swing all spring, and I was planning to coach your team..."

He doesn't need to complete his thought. "And I went away to Oxford."

My mom's prep school had given her a professional grant to study for two months at Oxford, and she wanted to take Scott and me with her, enroll us in the young scholars program. Up till then, my parents had done a good job keeping a lid on the tension in the house—a raised voice here or there, an occasional too-quiet dinner—but all hell broke loose over that. There were nasty fights, tooth-and-nail drag downs, and it always came back to this: my dad didn't want his boys gone for two months; my mom said it was his own damned fault he couldn't get vacation time to go with us and why ruin a once-in-a-lifetime opportunity just so he could take us to the park a couple times a week for baseball. Of course, they had no idea we heard all that—they thought we were outside or listening to music or sleeping—and ultimately left the decision up to us. My brother had his bags packed in an hour, but I wasn't so sure. After all, I was the one who'd begged my dad to help me with my swing—which he had—and to coach my team—which he said he would. I felt guilty about that. And I also felt sorry for him, the way my mom had ripped into him in all their arguments. But what about England, and the chance to walk the streets of Sherlock Holmes's London?

In the end, I rode a plane to England.

Something in my father's old face crumbles, and his eyes go dark, like it's happening again right now. "I can't explain it, Mitch, not in a way that won't make me sound like a pathetic old man. You were a happy-go-lucky kid going to a brand-new world, because what kid wouldn't? But it felt like you'd made some fundamental choice. Like you'd crossed over to the other side, to a place where your mom and Scott were, a place where I couldn't reach you anymore. You were gone. She'd won. I'd lost all of you."

I try to imagine those two months for my father, passing by Scott's bedroom, already closed off to him, passing by mine, empty now, too, waking up in a bed that'd been loveless for years—going through every motion of his day—and doing it all alone. I see him out in the family room, paging through our photo album, coming across pictures of Emily when she was alive, those "golden years" of our family; glancing at pictures of himself as a boy, those black-and-white prints of him at his father's tailor shop, when he was still young and wide-eyed and had all his life ahead of him. And now this was his life, and the only company he had was himself and the echoes of a family no longer there. Funny, but you always think of a kid needing his father. But what about a father needing his kids?

"The three of you were on cloud nine when you came back. Brimming with stories and inside jokes and souvenirs and laughter, and I wanted to take joy in all your excitement. I really did. But God help me, the happier all of you were, the sicker it made me feel. Because that wasn't my world, Mitch. The walls had gone up and the gate was closed and I was standing outside. And I knew that's where I'd always be. And I wanted to believe that there was still some bit of happiness out there for me, somewhere. So I left." His voice catches on that last part, and for a long time the only sign of life in the room is the hum of the overhead fan. Finally, he clears his throat. "I'm not proud of the way I handled it, Mitch. None of it, but especially after the divorce. But I didn't think you cared. You just shrugged a lot and said you were fine, and I left it at that. And by the time I realized there was so much more than indifference in those shrugs, it was too late: you'd learned to get along without me, and to hate me. And you were better off."

There's a photo of me on my First Communion, when I'm eight, and I'm standing with my mom and Scott and all my Catholic relatives, and my hands are stuffed with rosaries and prayer books and everyone's smiling and laughing, arms draped around each other like some kind of celebratory rugby scrum. My father's in the picture, too, but barely. He's off to the side, not part of the group, with some space between him and the rest of us, and he has an uncomfortable look on his face: *Should I be in this one or am I intruding?* And that's how he must have felt, all those years, but especially near the end: the outsider, a stranger in his own home, in his own life, and always believing that you could take a pair of scissors and cut him out — cleanly — without affecting anybody else in the picture. He didn't know how wrong he was.

The back door swings open and there's commotion in the kitchen. Leah's come in.

"Hey, Dad," I whisper, making a wiping motion with my hands to my eyes. "If Leah sees those, she'll kill me."

He dabs at his tears, unaware they were there.

Leah glides in a minute later, to a smiling father and son, no hint of anything amiss.

"Can I get you anything else?" she asks me, nodding to my glass.

"Uh, no. No thanks." I get up. "Actually, I was just heading out."

I go over to where my father's sitting on the sofa. We look at each for a long time, just stare into those eyes we've kept hidden from each other for what feels like a hundred years. Part of me wants to strangle him for what he did, tell him he's a stupid fucking old man who can go to hell. The other part of me just wants to cry.

"You comfortable with that pillow?" I ask.

He nods. "I'm fine."

"Good." Before I realize what I'm doing, I bend down toward him, but I know it's not going to be a hug, so I put my hands on his shoulders, and he lifts his hands to mine, and we wind up in something that almost looks like a wrestling hold. But the two of us know that's not what it is.

"Rest easy, Dad," I say. "I'll talk to you soon."

"Goodbye, son."

And then I walk through the front door of my father's home and into the yard, where the sun feels good on my face.

There are no famous faces at our lesson Thursday night, no Shandi or Tony or winners of *Dancing with the Stars* or *So You Think You Can Dance?* who we can sit around and discuss whether we'd like to star-fuck. Just the usual crowd. We have our group lesson, then Adonis works with Marie and me, then it's just Marie and I changing our shoes. That's when she blindsides me.

"Fran told us what you did for her. I think it was great. We all do."

We all do? Shit. Fran and her big mouth. "Hmm. Well, that kit was just lying around my place, collecting dust. She did me a favor by taking it off my hands."

"And the book? That was just lying around?"

I nod happily. "Yes, actually. At least my copy. All I had to do was go to the bookstore and pull another one off the shelf. I didn't even have to reach."

She gives me a look.

"I didn't. I swear." And I didn't. "Okay, look. She did something nice for me, I returned the favor. *Quid pro quo*. Scratch my back, I scratch yours. It's no big deal."

"But it *is* a big deal," she insists. "She's done something nice for all of us. I have some potholders and an apron because she knows I like to cook. Rosie has a poncho, with scissors and roses on it. And all she got from us was thank-you cards. You actually gave her a gift, something she could enjoy." Her look, combined with her tone, makes me very uncomfortable. "Do you know how thoughtful that is?"

And the answer to that is *No*. I don't. Honestly. Because buying books for grandmas who knit me things, and dancing, and putting gas in a car, and writing a book called *Catwalk Mama* that I don't hate, and eating popcorn with Sno-Caps and Milk Duds and Whoppers, and having a friend named Rosie, it's all new to me. I'm in uncharted territory. My GPS device is scratching its head, trying to figure out exactly where the hell I am. And the problem is, I need to get my bearings, *quick*, because if I don't, if I keep going around giving away possessions and books that could be traced to Mitch, and doing other things for reasons I don't quite understand, I'm going to find myself in a place I *know* I don't want to be: Disasterville.

The four of us head to Colchester's Friday night for my blind date, and I can tell straightaway she's the perfect girl for me. Her name's Trista and she's tall and lean and her jeans fit great, and she's a poet who's read both Brownings, and we talk about Donne and Milton and structuralism and postmodernism, and I don't ask but I can tell she knows it's "12 items or *fewer*," not "less," at the grocery store checkout, and if we got married and sent out holiday cards, she wouldn't put "Happy Holidays from the Samuel's" when all you need is the simple plural (*Samuels*), and, of course, she loves that I'm a writer and loves to hear me talk about what I've written, especially *Henley Farm*, and she gets all the themes and symbols and allusions that I've subtly woven in. In other words, she's a computer-generated, virtual-reality perfect match, but she's real, and I don't have to wear any hi-tech goofball visor glasses to see her.

Only I've dated this girl before. Her name is Hannah, or Stephanie, or Kristen, and she's always this way, or a version of it: cute, funny, polite, on the quiet side, intelligent, grammatically and academically impeccable. And guess what? It's never worked. And the reason it's never worked, I realize for the very first time tonight, as I listen to what I say, and the way I say it, as Mitch, *not* Jason, has nothing to do with them. It's me. Like Narcissus staring into a pool of water to get his own reflection, I've always chosen women who let me be exactly how I want to be—dismissive at times, maybe a bit condescending—which, if you think about it, aren't the most admirable traits. And while I think it's good that I've found women who accept me as I am—you shouldn't go into a relationship thinking you have to swap out every part of yourself: that's a recipe for disaster—it's also made me lazy and indulgent, and I haven't been asked to extend myself or evolve or improve.

A good relationship—love, frankly—should be a bit like manure. It should take something that's basically healthy and good and make it blossom and grow tall and strong and smell nice and have vibrant colors and bear lots of fruit. Love should make us bigger in all the right ways (and let's keep our minds out of the gutter; I don't just mean down *there*). It should be like the Grinch when he hears the Whos of Whoville singing and his heart grows three times its normal size and he lifts up the whole sleigh, dog with fake reindeer antlers and all. It should give us ripped muscles where they need to be ripped—generosity, compassion, good deeds—because if it doesn't, if it just leaves us in our same flabby old skin, why bother?

So...

I have a nice evening with Trista at the pub, but since I don't see us getting much beyond our mutual affinity for the Metaphysical Poets and other things grammatical and literary—my fault entirely—I mention that maybe the *four* of us can get together again, which, I believe, is the proper way of intimating that the *two* of us, Trista and I, won't be. Bradley shoots me a glance like "You gotta be kidding me," but I just shrug. How would I explain? He doesn't even like the Grinch.

CHAPTER TWELVE

I call Katharine Longwell on Saturday morning. I'm prepared to trot out a parade of details to jog her memory—St. Louis, Starbucks, cousin named Bradley, you gave me your card, your boobs were huge—but I barely get past my name when she cuts me off and says *of course*, she remembers me. She was hoping I'd call. I tell her Bradley has a hundred pages of a manuscript she'd love for Katharine to read, but she's too shy to ask, delicate creature that she is—an Emily Dickinson in that way, and no good with criticism—so I'm calling on her behalf, as her agent. Katharine's reply is breathtakingly swift: Absolutely, send it, she'd *love* to read it! This is a good week for her; she's in Chicago, not much on her plate. So I pack it all, take it to the post office, and just like that, *Catwalk Mama* is strutting her way to Chicago, to get the once-over from Katharine Longwell. In other words, *holy fuck*.

The winery crew meets at the studio lot at seven o'clock. We pile into three cars, having established who, by evening's end, will be in no condition to drive — Rosie, Dave, Gina — who will be perfectly sober — Fran, Steve, Vicky — and who will be somewhere in between — the rest of us. It's one of those scenic drives, over the river and through the woods, and the last mile or so is on a dirt road, and when we get there, the main house is ancient and bare-bones and really nothing more than a shack to order your wine. Where's the wine-making equipment? The bathrooms? But the outdoor patio looks better than fine, with lantern lights strung overhead and plenty of space, and a band is setting up.

There are twelve of us total, so we pull a couple tables together and start hauling our goodies out, since it's the kind of place that lets you bring picnic baskets as long as you buy their wine. I went simple, Brie and crackers, but Marie lays out a plate of pastries that look far more sophisticated.

"What are they?" I ask.

"Portuguese custard tarts."

I've never heard of such a thing. Krispy Kreme donuts, yes. "May I?"

"Help yourself."

It's the shape of a cupped hand but half as big, with a custard and blueberry topping. I take a bite. "Oh, man, this is good. Wow. Fruity. But not too fruity. And rich." (I realize I do not have a future as a food critic: "Fruity. Yummy. Me like!") "Not the kind of recipe you'd get off the back of a cereal box, is it?"

She gives a small laugh. "This was the dessert we made in my last cooking class. Iberian cuisine."

"Ah, so dancing classes *and* cooking classes for you."

"I have to. The cooking class meets once a month and we cook up all this food, with tons of calories. Then I have four weeks of dance class to work it all off." She pats her hips. "I could probably use six."

I take another bite of my tart. "So where do you go for that?"

"A place called Chez Henri. It's actually a restaurant open to the public, but they have two kitchens. Students cook up their dishes in one, then we all sit out with the other diners. It's a lot of fun. In fact, I have another class this Friday. Wanna come?"

I lick a splotch of custard off my finger. "If everything tastes this good, you bet."

The band launches into a swingy version of "The Girl from Ipanema" and the place gets hopping, people in sundresses and linen slacks and Hawaiian shirts pouring onto the dance floor, moving any which way they can. Those of us from the studio try to use our steps, and sometimes it works with some of the songs, but when it doesn't we just laugh it off and say we're glad Adonis isn't here to see. I dance with Fran and Marie and Jennifer and Rosie—who, true to her word, is well on her way to being in no condition to drive—and there's mingling of the tables and lots of "You gotta try this" and "Who made that?" and we talk about *Sideways* and what a great movie that was, and how it must've made it cool to order pinot noir because of that terrific scene where Virginia Madsen talks about the pinot grape, and how it must've made it uncool to order merlot, because, well, it's "fucking merlot," and did the movie really affect sales of pinot noir and merlot, which leads to a conversation about how Oprah got sued by the cattle ranchers a few years back because she said something about not liking beef, and we discuss whether Oprah's so powerful she could take down an entire industry with just a wilting glance. We agree she is: the woman makes presidents. And with all apologies to Bradley and Skyler and Trista, it's a thousand times more fun than last night.

Much later into the evening, after we've all had a chance to sample the wine and salads and sushi and Brie and custard tarts and whatever else has found its way onto our table, I ask if anyone *does* know where the bathrooms are.

Dave struggles to lift his bleary eyes from his empty wineglass. "Bathrooms? They have bathrooms here?" Apparently, Dave's been visiting the side of a tree.

Steve points over his shoulder. "Up that hill and bear to the left."

"Follow the signs," Jennifer cautions. "It's a bit tricky."

Marie nudges me. "I can show you, since I wouldn't mind stretching my legs."

We head up a grassy incline, and it's actually sort of quiet on top, since the band's on break and we're removed from the chatter. From here, everything lies below us—our friends at the tables, the swaying lantern lights that remind me of glowing bubbles, the silent vineyards rolling and tumbling as far as I can see. Overhead, a three-quarter moon is veiled by a thin layer of clouds, like a sheer curtain. A breeze stirs over my body and tickles the hairs on my neck, but not in a way that makes me want to scratch it, but in a way that lets me know I'm alive and I can feel things and autumn will be coming soon, with cool temperatures and pumpkins and color on the trees.

"It's beautiful up here, isn't it?" I say.

"Mmm. I love it."

From the way she says it, I can tell she's thinking the same—*feeling* the same—that life is wonderful in moments like this; and something catches in my gut, something sweet and deep and exhilarating, like a dip on a roller coaster, and what's pumping through my blood and warming every inch of my skin is the certainty that I want other moments like this with her, the two of us, alone, in the breeze, and the only way for me to have those times, and have them for real, is to tell her who I really am.

"Marie, there's something I need to tell you..."

She turns to me slowly, still feeling the breeze on her face, and she's something of a vision, in her halter top and billowy skirt, the bare skin on her shoulders tan and soft and glowing, her eyes catching a sliver of moonlight, her earrings shimmering and mingling with her hair; and I realize I can't say what I want to say, because if it doesn't come out right, or she doesn't hear it the right way, that's the end of us, and there's no way I can risk losing her now, because for the first time since the night we met, I'm not looking at Bradley's sister, or a woman I'd be embarrassed to introduce to my dissertation panel. Just Marie. So instead of the truth about me, I give her the truth about her.

"You look beautiful. You *are* beautiful."

She smiles, and even in this light I can see she's blushing. But from the way her gaze won't let go of mine, I can tell she has more on her mind, and she needs my help, so I lean closer and she brings her lips to mine, and we kiss.

Does the kiss last five or ten or sixty seconds? Don't know. Are her lips soft and warm and electric? Maybe. Is there a little tongue involved? Could be. The sad and unfortunate truth is, *I have no idea.* I'm so nervous and giddy and overcome and thrilled to finally be kissing this woman I've wanted to kiss *since the moment I saw her!* and only at this moment do I realize it's been since then, and now I'm actually doing it, and I'm so caught up in actually doing it that I forget to take notes on what it's like. Then it's over.

We stand and look at each other for a long time, in silence, like maybe we *have* swallowed each other's tongue. Then we look some more. Then finally I get some words out, and they're the words that every woman longs to hear on the crest of a hill on a beautiful summer's evening after she's just been kissed by the man she may or may not be falling for.

"I have to pee." Which I go and do.

When I get back to the table, thankfully she's out on the dance floor. We don't have much contact the rest of the evening, and when we do, we're overly polite ("The band is great, isn't it?"

"Wonderful!"), but mostly we ignore each other and try not to make eye contact, and we go back in separate cars, and barely wave goodbye across the parking lot. All of which is perfectly understandable when you really, really like someone. And you've just kissed them. And you're twelve.

Chances are good that somewhere along your TV-watching way, you've seen a doctor in a hospital utter a line that goes something like this: "The next few hours are critical." Maybe it was House of *House*, or Meredith or McDreamy or McSteamy, or even an old-school doc like Marcus Welby, and maybe they were talking about a guy who'd just been shot or hit by a car or had some preposterously confounding ailment that caused his heart to beat twice an hour, and it was touch and go whether he'd live or breathe on his own or ever walk again. The point is, whatever happened during those "critical" hours would go a long way in determining his fate.

Since I'm not a doctor (just a drug rep—ha!), I don't know how often this really occurs, or if it's accurate. How many hours are critical? And are they critical, or just really important, or is this just some trumped-up TV line to keep you coming back after the commercial? Whatever the case, I do know that when it comes to nonmedical conditions of the heart—such as saying I love you, or having sex, or making out with your best friend's sister—the next few hours *are* critical, in the sense that this is your chance to let her know it wasn't a fluke, that the alcohol had nothing to do with it, that you'd like it to be the start of something *big*.

Here's what I want to do when I get home. I want to call her. I want to call her and tell her that I'm lying in bed and can't get to sleep because I'm thinking about her and that kiss, and my head is still buzzing and my lips are still tingling, and I'm trying to remember exactly what it was like, and can you help me fill in the details? Better yet, how about I just come over and we can do it again. But I don't, since it's already late and she's probably in bed and there's no need to wake her; and I'm thinking a version of the same in the morning, that it's still too early and she's sleeping in. Besides, we all know there are rules about when to call a woman after a date, to send the right message that you're not overeager, but not uninterested either, so I've got that to consider (though technically speaking, this wasn't a date, and we're already friends, so probably this is different). Plus, I've got the entire day to make that call, right?

Only Bradley rings *me* up early and we head out to shoot baskets, then we go back to the apartment to watch football; and because Skyler has to work all day, this means the two of us making a marathon of it, watching all the games, which ordinarily would be great, but today not so much, since I need to have a heart-to-heart with his sister about where we stand, and is she feeling the same, and was that a French kiss, or not? Around five I feel the day slipping away; by seven, I have a panicky lump in the pit of my stomach that's telling me I should've called earlier. I finally get Bradley out the door at eight and make the call, but she's not home, which is disturbing: she didn't even bother to stick around to make sure she got my call. Then, she does call back an hour later and says she was out to dinner and a movie with a friend named Chris. But who's Chris, and is it Chris*tine* or *Christopher*, because suddenly I care very much. Worse, she sounds jittery, hesitant, a little strange (*guilty?*), which rattles me a bit, enough that when she asks about my day and I tell her I watched football, at a bar, alone, it all comes off sounding squirrely and evasive, like I'm trying to hide something, which, oddly enough, I am; and we wind up not talking about last night, and especially not the kiss, because by now I'm sweaty and uncomfortable and rambling. And then we hang up.

Monday night goes even better. I'm not sure how to greet her (handshake? kiss? *proposal?*), so I do nothing, just say hi, which means all the momentum of Saturday night is lost, and even worse, now we have negative momentum, since doing nothing signals a retreat from the kiss. I muddle through the lesson and our Showcase time with Adonis—stiff, formal, distant—and she's pretty much the same—like she hardly even knows me— and then it's over and I go home. A couple beers later, I figure out what's going on: before the kiss I was glib, spontaneous, playing with house money, with nothing to lose, but the kiss changed everything, showed me how much I like her, and now I'm getting nervous, uptight, self-conscious, wanting to be on my best behavior, and as a result, losing all my personality. It doesn't take a genius to figure that one out. But what's her excuse?

Ever since Saturday night, she's been as talkative as my belt. She hasn't said a word about the kiss, or her feelings, or *us*. Unless…this *is* her way of talking about the kiss, and her feelings, and us. Of course! It fits! All along, she's the one who's been making all the moves—inviting me out for drinks after the first lesson and to go shoe-shopping and to the movies and her cooking class. Now she's not making any moves at all. She's a statue. Which means the kiss meant nothing to her, but she's too chicken to tell me, and this is her passive-aggressive way of letting me know. Oh, that's rich. I give her the next couple days to call, to explain herself, but when she doesn't, I have my proof.

I consider not going to class on Thursday night, just skip the whole mess, but I do, to see if there's anything left to salvage. Apparently not. I tell an idiotic joke that's pathetic from start to finish—even giving you the punch line, "The pickle slicer got fired, too," without the rest doesn't damage the joke much, because there isn't much to damage—and no one else laughs, but Marie laughs like a fucking hyena. I know why she's doing it: it's her chance to pretend how supportive of me she is, that she'd fill awkward dead space with laughter to help me save face, so that later, if I tell any of them that we kissed and how poorly she behaved in the days that followed, she has witnesses who'll point out that she laughed at my stupid joke. It's a cheap stunt, and I almost tell her as much, right in front of everyone, but I don't. But I think she gets the message, because she keeps her distance the rest of the night, and I don't join any of them for drinks.

The next day my phone rings, and I assume she's *finally* worked up the nerve to cancel our cooking class date for the evening, probably with some excuse about having a cold, or headache, or malaria (the lengths some people will go to just to avoid saying they don't like you). But it's not her. It's Katharine.

"I got Bradley's story. I read it. I love it. I need to talk to her." She's saying all this in a rush, so that I hardly have time to process it. "Can you give me her number, Mitch?"

"Her number? Wow. You know, I don't think that's going to work. She never gives it out to anyone. No offense. Stalker ex-boyfriend. Besides, um, as I think I told you, she wants everything to go through me."

"That's right," she purrs. "I like that even better. Mitch, how about you fly up here tomorrow for dinner, drinks, and a little tête-à-tête about the book."

"Me? Fly up to Chicago?"

"Thirty-nine minutes and you're here. I'll take care of everything. Tickets, hotel for you..."

"But I'm here, right now. Let's talk."

"Oh, Mitch," she says, tickled, like I've said the silliest thing. "Some things I prefer to do in person." If her phone had one of those spirally cords, she'd be twisting a finger through it now. "Talk about books, of course."

"Of course."

Jesus. But what do I have to lose?

"Sure," I give in.

"Wonderful."

Tonight, dinner with my best friend's sister, who thinks I'm Jason. Tomorrow, dinner with the queen of chick-lit, who thinks my cousin has written a book and who quite possibly wants a boy toy for the night. Sunday, high tea with Prince Charles and Camilla, who think I'm the poet laureate. When did my life turn into a freaking soap opera?

I pick her up at her place at six, where we hug stiffly, and by the time we reach the parking lot at Chez Henri, I realize I've pulled into hell. There are Beemers and Audis and Infinitis, and I have a Malibu, which means my car is the skinny kid on the playground with duct tape holding his glasses together. It's not much better inside. These are beautiful people in beautiful clothes, and I have the type of outfit you'd wear to paint your bathroom, since I didn't want to get my good stuff messy. It never occurred to me that they might have aprons, since I've never worn an apron. My goal is to escape the evening without being mistaken for the janitor.

We take our places in a gleaming kitchen with stainless steel appliances and granite counters, and Marie explains the way this works: Chef Henri gives us directions, we do what he says, we put our concoctions in the oven, we sip wine as we wait. Simple enough. Except I've never heard of tournedos with champagne sauce, or dauphinois potatoes, or haricots verts au beurre, so my part is basically staying out of the way and handing Marie what she needs, or cleaning the cutting board, or fetching a fresh spoon, or sprinkling the minced parsley into the broth. Conversation is tough, too, since I don't know my wines, and Marie and the others do, thus I can't speak properly on the differences between the Salerno Merlot of 2003 and the Valencia Estate Proprietary Red of 2002. As a result, I keep my comments brief, crisp, al dente with these gems: "This place sure smells good." "Do you ever worry about chopping a finger off?" "Anyone else like the taste of raw green beans?"

Finally, when our creations are baking in the oven and we're seated out on the restaurant side, I spot my chance to turn the evening around, or at least get my footing.

"See that guy, over there by the window?" I nod to a man with gleaming white teeth and a chiseled chin. "That's Raymond Davies. He used to play wide receiver for the Rams. Now he does sports for Channel Two." I lean closer, hoping to impress her with my inside information. "I hear they call him RayRay at the studio."

As if on cue, RayRay looks over to our table and flashes a touchdown smile. At Marie. She gives him a familiar smile in return.

"Oh, you know him?" I ask.

She picks at her napkin. "Not so well."

"But a little?"

She shrugs like she's embarrassed to say it. "We went out a couple times."

"You did? How? *Why?*"

"He came into the shop a few months ago. We talked, he called, we went out."

Jesus. So she's dated the third most eligible bachelor in St. Louis (according to *St. Louis Magazine*), who probably just pulled up in his Mercedes convertible, and has satin sheets in his two-million-dollar condo, which she could probably describe in great detail. That's when it smacks me upside the head: I'm out of my league. I'm having dinner with a hairstylist who never went to a proper college, and with her knowledge of wine and gourmet food and the inside of RayRay's pleasure dome, I'm out of my god-damned league.

I'm not sure what my face looks like, but it can't be good if hers is any indication. She looks *miserable*.

"You don't want to be here, do you?"

No. I don't. Not for a second longer. But why should I? So I can feel even punier and more humiliated, if that's possible?

"What's that?" I say, raising my voice like I'm speaking over the roar of a jet engine in the next room.

"You heard me, Jason. At least give me the courtesy of an answer." She looks like she wants to cry. "You don't want to be here, do you?"

"No."

Now she actually does tear up.

"I'm sorry," I say.

"For what? For telling me the truth?" She starts dabbing at her eyes and her lips are quivering. "I knew this was all a mistake. That's what I've been telling Rosie."

Telling Rosie? "All *what* was a mistake?"

"This. A date. Us. The kiss last Saturday night."

She's losing me. "Who said it was a mistake?"

"*You*."

"Me? I never said that."

"Oh, come on, Jason. The way you've been acting all week at the studio. Barely talking. Trying not to dance with me. Not even looking my way. Pretending like you're enjoying yourself. You may as well be wearing a sign that says, 'Get lost.'"

A spasm of laughter spills out of me, despite myself.

"Marie, that wasn't because I thought it was a mistake. That was *nerves*. Last Saturday night was one of the best nights of my life. Kissing you was incredible. I haven't been able to string two sentences together because I was afraid the wrong things would come out."

I'm glad she's not holding anything, because if she were, it'd be on the floor right now, next to her jaw. She just keeps shaking her head. "But I thought..."

But she doesn't need to finish what she thought, because I know what she thought: that my awkwardness and inability to speak or be funny or make eye contact were obvious symptoms of my regret over the kiss; and I know this because I took her inability to speak or be funny or make eye contact for exactly the same. Suddenly, it's like McDreamy walked into the room, announcing that the patient who's been on life-support for the last five days—*us*—is now doing somersaults and cartwheels in his room, but the next *thirty seconds* are critical. I'm not going to blow it again. I lean over, and in front of RayRay and Chef Henri and whoever the hell else cares to be watching, I kiss her, full-on, ten seconds' worth, on the lips.

"What do you say we grab our food to go and get out of here?" I propose.

She leans over and kisses me back. And there's no way to misinterpret that.

We end up back at her place, and all the things I didn't notice when I was there to pick her up, since I figured why bother getting to know the place because I'll never see it again, now I do: the botanical prints and sky blue tapers and collection of sea glass on the shelf and the white lights draped over the curtain rods. Overall, not the kind of place you'd see on the cover of anything called *UberChic Monthly*; but it's warm and homey and I like it. After we finish dinner, I suggest we take a walk for ice cream.

"In a minute," she says. "I have a surprise."

She disappears into her bedroom, which gives me time to page through her *People*. There's a story about a seventy-year-old woman in Florida who beat off an alligator in her backyard with her cane. "He didn't like gettin' tapped in the snoot," she declares, and she looks like the feisty type who could manage a fairly brisk tap. But still, I'll bet that alligator's feeling stupid right now, especially when he gets a look at himself in the mirror, and sees all those teeth, and realizes all she was was an old woman with a wood stick that he could've used for a toothpick.

"*Aargh*. This is such a bad idea," Marie calls out from the bedroom.

"What is?"

"I can't tell you. Otherwise it won't be a surprise."

"But if you're not going to do it anyway, tell me."

"I'll do it," she says. "But only for a second. Close your eyes."

I hear her come out of the bedroom, and I can tell where she is by the creaking hardwood and the clicking from her shoes. Heels?

"God, I feel so stupid." She exhales. "Okay, you can open."

The first thing I think when I see her is that while I had my eyes shut and was sitting on the sofa, I actually got up and walked into another apartment, somewhere in Rome or Milan or Paris, or wherever the models live. Okay, maybe she's not that skinny (*thank God!*), since even she would tell you that she's still trying to lose a few pounds, but when she's standing there, in a way-up skirt and velvety top that's tight everywhere it should be, and her hair's dark and pulled back like a flamenco dancer, you'd have a hard time convincing me she doesn't make her living on a runway or in front of a camera.

"Take a look at you," I say.

She has her knees pressed together, almost like she's embarrassed to stand tall. "Would that be good or bad?"

"That's good. That's real good."

I look closer at the skirt. "Hey, that's the one from Dance Loft. The day we went shopping for my shoes."

She's pleased I recognized it. "After Adonis asked us to be in the Showcase, I went out and got it. This is the outfit I plan to wear."

"Then I guess no one'll be looking at me. Or anyone else." I still can't get over how great she looks. "Do a little pirouette, show the whole thing off."

She does a slow step-around circle, hands pressed against her sides, like she's shifting her feet through glue.

"No, not like that. A fast one."

"I can't."

"Because..."

She makes a face. "Can't you guess?"

I can't. "Ankle bothering you?"

"No, my ankle isn't bothering me." She raises her eyebrows, then glances down toward the skirt, ruffles it a bit to show how easily it flies out, and I realize what she's trying to tell me is that she's not wearing whatever it is you're supposed to wear underneath the type of skirt that flies out a lot if you plan to do lots of twirling.

"Got it," I say. "But a few steps, at least?"

"Sure. Slow ones."

I get up and we start doing something that's not very much like anything we've ever done at the studio—no sweetheart turns or pretzel or hammerlock—just the two of us swaying, arms on each other's back, and I'm disappointed, since I'd really love to throw her around in that outfit, try out some of our new moves. But there's a Faith Hill ballad on her stereo, maybe a bit sappy but okay, and we stare at each other, and I want to laugh and she does, too, because it all feels a bit like prom ("Let's get our pictures taken under the canopy after this!"); but then those laughy eyes turn deeper for both of us, more serious, on the edge of something, and I can tell we're thinking the same thing, that despite all the lessons and Showcase time and our kisses, we've never just held each other this way, allowed our bodies to touch, let skin linger against skin; and she presses her legs into mine, and my heart begins to thud in my chest, and I'm beginning to see that maybe this is the better dance after all, since I feel her breath on mine, and we kiss, and she's running her hands up the back of my shirt, and I'm running mine down that velvety top toward the back of her skirt, which is silky and smooth and filmy, her bare skin just beneath, and she starts to make a little moaning noise in the back of her throat and kisses me harder, and now she's tugging the shirt from my pants and the breathing has picked up for both of us, and neither one of us can seem to find enough of the other's lips, and this whole dance, it's getting easy to see, is heading for the bedroom, where the final moves will take place later tonight, or tomorrow, or both.

The only time I ever had sex and didn't compare it to any other time was the first time I had it. (What could I compare it to? My hand?) But every other time I've done it, I've measured up partners, in terms of the way she kisses, how she moves underneath, if she likes it on top, scratches her nails down my back, likes her wrists pinned down, likes to pin down mine, or does any of the million and six other things people tend to do during sex.

But not this time. This time there is only...*Yes.*

In the morning she tells me she'd love to close the blinds, unplug the phone, stay in bed all day, put the world on pause (except for us). But she's booked with a full day of appointments, starting at nine, and she doesn't want to disappoint. I'd expect nothing less. Besides, I have business of my own in Chicago, which I tell her is just for today. But at least we have time for a shower, together, which results in her leaving late for her first appointment. Sorry, Mrs. Blair.

CHAPTER THIRTEEN

Katharine told me she'd have someone waiting at the airport to pick me up. I'm expecting Morgan Freeman from *Driving Miss Daisy*, chauffeur's cap and all. What I get is Leonardo DiCaprio from *Titanic*. Only he's taller and blonder and his eyes are a deeper shade of blue. It's Brent, her assistant.

"Lovely to meet you," he says. There's British in his tone. "I had a feeling it was you when I saw you. Katharine gave me a spot-on description."

"Thanks for coming."

He's wearing a brown leather blazer and jeans with wine-colored loafers. "Any bags to collect?"

"No. Just my carry-on."

We make our way out to a Jeep Cherokee with buttery leather seats. Brent tells me he's been Katharine's assistant for the last six years and loves the job, and her, and sometimes she goes into Starbucks and gets the coffee for *him* (don't I know), and never throws cell phones at him, like a certain model named Naomi, or dumps her jacket on his desk, Miranda Priestly style, and I laugh because I get the reference (*The Devil Wears Prada*, don't you know). Plus, they shoe shop together. I tell him I have a shoe shopping buddy, too, and her name is Marie, even though it's only been for one pair of shoes, for dancing, but nothing's better, is it?

He drops me off at the Drake, and it's still early enough that I have some time to kill before dinner, so I cross Lakeshore Drive and take a stroll and watch the volleyball players and joggers and sailboats. I call Marie and tell her I made it in fine, and I wish she were here, or I were there, but we'll be seeing each other soon enough.

I get back to my room about six thirty and realize I've worked up a bit of a sweat, which I now regret since I'll be slipping back into the same moist khakis and oxford shirt after my shower. Oh well. At least *I'll* be clean. I get the shower going and I'm getting ready to step in when I hear a knock on the door.

"Front desk."

I throw on my plush hotel robe and open the door. It's one of the bellhops.

"Good evening, Mr. Samuel." He's holding a garment bag and a shoebox. "May I come in, sir?"

"Uh, sure."

He carefully lays the bag on my bed, the box on the floor.

"Compliments of Ms. Longwell. Good evening." He touches his cap and is gone, and I'm too stunned to realize I should've given him a tip.

I peel the wrapper off the garment bag. It's a navy pinstripe blazer with matching pants, a belt, and a powder blue shirt. Inside the box is a pair of black loafers. There's a note pinned to the lapel of the jacket: *Brent said you traveled light. We thought these might be your size, and look great on you. See you at seven thirty. K.*

Well son of a bitch: I *am* being wined and dined.

I shower and slip into my new duds, which fit perfectly, and style my hair the way Rosie did in the salon, best as I can. I think it works, because after the front desk calls and says Ms. Longwell is here for me, I pass a couple women in the lobby who give me a second look. I toss them a smile, like *ho hum*, just another day for me at the Drake in my Ralph Lauren Black Label pinstripe suit and Cole Haan loafers, but it doesn't feel that way inside.

Outside, in the early evening light, I look for the Cherokee from this afternoon, or a limo, or Brent, but see nothing of that sort. Only a vintage Jaguar convertible with the top down and Demi Moore leaning against the hood. Demi gives me a wave.

"Mitch!"

The first thing I notice is her legs. Tanned and slender and toned, and about six feet long. At least that's how they look in her dress, which is black and clingy and short. Her hair is down and straight and thick, and her sunglasses on top hold some of it back. She gives me a hug and I smell her perfume: womanly, sexy, expensive.

"Let's have a look at you," she says, holding me at arm's length. It's obvious she likes what she sees. "Brent has a wonderful eye for sizes, doesn't he?"

"He does," I agree, though I'm not sure I like the fact that Brent checked me out enough to get my size. But I should, since it all fits so well. "And you look . . . wow. Fantastic."

"*Merci beaucoup.*" She throws a little shoulder turn into the pose, model-like, which accentuates her, um, assets. I try not to stare, at either of them. "Shall we?" she asks.

We shall.

It's my first time in a Jag, and I'll tell you straight off it's no Malibu sedan. Not that we set any land speed records, because we don't: what we do is cruise along the lake, the wind in our hair, and it's a beautiful evening, the sun going down, and a ton of people are out, staring at us at stoplights, and what they're thinking, I'm sure, is, "Hey, it's Demi and Ashton," but I'd be flattering myself if I thought I looked half that good, so it's more like, "Hey, it's Demi and Ashton's cousin Shlomo." But I still feel pretty good about myself, if you want to know the truth.

We eventually get to a restaurant called Jimmy's and you can see it's a nice place from the lighting and all the woodwork and the jazz trio. Katharine is from the area, still has family here and lives here most of the year, and this is one of her favorite places to eat. The maître d' leads us to our table, and other patrons stare at us, as people did outside, whispering, nudging each other, but now it feels intrusive. It's one thing to do it when we're in the car, out in the open, on public streets; but we're here for dinner, so come on, people, give us a break. One woman a couple tables over actually pulls out a cell phone and I think she's going to call someone, but she snaps a picture. She's lucky I don't go over there and break the damn thing.

"Do you ever get tired of that?" I ask. "People more or less pawing you with their eyes wherever you go?"

She smiles as if I've said something terribly amusing, which I don't think I have. "No. I don't."

"Really? Never?"

"Really. *Never.*"

She can tell I'm having a tough time believing that, because she gives me another smile, this one sympathetic. "Let me explain something, Mitch. Do you have any idea who I was before I was this?" and here she makes a mock grandiose gesture to refer to herself.

It's a dangerous question (a thousand times more dangerous than "Does this make my ass look big?") because if I base it on how she looks today, then subtract fifteen or so years to get her back before it all started, I'm tempted to say something like "the highest-priced call girl in town," which, I believe, isn't the kind of thing a woman wants to hear. So I take the easy way out.

"I don't know. Fashion consultant for *Elle*?"

She just laughs. "No, not quite. I was a secretary for an insurance agent. The woman you'd call to give the make and model and year of your new car, and I'd quote you rates, depending on your age and zip code and what kind of deductible you wanted. Or maybe it was a boat or trailer or motorcycle. I did those too. I sat in front of a computer screen all day and took smoke breaks and was thirty pounds overweight. *That* was Katharine Longwell."

I've seen those before-and-after diet ads in magazines. She could *definitely* do one, if she still has the before pictures. Not that she needs to, with the writing career and all.

"Those were desperate days, Mitch. I wanted to kill myself. Not that I was actually suicidal, but I just wanted to put an end to that type of life. *This* is what I'd been so excited to get to when I was a kid and couldn't wait to grow up? So I started to write. I created a character just like me, a woman who was overweight, stuck in a dead-end career, with a history of bad relationships and no good prospects on the horizon. But then I gave her what *I* wanted: a fairy godmother, an escape, a way to change her life. She wins a contest to go to the Academy Awards with a celebrity date. Can I tell you it was Pierce Brosnan, even though I called him Brock? Anyway, she finds the willpower to lose the weight, become more assertive and self-possessed, so that by the time she gets to the Oscars and meets Brock, and he's a dud, she has become fabulous, star quality herself, inside and out, and her life takes off from there."

The story she's talking about is *Leading Lady*, her first novel. And bestseller. And movie. As if you didn't know.

"Let me tell you, Mitch, I had a great time turning the ugly duckling into a princess. And it was easy to do, because it was all in my head, and anything can happen there. But then one day I realized that it didn't have to be just in my head. I was alive, I still had dreams, and I could change *my* life, *if I wanted.* So I quit my job, did some freelance writing, started eating better and going to the gym and smiling more. And maybe I wasn't having tantric sex with my twenty-two-year-old hunky personal trainer or tying the hands of A-list actors to the bedposts, like my heroine, but at least I was getting second glances, having guys want my number, getting an article published here or there, *liking* myself. So that by the time I finished writing my book, I was looking people in the eye and taking chances and believing in myself. I'd created a different me, one that my ten-year-old self would be proud of, a woman who was strong and sexy and confident. I'd already won. And then the novel got published and flew off the shelves, and the rest, as they say, is history."

Here, she gives a delicious smile.

"Has some of it gone to my head? You bet it has. I love my clothes, my cars, my spa retreats, my ski trips to Tahoe, the fact that I can see a handsome young man in a coffee shop and flirt with him and fly him up to dinner on a day's notice because from the moment I laid eyes on him, I knew exactly the suit he'd look good in. And you do look good, Mitch." Here, Katharine Longwell—shopper, spa-hopper, and slope-dropper—gives me a smoldering gaze. "But beyond indulging my whims whenever and however I please, it's also given me the power to take on causes, adopt pet projects, like helping out Bradley with her writing. And I *love* doing that. Because in my heart of hearts, Mitch, despite the red carpets and Elton John Oscar parties and magazine cover shoots, that's what I am, too: a writer. And my greatest pride still comes from knowing that I'm able to lay a good story down on the page."

"Not according to critics." It's out before I can stop it. "I mean, that's what my cousin says. And she hates them for it."

"Ah, the critics. Well, with all due respect, when it comes to the critics, I made a decision a long time ago not to be a Keats."

"Pardon?"

"John Keats. English poet. Familiar with him?"

"Yeah. A little."

"'Ode on a Grecian Urn.' 'La Belle Dame sans Merci.' Sublime. Anyway, the critics hated his first book of poetry, he never got over it, and eventually it killed him."

"Uh, didn't he also have TB?"

"Sure he did. But the reviews crushed his spirit, took away his will to fight it. That's what I believe. In any case, I promised myself I wouldn't be one of those writers who lived and died by what the critics said. Great, if they loved me. But given the choice, I'd rather have my readers love me."

"But isn't that just pandering, appealing to the lowest common denominator?"

"Why? Just because the books sell lots of copies and people are entertained?"

"Yeah, basically. I mean, it shouldn't really matter how much people are entertained, or how many people read it. A novel should be art."

"And it is, sometimes. It's called literature. Artists do it, like Woolf and Faulkner and Flaubert. The rest of us are a different breed. We're storytellers. We're the ones who gather people around the campfire and spin yarns. Except we do it on the page."

I cross my arms.

"You don't think that's good enough, do you? That there's value in just weaving a good story and being entertaining?"

"No" is what I want to say, but I'm at risk of digging myself, and my cousin, into a bigger hole and blowing my cover, so I just sort of shrug.

She gives me a smile. "Let me ask you something, Mitch. You've heard of the Arabian Nights, right? Aladdin, Ali Baba, Sinbad the Sailor…"

I nod.

"Do you know who tells those stories?"

"Scheherazade."

"Good. And do you know why?"

I honestly can't remember. So I just shake my head.

"King Shahriyar's first wife cheats on him, so in revenge, enlightened soul that he is, he takes a new bride each day and executes her after the wedding night. Scheherazade is his latest, and she knows what's coming, so on her wedding night she tells the king a story, but she leaves it incomplete, promising to finish the next night. The king is so enthralled by the tale, he puts off killing her for one night, to hear the end. And the next night she does the same, and the next, and the next, until all her tales are told, and he's been so captivated by the thousand and one nights of her stories, Ali Baba and all the rest, that he permanently abandons his plan to kill her, or any other women. Armed only with her wiles and a collection of entertaining stories, she saves her own life, and the life of every other woman in the kingdom."

It sounds familiar now that she's saying it, so I'll assume she's not making it up.

"Mitch, you're a smart guy and you can probably see it yourself. But I think there's a moral there." She leans forward in her chair and I catch a whiff of her perfume, which still smells great. "Even those stories that *merely* entertain us have the power to touch us and delight us, and that goes a long way toward making us more human."

I'm sure I could rebut her if I wanted, come up with something from Goethe or Stendhal or Henry James that has nothing to do with stories as entertainment. But right now I don't feel much like trying. Sitting in my new clothes, listening to piano jazz, smelling Katharine's perfume, watching our waiter serve us our bottle of Bordeaux, I think I'd rather just kick back and enjoy my dinner.

Later, we drive back to her brownstone to "talk about the book." What this means, I assume, is that she'll grab some champagne and slip into a swimsuit the size of a shoestring and shuttle us out to her *Bachelor*-style hot tub for some one-on-one time ("Time to earn your flight up here, big boy"), so I already have my excuse: I'm allergic to champagne. And swimsuits. And water. But instead of stripping down to our skivvies and "talking about the book," we actually sit on the sofa in her living room and *talk about the book*. There are some minor changes she'd make — jazz up some names, tone down a drunken St. Tropez orgy, give the husband a redeeming quality or two (since why would Courtney go back to him, even temporarily, before she winds up with the other guy?) — but overall, Bradley is on the right track, her instincts are good, she's got a firm grasp of the genre, the writing is strong and funny. In other words, Katharine likes it a lot. So much, in fact, that though it's only a hundred pages, if Bradley keeps up as she's going right now, *Catwalk Mama* could find its way into print.

I nearly fall off the sofa. "You mean . . . as in published?"

She nods. "Of course, I don't want to get anyone's hopes up too early. This isn't the easiest business to break into, and even with all my connections, it's not like I can just wave a wand and get it published for her. But I think it has the chance to be something special. If the rest stays this clever, sexy, and good-hearted, I'd be happy to pass it along to my agent, throw a little weight around, see if I can't get something rolling."

Katharine Longwell as my fairy godmother? "This is great. I appreciate that. I mean, we both do."

"Don't thank me yet. I haven't done anything."

But we both know she has — in a big way. She smiles and reaches out to clink my wineglass.

I finish my sip, then stifle a yawn, but not quickly enough, because it catapults Katharine into one of her own, a long cat-like thing, as she arches her back and stretches her arms over her head, and the dress pulls tighter across her chest. Apparently, from the looks of things, she's sleepy *and* chilly.

"Mitch, this is the point where I'm supposed to drive you back to your hotel. But I'm just too damned tired. And Brent is off, doing whatever he does." She puts a hand on my thigh. "How about you just spend the night here?"

Oh, god: *now* it's happening. "Here?" I ask, an octave too high.

"Here, Mitch. My place. Casa Longwell."

"Oh, hey, Spanish. '*Mi casa, tu casa, sí?*'" I cough. "Hmm. Sure." I give a little bounce on the sofa. "Comfy. No bed for me. Right here is just fine."

She laughs. "You're not sleeping on the sofa, Mitch. I've got something much better in mind."

She gets up and stands in front of me and offers her hand, which I accept (*what the hell can I do?*), then leads me down the hallway, shoes in one hand, mine in the other. We stop in a doorway. She flips on a light. I squeeze my eyes shut.

"Well, what do you think?" she asks.

Nothing, since I'm still in the dark. But slowly I squint them open, till I can make out hardwood flooring, forest green walls, and *a bed*. It's humongous.

"You should find everything you need in the bathroom. Fresh towels, a robe, even slippers. Though the other guest room has a bigger TV."

Other *guest* room? My heart begins to beat again. "No, this is perfect. I love it."

She tilts her head, shakes out her hair, gives me a sidelong glance. "Of course, if you'd prefer to join me in my bed, that would be fine, too."

When I was a kid, I'd occasionally put up a stink when my parents told me it was time for bed, insist I wasn't tired, plead for another ten minutes of TV time, argue that Scott got to stay up later. Did it work? *Never.* Because when you're eight years old, you do as you're told.

That's how I feel right now.

"Katharine, uh, how do I say this? I'm extremely, um, flattered by the offer. You're a stunning woman. But the thing is, well, I'm sort of seeing someone at the moment."

"Ah. So what's her name?"

"Marie."

She gives me a smile. "I've always liked that name. *Marie.*" She says it with the care of a poet, gives extra air to the long *e* sound, and hearing someone say it that way makes me realize how much I love the sound of those syllables. "Is it serious?"

I freeze, since I'm worried it's some sort of trick question, like if I say yes, she'll ask me if my relationship with Marie is more important than helping out my cousin; but if I say no, then why won't I sleep with her? There's no good way out of this, not one that won't result with her hissing at me to give back the clothes I'm wearing, right now, on the spot, since she paid for them, and forget about getting any help with *Catwalk Mama*, because it's stupid and terrible, and did I think she was doing it out of the goodness of her heart; and I'll be left to hail a cab in my boxers and black socks and despicably reeking manuscript. So I just think of Marie.

"Very."

Her face warms. "Then she's a lucky woman." She grazes my wrist with her free hand. "Goodnight, Mitch."

She starts down the hall, but before she makes it to her room, she begins to unzip her dress, just to let me know what I won't be seeing. I don't even allow myself a look.

In the morning we go out for breakfast, and more stares, but after what she said last night about being grateful for the attention, I'm getting better with it myself, and I even smile a couple times. Let them wonder who I am. She gives me a hug, then Brent drives me to the airport, and by noon I'm on my way back to St. Louis. Sitting at thirty thousand feet, I recap my weekend. Jason made love to a beautiful woman. Bradley has a good chance of getting her novel published. Mitch, *well*...his luck hasn't changed a bit. But the people he lives with are certainly doing well.

CHAPTER FOURTEEN

You don't have to be Ebert or Roeper or even Gene Shalit to know what a montage is. It's that part in the movie where music plays and there's a collection of mini-scenes that zooms you around from place to place and you get the sense a whole lot is going on. The most famous one ever done, probably, is the training montage from the original *Rocky*, where Rocky jogs train tracks and back alleys and does one-arm push-ups and punches out sides of beef in Paulie's meat locker, and all the while that *Rocky* theme urges him on, horns blaring—da na NA/DA NA na—pushing him harder, faster, *higher!* till at last he bounds up the steps of the Philadelphia art museum two or three at a time, gets to the top, and looks out over the city and raises his arms in victory, and the gospel choir belts out, "Gonna fly now! / Flying high now" Watch it again sometime and see if you don't want to get up and throw a few jabs yourself.

But most of the rest are crap, cheap and lazy ways to push a story along, and the chief pushers, so to speak, are the romantic comedies and their pathetic dating montages. How many times have we seen a couple take a barefoot stroll on the beach, or end a slow dance with a kiss, or meander down the boardwalk eating ice cream, or have dinner on the rooftop of his apartment (with the obligatory scattered rose petals and ten thousand lit candles placed on the table and rooftop ledge and fire escape and every conceivable inch of the place, including the head of every pigeon, and how does this guy have time to light so many candles *and* cook a gourmet dinner *and* sprinkle all those rose petals *and* get his hair so GQ? You'd almost think he had the help of a movie crew).

That's why one of my all-time favorite movie scenes is the dating montage from *The Naked Gun*. Leslie Nielsen is a wrinkled old cop and Priscilla Presley is smoking hot, which means, of course, sparks fly between them when they meet, and before you can say, "He's a wrinkled old cop and she's smoking hot," she's calling him "Funnyface" and they're a couple. *Roll montage!* The music is Herman's Hermits "I'm into Something Good" and the two lovebirds run hand in hand on the beach...and clothesline another couple; he accidentally sprays a splotch of mustard on her blouse...and they titter their way through a condiment fight; they look out with wonderment from the bridge of a ship...that happens to be moored to the dock; they come out of the theater doubled over with laughter...and the marquee lets us know it's *Platoon*. And when the music stops and the montage is over— complete with song title and artist's name in the lower left hand corner, like it's a video on MTV—Priscilla turns to him and says, "I had a wonderful day." A wonderful *day!* A wonderful *day!* *Ha!* As if couples in love have nothing better to do than giggle and chortle and titter their way through the seconds and minutes and hours of their days, frolicking in frivolity and mirth and hilarity, acting like wacky kids.

Apparently they don't.

To my great surprise and embarrassment, this is more or less exactly the way it goes for Marie and me over the next few weeks. We spend all our time doing wildly fantastic and enjoyable things, it's all bliss and smiles, and I do feel like a wacky kid, and if I were watching any of this in the theater, I'd throw my popcorn at the screen and threaten to burn the whole place down unless I got my money back. Consider yourself warned, then, if you're the kind who can't stomach crappy dating montages (trust me, I understand) and turn away for a moment. For those still with me, here's a little something I'm calling "Marie and Mitch: October into November." I'll get it going with a little feedback from John's guitar, let Paul and George and Ringo jump in when ready, the tune is "I Feel Fine," and when you feel those harmonies start to get under your skin, go ahead and play the images, at your own pace.

Café Provencal: The two of us out for dinner, she wearing something sleek and form-fitting, me wearing something ironed, and we've had our entrées, feeding each other a sample of this and that off our own plates, and now the waiter comes by with the dessert cart and we give each other a delicious smile: we've got a taste for something decadent, but it isn't on his cart.

Her bedroom: Sex.

Dance studio: She wears shorts and a T-shirt, I'm in a T-shirt and jeans, and we're both sweaty, rehearsing for the Showcase, and Adonis is working with us, getting me to hold my lines when I complete a turn, arms fully extended, and I don't get it, I can't get it, it doesn't feel right; and then I get it and he claps and Marie claps and I polish my fingernails on my chest like it was nothing at all.

Her shower: Sex.

Art museum: We stroll through the modern wing, past the

Pollack and Lichtenstein and Warhol, and come across a pile of rusty pipes and plaster and nails, and we stand there and stare and scratch our heads: plumbing mishap or a piece of art?

Her kitchen: Sex.

St. Genevieve: We're out in her convertible, top down, and I'm driving, and the leaves on the trees are an explosion of crimson and gold and orange, and the dirt road we're on leads through miles and miles of the same, and I turn to her, and her hair is like a ribbon in the wind.

Bed and breakfast, on a blanket, in front of a crackling fire: Sex.

It may seem like we're making a porn flick, but we're not. That's just the limitation of the montage format, since it gives you the impression that the featured activity is happening every thirty seconds. Which it isn't. Most days. But since this is a PG-13 montage and we're talking about Marie, I'm not going to get explicit with any of the details—this is all strategically placed bedcovers and body parts and camera angles—other than to say that more often than not, we hit our marks at exactly the same time, if you know what I mean. Not the most stirring montage in the history of cinema—for sheer adrenaline, Rocky's your man—but as far as I'm concerned, you can have sweaty Stallone. I'll take my sweaty Marie.

Now, to answer a few questions. *Is he Jason or Mitch?* Jason, for a little while longer, till the time is right. (Think about it: you wouldn't tell your significant other about your fungus toenail on the second or third date, would you? "Hey, come here and look at this black stuff." Gross, inappropriate, a relationship killer. But wait long enough, till you're riding high and past the point where revealing minor flaws is anything to worry about, and then just mention it in passing, and you'll be lucky if your honey even raises an eyebrow.) *How is he handling that supposed job situation?* Simple. I set the alarm for six and get up and get dressed — business casual — and head off to my workplace, which happens to be my apartment or the library or my classroom, and I don't feel all that guilty, since I *am* working. In fact, I've never been so productive with the writing in my life. Finally, *Are they living together?* The answer to that is no. N. O. *No.* I do spend a lot of time at her place, maybe three nights a week or more (we never spend time at my place: "my roommates are *such* disasters"), but I've decided I'm not going to make the same mistake I made with Hannah, let a mostly behind-the-scenes accumulation of books and CDs and jeans and boxers constitute such a momentous step as living together. When that day comes, and let me tell you, it will, I'll gleefully blow a wad on champagne and dinner and some kind of expensive gift — jewelry, no doubt — because it means, finally, *Yes! We're living together!*

So, as you can see, from where I'm standing (or sitting or lying, depending on what the two of us are doing), things couldn't be better. But what about Marie? How does *she* feel about all this? Hmm. You really want to know? Then hit the repeat button on your iPod and listen to the lads from Liverpool one more time and pay attention to that second line. Better yet, let me sing it for you: "She's happy as can be, you know."

Yep, it's going that well.

A couple weeks into November, Bradley and Skyler invite me over for dinner. I'm happy to accept, since I haven't been spending much time with either of them: Bradley's been busy with work and Skyler; I've been busy with *work* and Marie. We're barely past the *hellos* and *don't you look greats?* when I realize something's off. Skyler's not much of a cook, Bradley can barely boil water, but tonight they serve an artichoke dip appetizer and roasted salmon topped with mango salsa, which you can tell took time, and there's a tablecloth on the table and no paper plates. And the two of them are so...*giddy*. I'm missing something. But none of it's so over the top—no Wedgwood china or Waterford crystal, no one's suggested a game of Twister—that I feel compelled to ask, *Why the better spread? What gives with all the giddy?* Besides, I don't want to give the impression that the food usually tastes like cardboard, or they're typically sticks in the mud. So I stay quiet.

Skyler talks about the nursery, and Bradley talks about the house he's working on, how his next project will be the attic. For my part, I try to be as honest as possible, which means I tell them the teaching is fine (it is), my family is doing well (they are), and I'm working on a book (I am), though I beg off sharing any of the details. The only time I'm forced to do anything that comes close to fibbing is when Bradley asks about my love life, and I shrug and grunt and make a face that, if you were really on top of it, you could easily recognize as "I'm in love with your sister, even though she thinks I'm someone else," but for whatever reason, he and Skyler take as "not so great." Do I want another go with Trista? No thanks.

After the meal, we settle in the living room in front of the fire with glasses of wine and Chet Baker on the stereo. My next move will be to lapse into a coma, since I'm warm and full and sleepy, and any misgivings I had earlier about the way they were acting or whether or not I should've noticed something have all been put to bed.

"See, I told you he wouldn't notice," Skyler says to Bradley.

Aw, *hell!*

I sit up and look at Bradley, but he's just shaking his head like, "Dude, you disappoint me," and then I look at Skyler, since it's obvious something *is* different—she just said so—but her hair and eyes and mouth all look the same, as do her breasts, which, I confess, I check out, because for some strange reason I'm thinking maybe that's it, though it hardly seems like the type of thing she'd expect me to notice in the first place and comment on, or point out herself if I failed to notice. But it's not those, or anything about either of them, or the room, and it's clear I've let everyone down.

Smiling, Skyler brings her hand up to her cheek, open palmed, more to display her fingers than anything. The firelight catches something on her finger, causing it to glint. It's a ring, on her left hand, on her ring finger.

"Holy shit!"

Instantly we're on our feet, hugging and spilling our wine and acting like kids who just found out school is canceled, and can you believe it? When we finally squeeze back on the sofa, Skyler tells me how it happened: two nights ago, he took her out for dinner at her favorite restaurant, then they came back here and sat on the back patio next to the terra-cotta firepot, a blanket between them, and he pulled out a ring box he'd made for her, and gave her the ring. No gimmicks, nothing hidden in a box of Cracker Jacks, no proposal emblazoned on the scoreboard during the seventh-inning stretch; just Bradley, a ring, and a question.

"May I see it?" I ask of the ring.

She reaches across Bradley with her hand and it's trembling, she's so excited. The center stone is a brilliant-cut round diamond, with trillions and a row of tapered baguettes on each side, and the band is platinum. I don't ask about the clarity or carat — VS1 at least and a carat and a half, my guess, but really it's none of my business. Besides, I'd have to explain how I know anything about engagement rings or the four Cs of diamonds, which would be from my chick-lit research, which I'd rather not get into right now. What's important is that the ring is classy and elegant and substantial. Like Skyler.

"Wow. I didn't even know the two of you'd been looking at rings," I say.

"We hadn't been." Skyler puts her fingers through Bradley's and rests their intertwined hands in her lap. "This guy got the bright idea to go out and do it all on his own."

He shrugs. "When you know, you know."

What he's talking about, I realize, is the ring, the timing, and the woman. And from the way light's shooting out from every pore of skin on Skyler's face, I'd say he got all three right.

We settle in for a new round of drinks, Bradley pouring, and he tells me I'm the first one they've told: his family finds out this weekend, hers when they go to Colorado for Thanksgiving. Of course, he needed to tell me now to make sure I was free on the first Saturday of October next fall. After all, what's a wedding without a best man?

The day of the Showcase arrives and I discover I'm doing fine. Fine as we pack up the car with all the things she spent so much time ironing last night, including my Zorro outfit, complete with mask and mustache (as opposed to a pair of slacks and a polo: I'm into not being recognized). Fine at the studio as we help rearrange tables and hang up streamers and blow up balloons. Even fine as the DJ sets up his equipment and does sound checks and plays snippets of Showcase songs. But not so fine when we finally do slip into our outfits, and there's an audience, and we're about to go on, and the studio is no longer the safe, cozy place where Marie and Adonis and I have worked so many hours, on our own, but has become a glitzier, fancier, Showcasier place. I'm nervous. Sweaty palms, heartbeat-in-the-throat, wobbly voice sort of nervous.

Marie is standing next to me in that sexy getup, which isn't helping matters a bit.

"You okay?" she asks.

"Yes. No."

She rubs my back. "You'll do fine. Think of all the time we've put in. Think of all the times you've done it perfectly in practice. Hundreds, probably."

"But not under these circumstances."

What I want to tell her is that when humans get nervous, our bodies get flushed with adrenaline—*for fleeing!*—which over-rides a lot of the body's other functions, and memory is the first thing to go. But then I'm not sure if it's memory at all: maybe it's hearing, or sense of smell, or peripheral vision. But since I can't remember, it must be memory, which is a terrible sign. Suddenly I'm quizzing myself about things I know for certain, just to reas-sure myself, but I'm getting mixed results, since I still remember that Shelley wrote "Ode to a Skylark" but I'm having difficulty remembering which Brontë sister wrote *Wuthering Heights*. And if I can't remember that, is there any way I'll remember to pass Marie on the correct side when we do our cape turn?

"What's the worst that could happen?" she asks.

"I could forget every move I'm supposed to do, then trip and fall and take you down with me."

"Fine. Say it all happens. Then what?"

I look at her in disgust. "What do you mean, 'then what'? That means we've made total fools of ourselves, and everyone laughs, and it's a disaster."

She shrugs. "So it's a disaster. Everyone laughs. Then we go home."

I'm not sure how this is supposed to help: so it's a disaster and everyone laughs and we go home. But then she squeezes my hand and smiles at me, *really* smiles, like this is one of the greatest days of her life, and I hear what she's saying in a different way. Not that we go home, in the sense of retreating from the scene with our tails tucked between our legs; but in the sense that, despite whatever happens tonight on the dance floor—whether we end up in a heap or not—when the final glass of punch is poured and last cookie eaten and all the balloons have gone soggy, *we* go home. Together. And because of that, this can't be so bad.

The music comes on and that's our cue to go out, and we get off to a shaky start, since I begin on the wrong beat; but after that we're good, solid, in sync, and it's over before I barely have time to realize I'm doing it; and then we're getting a loud ovation and taking a bow, and I'm already ticked off that I didn't jazz it up a little more, do something flashy with my cape, because I know I could have. But maybe next time. Then the rest of the evening is ours to clown around and cut loose and eat cookies and get flirty and laugh and kiss.

Back home, after a little celebratory sex, she tells me her brother is engaged. I don't want to play dumb, ask dopey questions as if I don't already know (What's his fiancée's name? What does she look like? Who's his best man?), so I ask a question that I could ask even if she knew I already knew.

"Are you happy for him?"

She rolls on her side and gives me a ridiculously happy smile. "Very. I know how much he loves her. He's exactly where he wants to be." Then she lays her head on my chest and nuzzles and does something that sounds like a purr. Which, I think, is her way of saying so is she.

Early the following week I meet up with my dad and Nathan for a round of golf at my dad's course. (My dad can't actually golf because he's still too sore from surgery; he's the designated cart driver.) It's about fifty-five degrees, the sun is out full-tilt, so the weather's just about perfect. My golf game is not. I haven't played in years and I'm rusty, spraying the ball all over the course. Nathan, however, is firing from the get-go, grooving his swing, so that by the time I turn it around and start playing better, it's too late; he beats me by a half dozen strokes.

Afterwards, we grab our sodas and sit outside, and my father seems to know everyone, coming or going, and he introduces me to some of the regulars. I feel like I'm the governor, shaking all those hands. Nathan talks about soccer and video games and school, and he doesn't sweat or choke or stumble on his words when he talks about girls, and I realize things have changed mightily from my day. A border collie mix named Shep hangs with us, but he's anxious to do some work, round up some cattle, perhaps, or golfers.

Eventually my father checks his watch and turns to Nathan. "I think someone needs to be heading home to get the table set for dinner."

"Can't Jessica do it? Or Mom?"

Not the right answer, from the look my dad gives him. Nathan trudges over to his bike.

"Please tell Mom I'll be there in a few minutes," my dad says. "And put your light on, son."

"But it's not even dark."

"I need you to light the way for me. Okay?"

He flips the switch and a taillight beats out a red pulse. As he leaves the lot, he calls out a goodbye, and Shep takes this as his cue for action—*finally!*—and tears out after him. They both dart out of view down a street that leads into my father's neighborhood.

The sun begins to slip past the horizon, and we both watch. It's the time of day when nothing is blanched or washed out by the intensity of the sun, and everything—the trees, the grass, the skin on my father's face—bears its truest colors.

"This worked out a little better for you, didn't it?" I ask.

He tilts his head a bit. "Oh?"

I nod, to out there. "This world. This life." I pause. "This family."

He remains silent.

"You can talk about it. It won't hurt my feelings."

"I've already told you, Mitch. Your mother and I did some hateful things to each other. And because of that, we failed you as parents. Or at least I did."

"You didn't answer my question."

He gives his head a helpless shake. "How can I? You want me to compare families? You're my son, sitting right in front of me. What do you want me to say?"

"The truth."

"Ah, the truth. 'What is truth?'" He says it in a voice slightly different than his own. "Pontius Pilate, right? At the interrogation, just before he hands Jesus over to be crucified. Your Jewish father remembers that, from his days with his Catholic sons and their religion classes."

He smiles to himself, as if despite everything, there's still a trace of something sweet and nostalgic about those days. But it all drains quickly from his face.

"Here's what I know, Mitch. I know there are nights when I have to get out of bed because I can't sleep, and the reason I can't sleep is because I lost a daughter and two sons, at least their hearts. I had one chance at that, to be their father, and I let them all slip through my hands. Then I think about Nathan and Jessica sleeping, and Leah in our bed, and I realize those children wouldn't be alive, and she wouldn't be my wife, if my first life hadn't failed. And that's when it hits me, the guilt, the shame, the gratitude, and I ride it out like a passing storm."

I stare at this sixty-year-old man, the pouchy skin under his mud-colored eyes, the age spots on his wrinkled forehead. My father. A man so miserable in one life, so happy in another. And what changed? There was no personality transplant, no conversion to Zen Buddhism, no red Corvette: he found a woman he loved, and she loved him back. And that, I suppose, is the beauty and tragedy of life. To bastardize a little Shakespeare, from *Julius Caesar*: Find the right person, and all of life leads on to fortune; choose the wrong one, and all the voyage of life is bound in shallows and miseries. My father found the person he was supposed to love, the life he was supposed to live, and the family he was supposed to be with. It just wasn't mine.

"Do you think much about her?" I ask. Then I add, even though I don't have to, "Emily?"

He smiles a pure smile. "Every day. That's Jessica's middle name, you know. And you should see Jessica's baby pictures. You'd swear it was Emily." He's lost in his thoughts for a moment. "Every time I look at Jessica, I see her. Both my girls."

My eyes start to sting and well up. I clear my throat. "I should probably be going," I say.

My dad rubs at his eyes. "Yeah, Leah's probably wondering where the hell I am."

The sky is washed in shades of lavender and pink, and if I had a camera, and knew anything about photography, it's the kind of sky I'd want to take a picture of.

"Thanks for coming out, Mitch," he says, shaking my hand. "I had a great day with you and Nathan."

He starts to shuffle away toward the clubhouse.

"Hey, Dad?" I call after him and he stops and turns. "Maybe next time we do this, you could bring Jessica. If she golfs."

"She doesn't," he says. "But I'll bring her anyway."

CHAPTER FIFTEEN

It's ten days before Thanksgiving and we're lying in bed, afterwards. This is one of my overnight stays, so I'm settled, content, dreamy, ready to welcome Mercutio's Queen Mab and her hazelnut chariot and whatever visions she might be bringing my way. Marie, though, has a little frowning look on her face.

"What do you want to do for Thanksgiving?" she asks.

I drape my arm across her stomach. "Spend it right here, with you."

"Right. And miss out on all the stuffing and pie?"

I've been waiting for the Thanksgiving moment, and dreading it, but I'm glad I've given it some thought.

"Well, let's see. You have a tradition with your family, I assume."

"My uncle Ted's."

"And I have two families to deal with, my mom's and my dad's." That's one bit of truth I've given her, that my parents are divorced. "So unless we want to be in one place all day and disappoint two other households, or spend the entire day running back and forth all over the city, I suggest we do our own thing."

This doesn't sit well with her. She leans up on her elbow. "Hey, what if we ask someone to have it a few days earlier, or later?"

I give her a look like, "You can't be serious." What I'm thinking is, "Jesus, I hadn't thought of that." "Don't you think that's a lot to ask, on such short notice, making everyone change their plans just to accommodate us?"

She gets one of those faces like she wants to fight it, but then sinks back into the bed.

I scoot closer and smooth her hair behind her ear. "Marie, listen. We have the big holidays coming up next month. Cookies and eggnog and a visit from St. Nick. Why don't we make plans for that?"

She doesn't respond.

"I promise we'll do it right. Spread it out, visit all the families. Okay? And as for *our* Thanksgiving," I whisper into the nape of her neck, "why don't we do something on Wednesday? Get a bottle of wine, cook up dinner or get takeout, watch a movie. Whatever you want to do."

She still doesn't answer, but does back her body into mine, so that now we're spooning and getting warmer by the second. That's a yes, by the way.

So I've bought myself a little time. A couple weeks at least. That should be plenty of time to come up with a thoughtful, sincere, and casual way to straighten out this whole mess. Or hop on a slow boat to China.

On Thursday I reach a milestone that under any other circumstances would be cause for trumpet blasts and cannon fire: I finish my novel. *Catwalk Mama* is done. Not done in the sense that it won't need a bit of tweaking here and there, but done in the sense that you could sit down and read clean through to page 316 and the story would be complete and whole and satisfying. I pack it all up and send it to Katharine, and to celebrate...I head to Bookzilla.

It's not exactly the way I'd prefer to mark the occasion. A celebratory dinner with my mom or Bradley or Marie would be a thousand times better, but a problem, since my mom doesn't know I started, Bradley doesn't know I finished, and Marie doesn't know who I am. But actually it's okay being here. This is where it all started, basically, and it feels good to come back for a visit that doesn't involve theft. In fact, with nothing on my mind, I grab a cup of caramel mocha latte, sit in the café, kick back, relax, and enjoy.

I watch the guy with the biography of John Adams and the older woman with a travel book on Venice and a couple with a book on infant care — though she doesn't look pregnant, so they must be starting this early — and the others with their paperbacks and hardbacks and bestsellers, and they all seem so absorbed and engrossed that I let myself imagine for a moment that someone in the not-too-distant future will take *my* book off the shelf and come here and sit and enjoy it, and if they do that, and get a laugh or smile out of it, or walk away feeling better than they did before, that would be good. Great, even.

Before I leave, I head up to the front counter to take care of some long overdue business. I don't know the proper protocol, so I jump right in.

"A couple months back, I walked out with a book I didn't pay for. I'd like to pay for it now."

The woman just looks at me. "So...you just walked out with it?"

"Yep." I smile.

"Hmm. I'm not sure how to handle that one."

"How about if I just give you the money for it?"

She gives her head a sad little shake. "Sorry, I can't do that. Then my drawer won't balance. Let me ask Val."

She asks Val, but Val just squints her eyes at me.

"I need to call my manager," my gal says, picking up the intercom phone. "MANAGER ON DUTY, PROBLEM AT CASH WRAP. MANAGER ON DUTY, WE HAVE A PROBLEM AT CASH WRAP." She hangs up. "Did that come through?" she asks.

"It did."

The manager comes over, and he's the kind of guy you'd expect to see leading the football team in tackling drills. I'm thinking maybe he'll make me run laps or do push-ups. The cashier explains the situation, and he looks over at me to make sure he's gotten it right. I nod.

"Well, sir, what we can do, I guess, is I can scan another copy of the book and charge you for it. That way the register comes out okay. It throws inventory off, but it's the lesser of two evils." He steps out from behind the counter. "What did you say the book was?"

At this point, Val and her new customer and everyone waiting in line are all looking at me, and I'm sure I'm blushing, because I feel like I'm blushing, all hot and prickly. I'm tempted to walk over to him and whisper the title in his ear, despite how *that* would look. But I don't. Instead . . .

"*The Cappuccino Club,*" I say. And then, just so he's got it, I add, "By Katharine Longwell."

"Yep. I know it."

And then he walks away to fetch it, no different than if I'd said *Macbeth*, and then he comes back and swipes it and I fork over the $26.85.

"Would you like a receipt with that?" he asks a little sheepishly, since now that I've coughed up the money and have no book in hand, he'd like me to leave with something.

"No, thanks," I say. Besides, I'm already leaving with something: the knowledge that at least in this small way, I'm still capable of telling the truth.

*   *   *

Marie has to work on Saturday, so we meet at the sandwich shop next to her salon for lunch.

"How about dinner tonight at Canyon Café?" she asks as we're finishing up.

"Sure."

"And I'll just meet you there," she half-mutters, trying to sneak it by.

"Meet? Why?"

"No reason." She uses her napkin to wipe her mouth, but it looks more like a bank robber's bandana since it covers everything but her eyes. "I just thought it'd be fun."

"Really. You wanna try that again, Jesse James?"

She lowers the napkin. "That obvious, eh? Fine. Just meet me there."

"Cool. A surprise. So what is it?"

"Like I'm going to tell you. That's the whole point of a surprise, now isn't it? To be surprised."

"I suppose. And you'd be surprised if I didn't show up?"

"Yep. And angry." She gets up and leans down to kiss me. "I'll see you at seven."

I spend the rest of the afternoon not knowing what to do with myself. With the book finished, I feel like I've quit a full-time job, one where I was putting in twelve-hour days, and now I'm bored. I get to the restaurant around six and sit at the bar, watching a hockey game. Around five till seven, my phone rings. It's her.

"I just pulled up at the restaurant," she says. "Where are you?"

So she didn't see my car. "Close. Now, about that surprise you were talking about. Wanna let me in?"

"Be patient. You'll see soon enough."

"Ah, so it's something I get to look at. Are you wearing it?"

"Not quite. But actually it's not an 'it,' it's a 'them.' And I have my arms through one of them right now."

"So, you have your arm through one of them, but you're not wearing it. Hmm." I get up from my stool and take a more covert spot, where I can still see the front door. My plan is to watch her walk in and impress her with my riddle-solving skills.

"Think about it," she says. "What can you put your arm through, but you don't wear?"

"Let's see . . . Oh, I know. The shower curtain. When you reach in to test the water."

"Exactly! How'd you know?" I hear another voice on her end, and she repeats what I said, "shower curtain," and then there's laughter. "*Arms*, Jason. You can put your arms through other people's *arms*. I've brought people. Two of them."

"Oh?" I say, and immediately my stomach flip-flops a little, because when we go out with people, they're usually friends from the studio, and there's no surprise in that, and there wouldn't be tonight. Which means she's brought another kind of people, which I'm not sure I like, and the instant the door swings open and I see the people she's brought, I like it even less. Bradley and Skyler.

Fuck!

I wheel around so quickly that I knock into a guy and he stumbles, but tough luck for him because I dash for the bathroom and duck into a stall.

"Jason? Are you still there?"

"Yeah, yeah, I'm still there," I say, panting. "It's just . . . there's an accident up ahead and I need to be careful here." My legs are shaking, so I sit down. I need to get off the phone before she hears someone whistle or fart or flush. "Hey, Marie. I have another call coming in. Let me put you on hold." I hang up.

Son of a bitch!

The simplest solution would be to climb out a bathroom window, and that's how it'd work in a sitcom, though depending on the sitcom, and the character I play, I would either make it out unscathed or I would get caught in the window, then the three of them would appear on the sidewalk, and I would throw my coat over my head to avoid being seen, but they would notice me anyway, which would have the studio audience in stitches. Unfortunately—or fortunately—there's no bathroom window. The only way out is the way I came in, and the way they came in: the front door. I wait till the bathroom is empty, then I peek out: all clear. I slip out into the hallway and inch my way toward the bar till I see them: they're sitting on the other side. Put my head down and run, or crawl: how about those for options? Then I spot a waitress, which gives me an idea. I signal her over.

"You okay?" she asks.

"No. Not at all. I need to get out of here without some people at the bar seeing me." I pull a twenty out of my wallet. "Do you think you could help?

She eyes me and my money suspiciously. "Did you do something bad to those people?"

"No, I swear. It's a long story and I'd love to explain, and I think you'd get a kick out of it, but right now I just need to get out of here."

She gives me another once-over. Maybe it's the sweaty forehead that convinces her. "Okay. Who is it?"

I point them out.

"I'll mistake the guy for someone I went to school with." She brushes the money away. "You keep that. Just come back sometime and tell me why I had to do this. And leave a big tip."

"The biggest."

She smoothes her hair back and straightens her blouse and walks to the other side. When she gets behind them, she stops, gawks at Bradley, and taps him on the shoulder. "Kevin!" she belts out over the din. Bradley turns. Skyler turns. Marie turns. I run, shielding my face with my hand, heart thudding in my chest, straight out the front door, and I don't stop running till I get to my car, and only when I'm inside, doors locked, slouched down on the seat, do I allow myself a peek back. No one. I wait until I'm off the lot to call Marie back.

"Sorry we got disconnected," I say.

"Is everything all right?"

"I'm afraid not. That was my mom who called. She's sick and she needs me to run to the drugstore." Then I add, because I know she'll be telling Bradley/Kevin: "Her fiancé would do it, but he's in Greece. Flying a plane. He's a pilot."

"I'm sorry to hear she's not well. You want me to come over?"

"No. That's the last thing my mom would want. To meet you under these circumstances. She could be contagious." I pause, breathe, put some nonchalance in my voice. "So anyway, who were the surprise guests?"

"Oh, no one. I'll save it for another time."

"Okay then. Well, I'll give you a call later on, let you know how it's going."

I give her a minute or two to break the news to Bradley and Skyler, then I call Bradley's cell phone. As expected, he has it turned off and I get his voice mail, and I leave a message that I'm at Colchester's grabbing a bite to eat, and he should join me if he can. Of course, I'm not holding out much hope that he'll show, since I get the feeling he's previously engaged.

Bradley and I shoot baskets the next day, despite the cold, because I want to feel him out, see if he suspects anything. He doesn't, of course. But why should he? Put the pieces together and the picture you get looks nothing like me: Jason is Jason, a pharmaceutical rep who drives a Malibu, who loves to dance and has his own shoes, who will watch chick flicks, who will go to malls, who will listen to Mariah Carey, and whose ill mother is engaged to a pilot. What signs point to me? That he has brown hair and brown eyes and his parents are divorced? That's half the male population of St. Louis, probably. Still, I'm paranoid and twitchy, and when Bradley asks me how Colchester's was, I'm glad I actually went, because I can tell him all about it with a mostly clean conscience.

I spend the rest of the afternoon reflecting on how absurd this has gotten. Maybe if I were a spy in a foreign country, breaking up terrorist plots or sabotaging hostile nuclear weapons programs; or maybe if I were an airplane pilot, like my mother's fiancé, with wives in three cities; or maybe if I were a mob-informant Donnie Brasco type; maybe then all the subterfuge and trickery and double-dealing would be necessary just to keep myself alive. But I'm just a PhD candidate in a mediocre apartment trying to carve out an unspectacular life with the woman I love. When did I become *The Fugitive*? But, of course, I know when I did: when I introduced the world to Jason Gallagher. One bad decision and it's the gift that keeps on giving.

I'd planned to tell her everything in a couple weeks, before Christmas, but it has to come sooner. This weekend, even. Just let me get through Thanksgiving, then I'll do it, before I wind up sleeping with the fish. Or worse.

Katharine calls on Monday. She's in Chicago to spend the week with her family, but she's gotten the manuscript and cleared all non–Thanksgiving related tasks from her schedule to read it.

"Is it good?" she asks point-blank.

"Um, Bradley seems pleased."

"Ah, ever the diplomat. But what about you, Mitch? Do you like it?"

"Honestly? Yeah, I do."

"Good. Because I trust your judgment."

She tells me she can't wait to read it and will call the moment she's finished.

So...she trusts my judgment. Would you think any less of me if I told you I like that?

Marie and I make an evening of it Wednesday. We don't want to do the traditional Thanksgiving foods, since we'll be getting our fill tomorrow, and Marie doesn't want to cook, so we pick up Chinese and a movie. It's her choice: *Pride and Prejudice*, the one with Keira Knightley. I know there was a big stink when the U.S. version was released, since they actually dared to let Mr. Darcy and Elizabeth share a kiss at the end and that's not in the book, and I'm prepared to be sufficiently outraged by the blasphemy, but it turns out to be a decently clever scene that I don't think Austen herself would've minded. The only awkward moment of the evening occurs when Marie calls Bradley to wish him well on his trip to Colorado with Skyler. I leave the room, since the thought of her talking to him while she's looking at me, or mentioning my name — Jason — makes me a little sick.

Thanksgiving Day goes off without a hitch. I stop in at my dad's around one, just to say hi and meet a few of Leah's relatives, then I get over to my mom's around three. It's a small group, just Scott, Melinda, Kyle, and my mom and grandmother. I toss the football in the yard with Kyle and Scott, then we settle in for the feast and tell Mom how great everything is, then we all collapse on the sofa and into various chairs and say we could sleep for a week and we'll probably never eat again. At one point, I steal away and make a call to Marie. I feel like a kid doing something illicit, speaking in hushed tones in the basement, but the queasy churning in my stomach, I realize, has less to do with the fact that my family might be upstairs listening in than knowing what I'm about to do this weekend. Namely, introduce Marie to a guy named Mitch.

CHAPTER SIXTEEN

I've never been much of a day after Thanksgiving shopper. Day before Christmas, sure. But Marie doesn't have to work and she wants to head out. Mind you, this isn't getting up at four AM to head to K-Mart for eight-dollar microwaves and Tickle Me Elmo dolls; this is bundling up and walking around and soaking up the holiday music and decorations.

I get over to her place around eight for bagels and coffee, and the morning gets off to a rocky start. I spill an entire cup of coffee, which I've never done in my life, and it misses my crotch by millimeters. A scalding hot cup, straight from the pot. I'm embarrassed of course, even though she says it's no big deal since it's only the kitchen floor and an old mug, but what bothers me most is knowing why it happened: nerves, the jitters, unease over my impeding confession. I sop up the mess—on my knees, appropriately, since I'm singing hallelujahs to my guardian angel for sparing me an agonizing stint in bed, in the fetal position, with an ice pack between my legs—and then we're off.

Marie selects a mall even farther out west than her apartment, one I'm not familiar with, so it'll be a bit of an adventure for me. The usual suspects are there — White House/Black Market and Abercrombie and bebe — but there are stores I've never seen before — Hollister Co., J. Jill, Torrid. Everything is done up right, all twinkly and bright and Christmasy, and the kids are visiting Santa and getting their pictures taken. We buy a few gifts for our families, and I see a sweater I want to get her at Ann Taylor, so I make her stand at the Starbucks kiosk while I double back and get it, and we have a great lunch at the Cheesecake Factory, and I'm filled with such a sense of felicity and well-being and joie de vivre that I'm certain this is another outing to add to our montage, and will, like most of the others, end with us in bed. And that's what I'm thinking just after noon, as we stroll hand in hand past the scarf-wearing mannequin at Banana Republic, Dean Martin crooning "Baby, It's Cold Outside," when I see someone I know coming straight toward me, saying my name, smiling, and there's no way to avoid her, unless I want to knock Marie down and sprint the other way, but even that wouldn't help, because Marie has already figured out that the woman's talking to me. And far *far* too late, somewhere deep in the back of my mind, I realize my guardian angel had nothing to do with getting me out of the way of scalding coffee this morning; he's the one who knocked it over in the first place, aiming it straight for my crotch, so that I'd spend the day in bed instead of being here.

"Mitch. Hey, Mitch!"

It's Hannah.

She stops right in front of us and gives me a hug and says she can't believe it's me, this far out west, and at a mall, and she's so happy to see me. I manage to mumble something.

"Oh, and this is my friend Alex," she says, presenting the guy with her. "Alex, this is Mitch, an old friend."

I shake Alex's hand. Alex has a firm grip. My grip isn't firm. I turn to Marie, who isn't blinking. "Marie, Hannah. Hannah, Marie."

"Nice to meet you," Hannah says. Marie just swallows.

"So how've you been?" Hannah asks me.

"Fine. Great."

"Any word on the book?"

"Um, no, no word, nothing. Just a rejection."

"Oh, sorry to hear that. But I assume you're still teaching."

"Teaching. Ha. That's funny. Yep."

She turns to Alex. "Mitch teaches at the university." Alex looks impressed. I'm not sure what Marie looks like, since I don't look her way.

"So...the two of you just out shopping?" Hannah says, moving things forward, beginning a new line of questions.

"We are. In fact, we're on a bit of a tight schedule." I scrounge up a smile for Alex and pat Hannah on the arm. "Great to see you both, but we've got to run."

I sidestep both of them and the throng of shoppers, and pull Marie by the arm like a child over to the bench, where we plop.

"Marie, listen—"

"No. Don't talk. Don't say anything. Just give me a minute." So I do. I give her a minute, but a minute turns into five, and still she's still trying to breathe, or form words, or blink. Finally...

"Why'd she call you 'Mitch'?"

"Because that's my name."

"Your name isn't Jason?"

"No."

"You're not Jason Gallagher?"

"No. I'm Mitch Samuel."

"And you're not a pharmaceutical rep."

"No. I'm a PhD candidate. And I teach and I write."

What she's trying to do, I assume, is process this, make sense of it, understand why I'd use a phony name and occupation, create a whole different person and life. Then she gasps. "Jesus, you're *married*."

"No, no, no. God no. Nothing like that. I'm as single as they come." This relieves her momentarily, and gives me a little momentum, which I decide to run with. "Though there *is* something else you should probably know. Actually, it's sort of funny." I manage a nervous stab of laughter, in case it's catching. It's not. "I know your brother pretty well. In fact, we share an apartment. In fact, even better ... I'm the best man at his wedding."

I've never slapped a woman in the face before (no great accomplishment). This is what it must look like.

"Oh my god oh my god oh my god. You're *Bradley's* Mitch."

It's clear I've miscalculated my momentum, since it's obvious she wasn't ready to hear that the guy she's been dancing with and sleeping with and saying "I love you" to was actually her brother's best friend. It'll be hard to get a word in edgewise, as appalled as she looks.

"I need to get out of here," she says, scrambling up from the bench.

"Marie, hold on. Let me explain—" I grab for the arm of her sweater and get it, but she spins around and pulls with such force and anger that I'm shocked into letting go, which sends her stumbling over her own feet and onto her backside, in a painful-looking spill. We're both stunned.

I get off the bench to help her, but she scoots the other way, kicking out at me. "Don't touch me," she screams, getting to her feet. "Don't you dare touch me!"

I hold my hands up to show her, and all the gawkers, that, indeed, I have no intention of touching her or coming any closer. She's free to do exactly as she pleases. Which, for her, means pushing her way through the crowd till I have no idea where she's gone.

I retreat to my spot on the bench, alone, since none of the other shoppers seems interested in joining me. This did not go as planned. In fact, the only way it could've gone any worse is if we'd had an earthquake, or we'd struck an iceberg and the entire mall began to sink. But I try to look on the bright side: Hannah was genuinely glad to see me. Which means bygones are bygones. Marie must've seen that too, that Hannah was not freaked out by the sight of Mitch, but actually excited and happy by the sight of Mitch. This has to be to my advantage. Plus, Marie ran off without any of her packages. Or her coat. And I drove. She has to come back.

So what'll happen, I decide, is that she'll take a stroll — probably down to the Macy's end of the mall — cool off, realize this is all a silly and ironic misunderstanding, and come back. She won't be happy, and she'll have a ton of questions, and there may be some accusations and finger-pointing, but at least I'll have the opportunity to explain. So I wait. For fifteen minutes. Twenty. Thirty. At forty-five I get off the bench and limber up: just because we had a spat, I don't need to be doubled up with back spasms for the rest of the weekend. At fifty I try her cell phone, but she doesn't answer. At an hour I reach this conclusion: she's not coming back.

I gather up all the packages and make my way out to my car, which I have trouble finding, since, if you want to know the truth, I'm a little rattled and can't remember exactly where I parked. But I need my mind to work. What's logical here? What's logical is that she found another way home. So I drive to her apartment. But her car is gone, which means she got home, figured I'd come looking for her, and split. That's disturbing. And now I have a sharp pang of regret that I didn't sit her down when I had the chance and *make* her listen to me, because now that she's had a chance to go off and brood and let monstrous thoughts whisper in her ear and tell her all sorts of horrible things, who knows what she's thinking? I need to find her, quick.

I call the salon first, but I'm careful to disguise my voice, use a British accent, pretend to be a customer, in case she's already warned them she doesn't want calls from me. But Samantha tells me, pleasantly, that Marie isn't working today. I call the studio. Adonis's voice is on the recorder saying the studio is closed for the day, but will be open for regular hours tomorrow. I don't know her parents' number, but I do know her father's name — Barnaby, a tough one to forget — so I dial information and get it. They put me through, and again I use the British accent and pretend to be someone from the salon, asking for Marie. I speak to a woman, her mom I suppose (fitting that the first time I speak to her, I'm pretending to be someone else), but she's not there. I've struck out. That's when the panic sets in.

Where else could she be? Anywhere, of course. It's a fucking city. But maybe I don't have to comb the entire city. Maybe my accent was too obvious, or she said she didn't want calls from *anyone*, Mitch *or* British guys, and she's actually at one of the places I already tried. So I go to the salon, but Rosie is there and smiling and teasing me about the state of my hair, which is shit right now, and no way could she be so glib about this if her best friend were hiding out in the back. Then I look up her parents' address and drive by the house, but there's no Volkswagen in the street or the driveway or in the garage, which is open. I even go by the studio, because maybe she just wants to sit in the lot; but the lot is empty. Gone without a trace. So I call Bradley, an option I'd forgotten about entirely, but his phone is turned off, which isn't surprising since he's in Colorado and probably out skiing or hiking with Skyler. At least Marie hasn't gotten to him either. Unless she has, and she's told him everything, and he *also* doesn't want to be reached by me. *Jesus.*

I drive around and look for silver VW Bugs and see a couple and tail them, get right up on their bumpers, till I can pull up alongside, but none is hers, so I go back to her apartment and the salon and the studio and her parents' house, and I sit in front of each one of them, all the while trying to stifle the sickening thought that she's doing all this—not answering her phone, not trying to get in touch with me, disappearing into thin air—because she has no interest in talking to me or hearing my side of the story, that she thinks I'm a jerk and a creep, and she never wants to see me or hear from me again. What part of "It's over" don't I understand?

My apartment is dark and freezing when I get back, but I don't turn on any lights, don't flip on the heat, don't even close the front door. I sit on the sofa. After a while my teeth begin to chatter, and I'm shaking, and I haven't peed for hours, and my bladder is about to explode, but I'm pretty sure this is the best I'll feel all evening. How can the planet continue to spin in moments like this? How can there be traffic outside, and planes, and how can the people in the unit above me just be going about their business, watching TV, like nothing's wrong? Then my cell phone rings and I nearly jump from the sofa. I stab my hand into my pocket and snatch it out.

"Marie, god, let me explain…"

There's a pause. "Sorry, Mitch. It's Katharine. Bad time?"

"Katharine, hi. No. I thought you were someone else, is all."

"I can call back."

"No, this is fine." I rub the skin on my forehead. "What's going on?"

What's going on, she tells me, is that she's finished the book and loves it, though a few issues need to be addressed, and even though it's short notice, and Thanksgiving weekend, maybe I can come up this weekend to discuss them. I'm sick and desperate and unhinged, and I need to shut my mind off and stop replaying the afternoon with Marie, and it's clear nothing is going to happen tonight, or anytime soon, or ever, and if I stay here, I might just do something stupid, like pee all over myself, or worse, so I tell her I have a better idea: I'll catch a flight and head up there tonight. Which I do. And then I promptly hop into her bed.

Here's a bit of good news/bad news for all you ladies who've had boyfriends or husbands or otherwise significant others jump right into bed with another woman after an argument. Bad news first: he jumped right into bed with another woman. No matter how you look at it, that's a bad thing, and to pretend otherwise is foolish and ultimately counterproductive. But here's the good news: he may have done it because he's desperately in love with you.

When a man loves a woman (and yes, we all hear Percy Sledge crying out in that lovesick man-wail voice of his right now) and he thinks it's over, especially because he's done something stupid, he's liable to be off-kilter and unbalanced and do any number of ill-advised or rash or destructive things. He might drink till he's sick, or drive his car off a bridge, or slam his fist into a wall. He will do these things because he's down on himself. Because he thinks he's an ass. Because he has sunk to the bottom of a dark pit and there's really no way out, and he needs to grasp onto something that will make him feel better about himself. Sleeping with the first available woman is often just the thing.

I'm not saying it's like this in all cases. Sometimes the guy really is just a prick, and he's had this other woman on the back burner all along, and your argument or breakup is just the excuse he needs to get to knocking the boots with her. But I do know that there are guys who go out and screw random women because they can't stand the thought that they've just gone and ruined the best thing that's ever happened to them, and they need to escape that feeling quick. That's how it is for me.

Here's what happens in Chicago. Katharine picks me up from the airport and we go straight to her place. We talk about the novel and have drinks. We get comfortable on the sofa. I get buzzed. I tell her she looks great. She kisses me, I kiss back, we get to touching and stripping and end up in her bed. I don't want to say much about it—Katharine has been very good to me and doesn't need her preferences between the sheets broadcast to the general public—but I will tell you she does things that a forty-two-year-old celebrity millionaire really doesn't need to do to a twenty-eight-year-old nobody, but she seems to enjoy herself, and my body, despite itself, seems to enjoy it too. Of course, I'm thoroughly disgusted with myself afterwards, which thankfully I manage to hide from Katharine by pretending to be asleep, and it's only later, after she's asleep and I've gotten up to pace, that I throw up.

In the morning there's no repeat, or suggestion of a repeat, or kisses like we're a couple. She doesn't refer to it again, other than to say she enjoyed the evening, and I smile, even though that vomit taste is working its way up my throat again, which I swallow back. We go to breakfast, then she drives me to the airport because I want her to think I'm going home. But I don't. I get on the El and ride it around the city, then get off and wander around for most of the afternoon, and finally wind up at the art museum, standing in front of Seurat's *A Sunday on La Grande Jatte*, the painting from *Ferris Bueller's Day Off*. I stare at it, like they did, and wish I could climb inside, because everyone in the painting looks so jolly and happy and light in their parasols and top hats and sailboats, or maybe I could just be one of the dots of color, since that wouldn't be so bad, and I wouldn't feel like shit, or anything at all.

Only when I'm back on the ground in St. Louis and in my apartment do I turn my cell phone on. It rings immediately. Bradley, from Colorado.

"Finally. Where the fuck've you been?"

"Um, out. Doing stuff."

He gives a short, mirthless laugh. "You got that fucking right."

From the intensity and frequency of his f-bombs, I'm glad he's in Denver and I'm in St. Louis. So are my nose and the other breakable parts of my face.

"So you're Jason," he snorts. "This is fucking unbelievable." I know what he's doing: trying to piece it together, connect the dots, string together conversations he's had with Marie and me about boyfriends or girlfriends to make sense of it all. Good luck with that. "Jesus, Mitch. Do you even want to try to explain why you've been posing as a goddamned pharmaceutical rep and shtupping my sister behind my back?"

In truth, no. But since I wouldn't put it past him to send a guy over with a tire iron to make sure I do—and, more importantly, since we're way past the point where he deserves to know—I tell him. I keep it short, sweet, an exercise in economy: I hate dancing, Jason was an out, I got in over my head. Then I fell in love with Marie.

"Christ. I can't even believe I know you." He's disgusted, of course, but I think the whole falling-in-love-with-your-sister got him, because when he speaks again, I don't feel his hands clamped around my throat anymore. "Why didn't you tell me?"

"I don't know. I wanted to. I should have. I didn't." Because I was a fucking chicken. "I'm sorry, Bradley."

"Yeah, I'm sure you are. But save those apologies for Marie. You're gonna need them."

Neither one of us says anything for a good long time, mostly because, though Bradley and I have been through a lot together, the one where I pose as a dance-loving man of medicine and, uh, *date* his sister behind his back is new to everyone. Finally, he speaks.

"Mitch, this is my last evening in Colorado with my fiancée's family. I'm going to get back to enjoying that now. As for your . . . *situation*, I wouldn't mind seeing your ass twist in the wind for a while on this one. You deserve it. But my sister's involved, so I'm not going to do that. I've got a few ideas. But before I do anything, and I mean fucking anything, I need to know something, and you better not give me any of that lying through your teeth Jason bullshit. You hear?"

"I hear."

"What you said before about loving Marie: is that true?"

I couldn't lie about that one even if my life depended on it. "Bradley, she's the one."

He lets it sink in for a minute. "Okay. Then what you need to do is just lay low for a while. She's a mess right now, really confused. Give her some time to calm down, sort this out, get a perspective on things. In the meantime, I'll talk to her, tell her I know you and you're not some loony, just a part-time schmuck. Who knows: it just might find a way of working itself out."

After we hang up, I'm buoyed by the thought that maybe he's right, maybe I just need to lay low for a while, give her time to sift through this and realize how silly it all is, let her see that whatever I may've called myself—Jason or Mitch or Twinkle Toes—it doesn't matter, since I love her and she loves me, and that's why this will all work out. Love Will Keep Us Together. Love Is the Answer. All You Need Is Love. But somewhere between taking my Chicago clothes out to the Dumpster—I don't need to see that shirt or those jeans again—and taking a shower—I already took one this morning, but that was in Katharine's shower, with her soap, and I'm sure there's still some trace of her on me somewhere—the bubble bursts and my umbrella of cheery pop-song optimism snaps itself inside out (You Give Love a Bad Name; These Boots Are Made for Walking; Hit the Road, Jack), and a tidal wave of clear-headed, sober-eyed, grizzle-toothed reality crashes down on top of me, and I realize that Bradley's advice about laying low, though well-intentioned, is, if you'll pardon the French, shit.

I've misled her and tricked her and lied to her. I've fucking pretended to be someone else. I've let her call me by another name—*during sex*. And symbolic gestures like trashing my guilt-stained clothes and scrubbing off a layer of skin and crossing my fingers and wearing my lucky underwear and sitting around waiting for her to call and say she's worked through her feelings and all is forgiven—in other words, laying low—aren't going to fix this. It's not that easy. It shouldn't be that easy.

So I call her. She doesn't answer, which is no surprise, but I call again. She doesn't answer again, and we're back to yesterday, me trying to reach her, her not wanting to be reached, and I suppose I could keep calling her, and each time she doesn't want to speak with me, I could fly to Chicago and sleep with Katharine, though this would ultimately get very expensive (unless I just start living with her; but even though she gave every indication she enjoyed our rendezvous, she said nothing about making the two of us a permanent arrangement). Or, I could grow a pair, act like a man—or even better, act like a human being—and do what I should've done yesterday, at the mall, never mind who was watching and what they might say and how big of an ass I would've made of myself, and how much dignity and self-respect and pride I would've left puddled on that glossy tile out in front of Banana Republic: I could fight for the most important thing I've ever had in my life.

Dignity is overrated. I'm ready to go down swinging.

* * *

Sunday afternoon, I show up at the salon around one, but I don't go in. I walk by a couple times, till I get Samantha's attention. When she sees me, she gets one of those deer-in-the-headlights looks, like she's not sure what to do: tell Marie, call the police, grab her Mace. But I just sort of smile and nod, then make sure she's watching me as I go directly across the street and into the coffee shop and take a window seat. Sure enough, Rosie comes to the salon window a few moments later, scissors in hand, and scowls at me. Even through two panes of glass, across two lanes of traffic, it's scary. And so it begins.

I've decided I'm not going to go barging into the salon like a madman, or follow her home, or show up at the studio, or pop up in her shower, or do any other type of TMZ paparazzi stalking or shadowing or hounding. It's not a good strategy, since that would probably piss her off even more, give her a reason to fume and rage against me, even take legal action (restraining order, anyone?). More importantly, she doesn't deserve it. Instead, my plan is to show up every day in this coffee shop, sit in this seat, let her know that I'm here and I'm thinking of her and I just want to talk. I'll be like a tree that's outside her back window—patient, nonthreatening, ever present—and when she's good and ready, she can come over and sit for a spell, get relief from the glare of the sun. Or chop me down. I've also decided to send her something in the mail every day, to let her know how sorry I am.

So I come back on Monday and Tuesday, same spot, drinking coffee, grading papers, passing time, watching commerce along the street, signing myself up for the "Java Junkie" frequent drinkers program, knowing that in those two days Marie has received, respectively, a bouquet of Mokara orchids—her favorites—and a Tiffany's bracelet, and I, in return, have received the back of her head a few times in the salon, since she's on to me and apparently wants no part of being seen. On Wednesday, Coach clutch day, Rosie makes a mid-afternoon run to the Thai place for carry-out, and on her way back she acknowledges me, which I take as progress, even though it's only with her middle finger. On Thursday, I know Sylvia's Double Fudge Peanut Swirl Macadamia Mud Pie should be arriving from the Magnolia Café in North Carolina, which Marie had told me was the best pie ever; but no one calls to invite me over for a slice, not even to ask for extra napkins. On Friday Bradley and I talk—he still thinks laying low would've been better, but gets why I'm doing what I'm doing—and he tells me, in fact, that he and Marie are getting together later that evening for drinks. Back at the apartment, I'm a nervous wreck all night, sitting with my phone in hand, waiting for word of a breakthrough, an accord, a truce, but no call comes, which means there's nothing new to report, my status remains unchanged, and I'm as fucked as I was last week.

I spend a miserable Saturday at the coffee shop, taking stock of everything. I'm nowhere closer to getting back with Marie than I was a week ago—maybe farther—and, from a financial standpoint, bleeding myself red. Maybe I made a grave error, starting too big with bracelets and handbags and overnight pies from another state, since, if I keep escalating the worth of what I send, by the end of next week I may have to buy her a Vespa, or a small island. Maybe I should just show up here on Monday with a Java the Hut apron, since I already know everyone who works here and comes in, and even though it wouldn't be much money—minimum wage, do you think?—at least I'd get my coffee free. And apparently I get lost in some calculations about hours worked and gross versus net pay and what cut of the tip jar I'd get, because the next thing I know, the front door flies open and Rosie storms in and marches over to my table.

"Why do you keep hanging out here?" she growls, hands on her hips.

A week to prepare for it and I can't find my tongue. I shrug. "I just want to talk with her," I say weakly.

"She doesn't want to talk to you."

"Why not?"

She rolls her eyes disgustedly. "What do you mean, 'why not?' How stupid are you. *Jason*. She hates you."

"Did she say that?"

"She didn't have to. I know her. She hates you." She glares at me. "We all do." Her eye catches something on the table. "What's in the bag?"

"What? Oh, Noni's".

"Duh. I can see it's Noni's. What did you get?"

I look inside. "Brownies, a cinnamon roll. So she didn't say she hates me, she just doesn't want to talk to me?"

"Sounds familiar."

I take a breath. "Look, Rosie. I know you don't like me right now. I get it. But I need your help. I need you to convince her to talk with me, so I can explain some things."

She snorts. "And why would I want to help *you*?

"Because I'm an ass. And I want to tell her that. And that I love her."

She grits her teeth and balls her hands into fists, as if I've given the only possible answer that would force her to grant my request. And she hates that.

"Rosie, listen. If she doesn't like what she hears and never wants to see me again, I'll accept it. I'll stop hanging out here, and I won't bug anyone, and you'll never have to see me again."

She narrows her eyes. "Promise?"

"Promise."

"Fine. I'll talk to her." She starts to leave, then clomps back to my table. "Give me those," she says, snatching the Noni's bag. She charges out and across the street, and returns a few minutes later.

"All right, buster. She'll talk. Her apartment, in an hour. Me, I would've chosen someplace neutral, like a bridge, so I could throw you off. But that's her business. But just so you know: I'm on standby. And I'm warning you: if you try anything crazy, I'll be there to kick your ass."

So, finally, a chance for a one-on-one. And just like that my stomach drops, my blood goes cold, my skin gets clammy. A one-on-one with Marie. As Mitch. Jesus. Can't I just send her another pie from North Carolina?

I'm ready for just about anything when I get to her apartment. Angry Marie. Bitter Marie. Detached and apathetic Marie. Vindictive Marie. Maybe she already has a guy over and they're having sex right now, and she wants me to walk in and see what I won't be getting anymore, and *that's* why she chose her apartment. Maybe she's gathered up everything I sent her this week and plans to torch it in front of my eyes, and laugh. Or maybe she's not there at all. Ha! Talk about the ultimate way to get a message across: invite me over, then don't bother sticking around. But I knock on the door, and she's there, and she lets me right in.

The place looks pretty much the same as it did last Friday when I picked her up for our trip to the mall. No well-endowed naked strangers, no gifts heaped in a pile next to a gasoline can. Just Marie in jeans and a sweatshirt. And maybe she looks a little tired and strung out, but overall, she looks good.

We don't kiss or hug.

"Drink?" she asks.

"Water would be great."

She returns from the kitchen with a glass for me and something with a straw for her. She settles on the sofa, I take a chair across from her, and for a long time we just look at each other. In fact, we do this for such a long time that I realize this is an incarnation of Marie that I hadn't anticipated: Stare Marie. Finally I look away, like I have important matters to tend to in the room, such as counting the colored glass bottles on the shelf, or making sure the Latin names on her botanical prints are correctly spelled, when all I'm really doing is trying to keep track out of the corner of my eye whether she's still staring at me—which she is—and trying to figure out if this is some kind of passive-aggressive evil eye interrogator thing, her attempt to get me to own up to a whole litany of criminal misdeeds. It's starting to work, because I'm beginning to sweat and think I may have to tell her about the time I was five and swiped a Snickers bar from Walgreens, or when I cheated on a geometry test freshman year, or god help me, I may just have to blurt it all out, that I went to Chicago and slept with Katharine; and that's the thought I'm trying to beat down when, unbidden—*horribly!*—Katharine Longwell's breasts pop into mind, her naked, glistening, and not-so-fake-as-it-turns-out breasts, and I realize I am sitting in a car with no brakes, and I'm about to go off the cliff.

"What are you thinking about?" she finally asks.

"Me? Nothing. Bunnies. The weather."

"I'll tell you what I'm thinking. I'm sitting here thinking that we've baked cookies together and danced together, and taken a bath, and had sex I don't know how many times, and I've told you I love you, and you've done the same, and I can't even get myself to say your name. Your *real* one. So I keep saying it in my head, trying to get the face to match the name. 'Mitch Samuel. Mitch Samuel.'"

"That's me," I want to say, like we're taking roll. I don't.

"That other name, 'Jason Gallagher,' where'd that come from?"

"My middle name, plus my mom's maiden name. It's Irish."

"Bradley didn't recognize it. Of course, that's probably why you chose it."

Exactly, I nod, a little proud of my cunning. Then I stop.

"And you teach at the university, and you write."

"And I'm also working on my PhD. *The Canterbury Tales.* Chaucer. English poet from the fourteenth century. 'Father of the English—'"

"I got it. I know who he is."

"Sorry."

She takes a thoughtful sip from her drink and places it deliberately back on the table. She smoothes some wrinkles from the sleeves of her sweatshirt. "So tell me…Mitch." The name sticks on her tongue an extra second. "Why'd you do it?"

"Go to the studio?"

"No. Bradley already told me about the book, and doing research, and needing to be around a bunch of people who get worked up over the label on their purse. Which I want to discuss later. I'm talking about the phony identity. Jason. Why'd you do that?"

I think about Snoop Dogg and Bono and Jon Stewart, and I'd like to explain the idea of a stage name and tell her that it's really not that uncommon. But I know better. "Fear," I say. "I hate dancing, or at least I did, and I thought I was terrible at it, and I really couldn't stomach the idea of putting myself out there on display. So I made up Jason to take the heat off Mitch. Besides, I figured I'd only be playing Jason for a day or two, just long enough to get what I needed at the studio and be gone."

"But when you realized it wouldn't be so quick. Then what?"

"Then it got hard. I was having so much fun, dancing, getting to know Rosie and Steve and Jennifer and Fran and the whole crew. And the next thing I know, I'm past the point where I can just say, 'Hey, guys, my name's not really Jason, and by the way, I've been spying on you.' I decided it was better just to keep quiet as Mitch and let Jason do all the talking."

"Even to *me*? That didn't bother you?"

"Of course it did. But to be honest, Marie, I just saw you as one of the group. The last thing on my mind was starting anything with you."

She gives me a withering look. "And why's that? Because I'm a *hairstylist*?"

I hate the way she sneers it, because it's exactly the way I would've sneered it before I got to know her. "The first couple lessons, sure, maybe that's what I was thinking. What could we possibly have in common? But beyond that, *way* beyond that, you were Bradley's sister. That was the built-in safeguard. You were off-limits. Of course nothing could happen. No way anything could happen. Then it happened."

"As in, we started sleeping together."

"No. Before that. It was the night we went to the winery, and we were standing on that hill, and I looked at you and realized that I didn't want to be without you. Without trying, without wanting it to happen, I was falling in love with you, Marie. I *had* fallen in love with you. And I couldn't risk losing you."

Her face softens and I can tell she's gone back to that night, to the moonlight, to the kiss, and even in a sweatshirt and ponytail, she looks as beautiful as she did that night, and I want to kiss her right now. But I can't. And I can't believe it's come to this, that I'm sitting on her sofa, with her, as I've done hundreds of times, and I'm afraid to touch her or kiss her, not knowing if this is the last time I'll ever be sitting on this sofa. But I can't think that way.

"Did you like the pie?" I ask brightly.

She nods, grimly. "I did. And the flowers and clutch and bracelet. All very nice. But you can't just buy me things and throw them my way and expect all the bad stuff to just go away. Do you get that, Mitch? Do you understand that's not the way this works?

"God, Marie, yes. I get it. I swear. I didn't send all those things to try to buy you back. You wouldn't talk to me. It was the only way I could get anything to you, to let you know how sorry I was. How sorry I *am*. I was desperate." I feel slivers of that same desperation creeping up my spine right now. "Look, I even did something that didn't cost a dime. I made a list of all the things I promise to do, or not do, if you'll just give me another chance."

That bit of news catches her off guard. "You made ... a list?"

I nod. "Ten items. Sort of like a Ten Commandments, minus anything about the Sabbath. Or killing."

She looks at me like I'm joking. Which I'm not. Though now I realize I should be, since her face is telling me that anyone who would actually make such a list, and admit it, *must* be joking.

"All right, then," she says, settling in. "Proceed."

"Um, on second thought, I didn't make a list."

"You made it. Let's hear it."

I suppose at this point I could clam up, refuse to read it, maybe fly out in a huff, but I can't imagine she'd be ringing my phone off the hook begging me to come back, since I'm the one who had to beg her for this get-together in the first place. This is my best shot. So I pull it out of my back pocket with as much of a flourish as I can muster, but what I really need now is a couple of stone tablets, like Charlton Heston had, even parchment, instead of a folded up piece of loose-leaf

"It's still a little rough," I say as a disclaimer. "More in the draft stages, really."

"Read."

I clear my throat. "'Marie.'" I look at her, then back at the list. "'I promise I will never lie to you again. I promise I will never pretend to be someone else. I promise I will never be dis-honest. I promise I will love you, love you, love you. I promise I will never take you for granted. I promise I will respect you. I promise I will always put you first. I promise that I will always forgive you, especially if you do something odd or wacky that I don't understand at first, but then, when you explain it, I do.' "

She lets it all sink in for a moment. Then: "That didn't sound like ten."

"Oh, it is. Trust me."

I can tell she's still not convinced, so I hand her the list. "The 'love you, love you, love you,' those count as three," I point out.

She looks it over. "So, three to say the same thing, you won't lie. Three to say you'll love me, with those words. Three more to say you'll love me, with different words. And one to forgive me for a hypothetical wrongdoing that I'd never do, perhaps on the off-chance that should you ever do something that stupid, which you have, I'd forgive you. Do I have it?"

"Pretty much."

The whole thing makes her smile — me too — and for a moment it's back to old times, Mitch and Marie, or Jason and Marie, smiling, joking, ribbing each other, but most of all, delighted to be with each other. Then, as if she realizes the very same thing, her look goes hard — toxic, really — and it's back to new times.

"Do you know what a week I've had?" she fumes, flinging the list back at me. "Going from being in love with you to finding out you're not who I thought you were, crying my eyes out, hating you, wanting to rip your throat out, wanting it all just to go away, wanting to be back with you. Do you realize what you've put me through?

"Sorry."

"Sorry. *Sorry.* Fuck sorry. I hate you for putting me through this, you know that? I hate you for making me feel this way about you. Fuck you, Mitch. Fuck you."

I sit there and endure her fury, and it's killing me to see her look at me that way, face red, eyes wide, furious, blazing holes through my skin, but I deserve every ounce of it, so all I can do is sit there and absorb it and let her do what she needs to do. Slowly, mercifully, the anger leaches out of her, like a fever, till her breathing and complexion and eyes return to normal and she looks like Marie again—a sad, pissed, torn version—and she collapses back into the sofa, woman wronged and hurt little girl, all at once, deflated in a sea of cushions.

"Oh, Mitch. I don't know what to make of any of it. Maybe I get it. Maybe I understand why you'd do all this, how one thing led to another. Maybe. But here's what I'm left with. Not knowing if you're Mitch or Jason, what parts were real. The bottom line is, I don't even know who you really are."

I move to the edge of my chair. "But you do, Marie. Beneath all the hang-ups and stupidity, it was me, every step of the way, getting to know you, wanting to spend time with you, falling in love with you. And yeah, if I could do it all over again, I'd march right into that studio and say I was Mitch Samuel. But the irony is, I couldn't have done that. Not three months ago. I was ready to turn around and go home that first night. It took Jason Gallagher to lead me to you."

Despite the mental gymnastics it takes to understand that one, I think she does, because she looks like she's ready to cry. Or hug me. Or throw the table at me. I can't be certain.

"You should go now," she says.

So I do.

Back at the apartment I watch TV, then listen to every Nirvana CD I own (which is a mistake, given that I already don't feel so great and look what listening to too much Nirvana did to Kurt Cobain), then watch more TV, then go for a jog at midnight, then listen to something happy—Elvis—then take a shower and watch TV. It's after two when my phone rings.

"What are you doing?" she asks.

"Not sleeping. You?"

"Staring at the walls." There's a long pause. "Do you want to come over, so we can both get some sleep?"

Abso-fucking-lutely I want to come over.

"And bring that list and a pen," she says. "We're adding a few things."

I have the car started before we say goodbye.

CHAPTER SEVENTEEN

At last we're a couple in the way God and the universe intended: Mitch Samuel and Marie Colson. The next two weeks are a series of firsts. 1) She meets my mom. We go to the student production of *The Imaginary Invalid* at my mom's school, and even though Marie has never heard of Molière, she gets all the jokes and laughs a lot, and we go out for drinks afterwards, and it's obvious my mom likes her, and she likes my mom, and I like that a lot. 2) She comes over to the apartment. I give her the grand tour, and I can tell it's a little weird for her, seeing how Bradley and I shared this space and she had no idea, but by the end of the visit she gets over it, enough to fix up a meal using pots and pans that, between Bradley and me, have likely never held anything in them. 3) I give my real name at the studio. I announce that I'm going by Mitch now, and they give me a funny look and shrug, because at age twenty-eight, people usually don't start going by something else; but they go along with it, even Rosie, who, after making a big show of forgiving me for all I've put her through, announces she

has news of her own: she's no longer going by Rosie but by Angelina Jolie and has Brad called yet? 4) We double date with Skyler
and Bradley. We go to Colchester's for dinner, and Bradley has the
line of the night when he sizes up our group, gives me an extra
once-over, and tells the hostess we're a party of five.

Most importantly, Marie reads the book. I give it to her on a
Friday night and she reads it straight through the weekend, and
the entire time I'm nervous, like an expectant father who's got
nothing to do but pace the floors and wring his hands and have
unsettling thoughts — the baby's out, and it's a seal or zebra or
loaf of bread. She finishes on Sunday evening.

"I loved it," she says, not holding back her smile, and my heart
starts to beat again. "I was worried you'd stolen all our identi-
ties, just changed the names, and slapped us into print. But you
didn't. I see bits of all of us, but these are new people. It's a world
I recognize, but it's different."

We talk about this and that concerning the characters and
the plot and some suggestions she has, but it's all good and fun,
and I realize that there ain't no stopping me, now that Marie's on
board. But then this:

"So you really met Katharine Longwell?"

"Um, a little."

"What do you mean, 'a little'? That doesn't make sense. Either
you did or you didn't."

"No, right. Of course. I did. Yes."

"What's she like?"

"Not much of anything. Not as good-looking as you might
think, that's for sure."

"Anything else?"

"Sweet. Boring. The matronly type."

"She doesn't seem that way, not from her books and what I've
seen on TV."

"That's all an act."

"Interesting."

"Yes, it is."

And so we leave it. Till the end of our natural lives, I hope.

The last day of classes arrives, and the students are ready to be done. They've only to turn in their final research paper, on the topic of their choice. A few of them volunteer to read excerpts—no aliases this time, since it's the last time I'll see them—so we hear a little about opera and Gothic cathedrals and Bob Marley and NASCAR, and when it's over, after I've wished them well on their upcoming exams and collected the papers, I head to my office. Grading time. I'm not there long before I'm interrupted by a knock on the door. It's Molly.

When the weather turned cold, Molly turned to sweaters, and she's been sporting an assortment of styles and colors and textures these past few weeks, all with this common thread: hello Molly's body. But today, the coup de grâce: a painted-on baby blue, paired with hip-hugging low-rider jeans.

"Mind if I shut this?" she asks, of the door.

"I'd rather you left it open," I say quickly.

She gives a small laugh. "I'm harmless, Mitch. Really." She slides into the chair across from me, looking anything but harmless. "Besides, I already have a boyfriend. Pete."

"Pete? From class Pete?"

"Yep, Pete-from-class Pete. Don't look so surprised."

Surprised? Me? I'm not surprised. Dumbstruck, astounded, flabbergasted, yes. Molly could be modeling swimsuits in *Sports Illustrated*. Pete...well, Pete probably *has* a swimsuit, and I'm sure he looks fine in it, but I don't imagine anyone'll be taking pictures of him in it and splashing them across the centerfold of a magazine. "I just wouldn't have put the two of you together. Based on the way you go at it in class," I throw in.

"He challenges me and I like that. Plus, he's the funniest guy I know. And smart. Don't let the stupid grin fool you."

After today, I won't. "So, what can I do for you?"

She picks at the corner of the chair. It's the most submissive gesture I've seen from her all semester. "I just wanted to tell you...I didn't turn in my paper."

"Oh?" I don't have to remind her she loses a letter grade for each day it's late. I've been reminding them for the last month. "When can I expect it?"

"See, that's just it. You probably shouldn't expect it at all."

"Meaning..."

"Meaning, well, probably never."

I let that settle for a moment. "Never. Wow. That's a long time. You do realize it counts for a fourth of your final grade."

She drops her eyes and nods. "But I'll pass, right?" She actually seems a little worried.

"Assuming you were getting an A going in, which you probably were, then yeah, you'll pass. Barely..." C minus or D barely. How about that? Ms. When-are-you-going-to-write-something-real-like-a-novel pain in my ass just screwed her own grade, and I didn't even have to blink an eye. A few months ago, I would've been rejoicing. I would've done cartwheels. But now, I don't feel so good about it.

"Do you need an extension?" I've told them I *might* be willing to provide one, in extreme circumstances—like loss of limb.

"Thanks, but I don't think it would help."

We sit there and look at each other, and there's really nothing I can do. She doesn't want to write the paper, she's willing to accept the consequence, so that's pretty much that. But I don't want to let go.

"Look, Molly, I know we didn't see eye to eye on everything this semester. No secret there. But you were a good student—a great student—and I respect that. You don't seem much in the offering mood, but I'm going to ask anyway." I lean forward and give her as intense a look as I can manage, without having it come across as one of those "I'm deep, I'm concerned, now why don't you let me separate you from your panties" looks. "Why didn't you do it?"

She shakes her head. "But that's just it. I did do it. Most of it, anyway. I'm doing it on Mount Everest because I want to climb it someday. But then I started thinking about why. It's dangerous. Irrational. People die there every year. One wrong step, or freak storm, or unstable piece of ice could do me in. Am I that much of a thrill seeker? Or is it that sometimes I don't really like myself or some of the things I do and wouldn't mind if it all *happened* to end." You can tell that she'd planned to say some of it, but not all of it, and that it's upsetting to her own ears to hear it, but now that she's started, she doesn't want to stop. "I don't have the answers, Mitch," she says, her voice starting to crack. "I think it's the thrill-seeking thing, but there are enough days when I think it could be the other. And it scares me. That's why I had to stop, because I'm not ready to stare at those things too hard right now, if you know what I mean..."

I look at her, this beautiful, scared, sexed-up, mixed-up, intelligent, trembling teenage girl, and realize that, despite the obnoxious T-shirts and skintight sweaters and form-fitting jeans and everything I think I may know about her, I have absolutely no idea who she is. *None.* What's more, I can see she's getting ready to do something that I never in a thousand years would've thought possible from Molly Schaeffer: she starts to cry. Big tears. Big big tears.

My impulse is to push her chair out the door, or crawl under the desk, or run, because I am immediately back to the night with Hannah, when I saw her on the bathroom floor, sobbing, and did nothing, and how can I be expected to do anything for a girl I've spent the better part of four months cursing under my breath when I didn't even do it for a woman who made the coffee for us every morning? But then something else kicks in, and I can only say that it's the Marie in me, which is an odd thing to say under any circumstance, but even odder in this situation, since we're talking about a gorgeous eighteen-year-old girl, and that the Marie in me is telling me to give her a hug. So that's what I do.

I don't say anything, because I'm not sure what I'd say, but I just sort of hold on, and she buries her head against my shoulder and I let her do it, and I will myself not to have any impure thoughts, or notice how good she smells, and I don't know if anyone passes by, but I don't care either, because whatever it may look like, I know it's the right thing to do.

Finally she pulls away and wipes her eyes. The storm has passed.

"Do you wanna talk more?" I ask.

She laughs. "And have you try to analyze me any more than you are right now? No thanks, Dr. Freud."

She takes a moment to compose herself—straightening her sweater, sweeping back her hair, smoothing the fabric on her jeans—all in a way that makes it clear that even though there may be some chipped or dented pieces inside her soul, and she doesn't have it all figured out, life goes on and she needs to be ready to face it. And be sexy. The swagger is back. Honestly, I'm glad to see it.

She stands. "It's been a good semester, Mitch. I'm not just saying that to kiss your ass. I enjoyed it."

"Take care of yourself, Molly. Okay? And have fun in San Diego."

"Oh, I will." She gives me a smile that's laced with flirty (Molly is Molly, after all), and she's gone.

Early on in *Hamlet*, there's a scene where Hamlet's friend Horatio is trying to make sense of all the crazy goings-on in Denmark—like ghosts of dead kings wandering through town—and he says it's all so "wondrous strange." That phrase is looping in my head right now. A student who bugged the hell out of me all semester just cried in my arms and I comforted her—I think—and even though I have every right to give her a D for the class, I'll split the difference and give her a B. What's more, I've danced as Zorro and golfed with my dad and written a chick-lit novel and fallen in love with my best friend's sister. I realize we're not talking ghosts of murdered fathers coming back with tales of fratricide and incest and wife-stealing, but there's no other way to put it: it's all so wondrous strange. But then again, with all apologies to Master Will, maybe it's something else altogether. Maybe it's all so strangely wonderful.

Later that night, we're sitting on Marie's sofa watching *Frosty the Snowman*.

"I'm not really a fan of this one," I tell her. "I don't like the way they added the jealous magician, Professor Hinkle. He's not in the song."

"But they had to add things. If they kept to the song, the show would be two minutes long. Even less, because of all the thumpety thump thumps."

She's right, of course. Sometimes you have to tweak the source material, especially when it has no plot whatsoever and the only characters are a snowman, children, and a traffic cop who hollers, "Stop!" So I get to the crux of my problem with *Frosty*, which I've never told anyone. "I don't like the way they let Frosty melt in the greenhouse. When he dies."

"He doesn't die."

"He dies. He melts. For a snowman, that's death."

"Fine. He dies. But Santa brings him back to life."

"But he was dead first. And that's tough to get out of your mind, that puddle of water, and the corncob pipe and hat sitting on top of it. So every time I hear the song, that's what I think of. Dead Frosty. Puddle of water Frosty. They should stick with the song, even if it's only a two-minute show. I like the Rudolph special better."

"Oh, like that one sticks to the song. The dentist. The Isle of Misfit toys. Yukon Cornelius. Burl Ives as a snowman with a plaid vest. And that one's an *hour*."

"But no one dies."

"But they *think* Yukon Cornelius does, when he falls off the glacier ledge with the Abominable Snowman."

"But not Rudolph. He doesn't die and come back to life."

We stop there, because it's clear she really likes Frosty and I don't, and I want her to enjoy this.

"Charlie Brown?" she asks.

"Love it."

"Good."

We watch a little more, and get through the part where he dies and comes back to life, and I tell her it's not so bad after all, even though it is, especially when that little girl cries. Ask *her* if Frosty was dead.

"You know, the TV at your place is nicer than this one," she says, when Frosty is safely on his way to the North Pole with Santa. She half turns my way. "Are you planning to bring it over someday?"

I do a half turn myself. "Maybe." But even without a mirror I can tell I have a huge smile on my face when I say it.

* * *

When I came back from Chicago with the manuscript, I had Katharine's comments. Now Marie and Bradley have read it and offered theirs, and I've considered what everyone's had to say and made my changes. It's finished. I call Katharine to let her know it's on the way.

The conversation is brief and cordial. She tells me she's looking forward to reading it, which is nice, and that her agent will probably want to start shopping it around to publishers, which is great; and when she asks about my plans for the holidays, I mention that my girlfriend and I will be celebrating our first Christmas together, which, in my opinion, is the best news of all. There's a pause, and I can tell her mind goes back to my first trip to Chicago, when I said I had a girlfriend and we didn't sleep together, then to my second trip, when I said nothing about a girlfriend and we *did* sleep together, so she must realize we've patched things up and we're back on track and everything is going well.

"Good for the two of you," she says, and she sounds sincere. Which means, if I'm reading her right, the fact that we slept together will never be mentioned again, by either of us.

Now I need to get to work on that letter to Virginia and tell her there really is a Santa Claus.

Hanukkah starts on the eighteenth, and my father has a party. He's had this party every year and invited me each time; and each time he's invited me, I've never gone, usually without the courtesy of a reply. This year is different: he invites, I reply, it's a yes, for two.

The house is filled with people I don't know: brothers and sisters and nieces and nephews on Leah's side, friends of my dad and Leah, a few faces I recognize from the course; but everyone is warm and friendly. The kids run around and play games and quote lines from Adam Sandler's "Hanukkah Song," and there is every conceivable shape and style of dreidel, from glow-in-the-dark to wood to pure chocolate, and the kids take turns deciding who will spin which one—or eat it, as the case may be. We light the Hanukkah candles and Nathan leads us in the prayers; he's a year away from his bar mitzvah and intent on getting his pronunciation correct: "*Baruch ata adonai elohaynu melech haolam…*" My dad helps him when he stumbles, which isn't often.

After dinner, the adults play a gift-stealing game. We've all brought a wrapped gift under ten bucks, gag or serious, and we throw all of them on the dining room table. Low number chooses the first gift and unwraps it, then each subsequent person opens a new gift or steals one already unwrapped, which gives the person who lost a gift a similar option, steal or unwrap. It's a surprisingly lively game, and we ooh and ahh a lot, and haggle and barter and groan, because there are a few desirable gifts that everyone tries to get—a six-pack of microbrewed beer, a tin of gourmet biscotti, a coffee thermos; a handful of duds—a Chia Pet, a porcelain clown, a squeaky mouse toy; and some that are too wacky to classify—a rubber fireman puppet, The Complete Pizza Party in a Can. In the end, Marie and I wind up with a bottle of sparkling wine and an Aquaman toothbrush holder, which I actually like, but then Kyle sees it and wants it, so I give it to him.

At the end of the evening, my father escorts us to the door and helps us into our coats.

"How'd you make out?" he asks.

We show him our lone bottle.

"Hmm, not so hot. Then take these." He shuttles two gift bags our way, then adds conspiratorially, "Don't open them here. I don't have enough for everyone."

We wait till we're back at Marie's to open them, and I figure he just felt sorry for us and gave us something generic like cookies or a fruitcake. But Marie opens hers, and it's soft and feminine, a bath set, with salts and a candle and an array of scented lotions and creams and washes, the good ones, and it seems just right for her. And mine, well, mine is a book, leather-bound with gilded pages and fancy endpapers: *The Collected Stories of Sherlock Holmes.*

"You like those?" she asks.

I nod, and despite myself, I'm a little choked up. "My favorites when I was a kid."

I call my father the next morning to thank him for everything: the evening, the gifts.

"My pleasure," he says, and there's a long pause, and when he speaks again, his voice is a little emotional. "I'm glad you brought Marie. She's a special one."

It's only much later, after Marie has gone to work and I've graded the last batch of essays and I'm on my way to school to drop off my grades, that I understand his shaky voice: of all the girls I've ever dated—the high school crushes and fellow summer camp counselors and art majors and working girls, like Hannah—this is the first one he's ever met.

CHAPTER EIGHTEEN

With Christmas only days away, we plan one final trip to the mall. All the heavy lifting is done — gifts for my mom and her parents, Bradley and Skyler, Rosie, Scott and Melinda and Kyle — and now we're left with a few odds and ends. We finish up in the early afternoon and bring all those goodies to the car, then trek back inside and go our separate ways, to *browse*. Of course, when we reconvene at six, we've browsed our way into a hundred or so bags whose contents we can't share with each other at the moment. We head back to her place for dinner, since we're so poor now that we may never eat out again. Even so, that doesn't stop me from going out the next day, while she's at work, to make one more purchase, something that wasn't on any of the lists she gave me.

Thanksgiving was a slipshod affair, thanks to Jason, but Christmas will be a different story. We've got it all mapped out. Christmas Eve: Mass, then over to Skyler's for dinner, putting up a tree, watching *It's a Wonderful Life*, and a sleepover. Christmas morning: opening presents at my mom's with Scott, Melinda, and Kyle. Christmas evening: opening presents at her parents with all the relatives. In fact, there's only one thing that could ruin our plans, and it has nothing to do with Jason.

Mass is at five, and it's festive, upbeat, a celebration. But how can it not be? It's a birthday party. The church is decked out with Christmas trees and lights, swags of evergreen, and wide-eyed kids in velvet dresses and clip-on ties who know what happens tonight; and every ten minutes or so we're singing carols (not "Santa Claus Is Coming to Town" or "White Christmas," but "Hark! The Herald Angels Sing" and "Joy to the World," which put you in the mood just the same). Marie isn't a very good singer, but it doesn't really matter because she enjoys herself and sings along just fine. The service lets out around six fifteen, and it's still snowing, which means everything is frosted over like cake icing, glittery and white. Since we have time to kill—we're not due over at Skyler's till seven—I suggest, nonchalantly, that we drive a couple blocks over to Forest Park for a stroll.

Forest Park is thirteen hundred acres of zoo and art museum and outdoor amphitheater and ponds and jogging trails, and on a summer's evening, the place is swarming with people. Not so tonight, on Christmas Eve, in the snow. As we make our loop around one of the ponds, the Grand Basin, Marie leaning into me for support, which I like, snow crunching under our shoes, the only other spot getting any action is the hill that sweeps down toward us. A few kids and adults are out on sleds and saucers, giving it a go.

I gesture to a bench. "Shall we?" I suggest, and she nods.

We sit with our shoulders together, hand in gloved hand, quiet, listening, watching. I start to get the feeling we're in a Norman Rockwell painting: the sledders laughing and hollering and making their runs, the silhouette of the art museum at the top of the hill, the snow splashing around us, tumbling into the dark waters of the pond and rippling the surface. I realize this is my moment, my perfect opportunity to tell her all the things I've rehearsed, how I love her kindness and generosity and forgiving and caring heart, and just her, plain and simple, the whole package, the way she walks and hitches her thumbs in her jeans and tilts her head and flicks her hair out of her eyes and lets her eyes bug out sometimes, on purpose, to express cartoon-like shock, the way she sits and sleeps and picks up the phone, and if I were God or whoever and had the power to start the whole human race and base it on one person, it would be her, with every feature and expression and trait, and I couldn't love her any more than I do, even if I had a thousand more years to try. And then I open my mouth to say it.

"Cold, isn't it?"

She shrugs. "A bit."

Son of a bitch. "Do you want me to grab a blanket?"

"I'm fine. Really."

"I have one in the car. It's no problem for me to get it."

"Mitch, I'm fine. I swear."

"Are you sure?"

"I'm sure."

Jesus. I need to stop talking. And breathe. And regroup. I start small. "The sledders look like they're having fun."

"Yeah, they do."

"Ever come sledding here?"

"Not really. We had a great hill near our house, so that's where we went. I came over with Rosie a couple times in high school, so she could meet guys. Never on Christmas Eve, though."

Ah, Christmas Eve. My way back on track. "Remember what you were doing on Christmas Eve last year?"

She narrows her eyes. "Hmm. I won't swear to it, but I think I was still driving in from North Carolina. I might've just been getting in around this time, or a little before. How about you?"

"Over at my mom's. We did Christmas Eve there, then Midnight Mass."

I take a deep breath, one that's a little shaky on the exhale part, and my heart knows what's coming next, so it starts jumping around in my chest.

"Marie, I know we have lots of separate memories about our past Christmas Eves, which is natural, since we didn't know each other till this one. But what I'm thinking is that I'd like it if we didn't have any more Christmas Eves, or any eves, really, where we didn't have the same memories. Though not that we won't remember some things differently, because two people can go through the same experience and have different memories about some of the details, like did I wear a brown shirt or blue one to the party, and maybe you think it was brown and I think it was blue, so we have to try to remember which shoes and pants I wore. Which really isn't a big deal, though, even if we never agree on which it was." Jesus. I'm sweating despite the snow. "Do you have any idea where I'm going with this?"

Her hands go up toward her mouth, and they're trembling. "Maybe. I think."

"Good."

I get down on my knee in front of the bench and pull out a small box and flip it open, and it's all by the book and utterly cliché—a thousand proposals from a thousand stories and books and movies, and this is the best I can come up with?—and I'm about to pass out, but I'm also about to cry.

"Marie, will you marry me?"

For a moment I'm not sure she heard me, because nothing happens, but then her nostrils begin to flare and her lips quiver and her eyes well up, and her hands don't know what to do with themselves, so they just tremble even more, and do something like a clap, then grab for the ring and stop, and we both laugh, and we both start to cry a bit, and finally she gets it out, as if she had to.

"*Yes.*"

I'm sure there will come a day when I tell her all those things I had in my head, about how much I love her, and why I love her, and how wonderful she is, and how lucky I am to have her. But not now. Now we just hug. And from the way I'm hugging her, and the way she's hugging me back, I get the feeling that even if I meet with some freakish tongue accident tomorrow and lose my power to speak and never get those words out, she'll know exactly what I was trying to say.

The next twenty-four hours are a blur. We go to Skyler's and my mom's and her parents, and uncork the announcement each place, and get showered with kisses and hugs and handshakes and women clamoring to see her ring and men clapping me on the back to offer *Congrats!*; and there is so much of this over the next few days—at the studio, her salon, New Year's parties— and I'm so proud and exhilarated and tempted to sprint straight to Chicago to ask Oprah if I can hop up and down on her sofa and say "I'm in love I'm in love I'm in love" that I decide the early days of an engagement should have their own name. I tell Marie.

"Honeymoon," she says.

"How so?"

"It's the 'honeymoon phase' of our engagement."

I try to be gentle. "Nope. Won't work. We already use honeymoon for marriage."

"So."

"So? Put it this way. You won't be planning for the 'Fourth of July' of our engagement, will you? It's our *wedding*. And we won't celebrate the 'birthday' of our marriage: it's our *anniversary*. Important ideas need their own names, not one borrowed from something else. Make sense?"

"No. Not really. I still like honeymoon."

But not me. I decide to take a Native American approach. They had a great knack for calling things the way they saw them. For example, they noticed that a big river seemed to stretch everywhere, so they called it the "father of all waters": Mississippi. Or they noticed a guy who liked to dance with wolves, so they called him "Dances with Wolves." So what's this early stage of being engaged like? It's like waking up every day and noticing something different, or fresh, or changed from the night before, that there's a new bud or bloom or splash of color, and life seems bounteous and bursting at the seams, and it makes you want to be a poet, even if you should stick to fiction. It's like spring. *Springtime days!* Only that doesn't do it. So I go for the Spanish. *Primavera days.* But that sounds like a sales pitch at the Olive Garden. So I narrow it down to the element of spring I like most: the smells. Flowers, sure, and honeysuckle and jasmine and lilac, but just the smell of grass clippings and wet earth, Mother Nature spritzing on a bit of fragrance. Perfume days. *Dias perfumados.* Perfect.

Katharine calls from New York a couple weeks into January. At first I think she's calling to congratulate me on my engagement, but I'm getting my worlds confused. How would she know? Rosie? Marie's Uncle Ted? *Page Six?* We chat about the holidays, which I tell her were great, and she says hers were very nice, too, though it wasn't all fun and games. She had some work to do.

"We found a publisher," she says.

"Pardon?"

"We found a publisher. For *Catwalk Mama.* My agent's on the line with us and she can explain all the details, since she did all the work. Say hello to Susannah Berg."

I say hello to Susannah Berg.

"I'll get right to it, Mitch," Susannah says in a voice that belongs on radio: rich, sonorous, confident. "I made the rounds with *Catwalk Mama*, and let me tell you she caused quite a stir. People talking beach book of the year. Blockbuster. Movie rights. I almost took it to auction. But I think I found us an excellent fit: Sheldon Leifer at Regency House."

Beach book of the year? Blockbuster? *Movie rights?* "Uh, sounds good."

"And Bradley?" asks Katharine.

Bradley? Who cares about Bradley? Oh, *Bradley.* "I can't speak for her, for certain. But I think she'll be pleased."

"Excellent," Susannah says. "Then we need to move quickly on this one, because Mr. Leifer is over the moon about it and wants it ready for an early summer release. You know how it works from here, right?"

"Like the back of my hand." I pause. "A refresher would be good, though."

"Okay, I'll break it down. As the agent for the book, I'm the one who'll negotiate a deal with the publisher. In ordinary cases, an agent would directly represent the writer, Bradley. But in this case, since she already has an agent—you—both of you are my clients. Make sense?"

"So far."

"Good. Now, when I strike a deal with the publisher, he cuts me a check for the full amount, called the advance. Let's use real numbers here, just to keep it simple. Let's say half a mil."

"Half a what?"

"Half a million. Five hundred thousand. That's probably not the exact amount, but I want to keep things round. From that check, I take my share, seven and a half percent. Thirty-seven thousand, five hundred. Then I cut a check to you for the remainder, you take your thirty-seven five, and Bradley gets the rest."

"You do have a contract with her, don't you?" Katharine interjects.

"Oh, sure. No doubt."

"Smart man. Sometimes people assume just because it's family, they don't have to worry about that. But money makes people do strange things. Sorry, Susannah, back to you."

"Not much more to say. Other than, after the publisher has recouped the advance amount, based on books sold, we all get a percentage on each book sold thereafter, called a royalty. And that's how it works. Any questions?"

"Just one. You used half a million as the advance amount. Why that number?"

"Because I think that's what we can expect. Probably a little more, but not much." She pauses. "Unless you want to strike out on your own with this. If you think you can do better, more power to you."

"No, no, not at all. That amount sounds good. I was thinking in that range anyway so, no, let's just stick with it."

"Great. Now, all I need is for you and Bradley to come up here next week and meet with the publisher to seal the deal."

All the air gets sucked out of the room. "You mean both of us come up? Bradley *and* me? In person? Aren't these things usually handled through the mail?"

"Typically, yes. But this is *far* from typical, Mitch. We're on a crash publication schedule. There's a half-million-dollar advance in play. We have an author with two agents." She pauses. "There won't be a problem with that, will there?"

"Well, now that you mention it . . ." Then I explain to Susannah all the Emily Dickinson stuff about Bradley, shy bird and all. Which means she might not come.

"Oh my," Susannah says, making no effort to mask her impatience or alarm. "Uh . . . Katharine, a little help?"

"Look, Mitch," Katharine steps in, her voice a skosh to the good side of scolding, "I get it that Bradley's reclusive and sensitive. And to be honest, Susannah and I both like the mystery-author-veiled-in-shadow part of it. Sheldon does too. But mystery author or not, Sheldon wants to meet with everyone face-to-face before he signs off on this. And trust me: he's not going to budge on that. If you don't show up with Bradley, the whole deal goes kaput. She needs to be here."

"I'll try."

"Don't just *try*, Mitch. Do it. I've gone to bat for her in a big way. So have you. Susannah has worked her rear off. I don't think that's asking too much. Do you?"

"No." I feel like a reprimanded schoolboy.

"Great. Then I'll let you talk to Susannah about the details, when and where we're going to meet. You get the two of you up here, I'll take care of the hotel. Fair enough?"

"Fair enough."

I am that close to half a million dollars. And that far away.

When I tell Marie I'm getting published, she throws her arms around me and starts jumping up and down and nearly gives me whiplash. When I tell her the amount Susannah tossed out, suddenly all the jump is gone and she's quiet as a monk at a morgue.

"Oh my god," she finally whispers. Then she looks around the room, like she's checking for spies or surveillance devices or hidden cameras. "You're not serious, are you?"

"I am. And all I have to do is fly out there and meet with the publisher..." But here, where my voice should be shooting to the moon with excitement, it trails off.

"Except..."

"Except...I have to bring my cousin with me. My female author cousin. Bradley."

For a long time neither one of us speaks.

"What're you going to do?" she asks.

"I don't know."

I remember an old comedy skit where a guy wore half a tuxedo and half an evening gown, split right down the middle, and he could be a man or woman, depending on which profile he showed. There's also Robin Williams in *Mrs. Doubtfire*. Those two got away with it. But something tells me none of that will work for me.

"Mitch, let me ask you something." She rubs her hands on her jeans, a little uneasy, like she's not so sure about what she's about to do. "Does the name Edward Lewis ring a bell?"

"Not at all."

She gives me a small smile. "Actually, I'd be kind of worried if it did. It's Richard Gere's character in *Pretty Woman*. You've seen it, right?"

"Yep." And I want to add "unfortunately," but I realize just in time that it's her favorite movie.

"Remember what Edward does?"

I think for a minute about the scenes I actually remember. "Punches out the guy from *Seinfeld*?"

"Way before that. What he does to get the whole movie going."

"Uh...hires a prostitute to pose as his girlfriend."

"Exactly." She pauses to let me make the connection.

"You want me to hire a prostitute to pose as Bradley?"

She just stares at me. "You're so clueless sometimes." She puts a hand on her hip and does something I think is supposed to be a hooker pose, but Marie doesn't have much of an inner hooker, so it looks more like she threw her back out. "I was thinking maybe someone closer to home."

"Ah...*that* close to home."

I believe I've found my cousin. And a kissing cousin at that.

CHAPTER NINETEEN

I know a lot about New York City, since I watch TV and I've been to the movies, and it's the setting for basically every other TV show and movie ever made (except *Shrek*; I think that was upstate New York). Even so, I wasn't prepared for this. Just from the limo (that's right, *limo!*) ride from LaGuardia to our hotel in Midtown, past the Chrysler Building and Grand Central Terminal and St. Patrick's Cathedral and MoMA, it's better than I ever expected.

I have three goals for tonight. First, dinner. We go to a place called Reuben's (yep, it's where they invented the sandwich) and it's great. Second, I want to take a dry run to the place where we'll be meeting tomorrow, Michael's, to make sure we know how to get there and how long it'll take. So we swing by. And last — touristy, stupid, I know — we go skating at Rockefeller Center. It'd be great if they still had the Christmas tree up, but it's still just fun to be out there knowing you're not on a pond in the middle of the woods, you're in a city, and if you want to walk across the street to Saks in your skates, you can. Marie spends most of her time sipping hot cocoa, while I do some laps to burn off nervous energy.

Back at the hotel, I take a shower, and when I come out of the bathroom, I expect to see her sprawled on the bed, cozy and comfortable, doing her nails or combing out her hair or lying on her side, modeling a satin teddy or leopard print v-string that she had time to buy at Hermès when she slipped away at the restaurant and pretended to use the bathroom, since she is, after all, pulling a Julia Roberts for the weekend. Instead, she's sitting on the bed, not so cozy or comfortable, in a flannel shirt and sweatpants that are definitely not lingerie, with her knees pulled up to her chest.

"What's going on?" I ask. "Did I miss something?"

"Uh-uh," she mumbles. She's staring over her knees, at a spot on the bed.

"Then what's wrong?"

"Nothing."

"Right. Nothing. That's why you look like someone just died." I lay myself across the bed, next to her. "What is it?"

She pulls her arms tighter around her shins. "You'll think I'm a baby."

I rub the small of her back. "I already do. Baby." Cheesy and silly, but that's how I feel. "Now tell me."

She does a little rocking thing like an upset child might. "I was just thinking about tomorrow. I'm not good at this kind of thing."

"What, lying? It's easy, once you start. Just ask Jason."

She doesn't laugh.

"I'm kidding, I'm kidding."

But she can't even work up a smile. "I'll be walking in there pretending I'm someone I'm not, that I did something I didn't do." She picks at the hem of her pants. "I don't even know if I'll be able to get the words out."

"Then don't. I'll tell them you have laryngitis. Wave for hi, thumbs-up for thank you, wave again for goodbye. Hell, I'll even tell them you have the bird flu. They won't want you in there any longer than you have to be. How's that?"

But she just buries her head deeper against her knees.

"Marie, listen, it's not that big of a deal. It's my book. I wrote every single word, so it's not like I'm stealing it from anyone or claiming something is mine when it isn't. I'm just using a pseud-onym." I've already told her all about O. Henry and Mark Twain and George Eliot and she seemed to get it. "Besides, they don't care if my shoe wrote it. They like it, they want to publish it. No one's getting hurt here."

I give her a moment to come around, but she doesn't. Then I hear little noises. Sniffling noises. "Hey, are you crying?"

"No," she says thickly. She wipes her eyes and sniffles.

"Jesus, I had no idea this had you so worked up."

"I'm sorry, Mitch. I thought I'd be okay with it. But I keep thinking about how it'll be, me trying to laugh and smile and act like this is one of the happiest days of my life." She gives her nose a sloppy wipe on the top of her knee. "I can't explain why it bothers me so much, you seeing me lie like that, even though you know why I'm doing it. But it just . . . it just makes me feel like such a . . . *fake*."

I put my arms around her, and as she just sort of collapses into me, I know what this means: I'll never have to worry about her being dishonest, or cheating on me, or deceiving me in any way (the only downside being that I'll never get one of those grand surprise parties for my birthday, since pulling off one of those requires at least a small measure of trickery; but it's a small price to pay, all things considered). She's too genuine and honest, and ever since the first night in the bar when she found a way to tell me I was handsome, to this day she's never given a hint that she's

capable of anything less than the truth. Not till I needed a flesh-
and-blood Cousin Bradley and she got roped into this mess. She's
not like my mother or father, capable of hanging on to a secret
for years, and she's especially, *especially* not like me. Or Jason.

That's when I realize I'm fucked.

Back when I was still with Hannah, we played a "would you
rather?" game called Zobmondo one night with some of her friends.
It's a pretty crude game, with questions like, "Would you rather get
a paper cut on your eye, or have a toothpick shoved underneath
your fingernail?" or "Would you rather eat a bowl of live crickets or
a tarantula's legs?" But some of the non-gross-out questions were
actually provocative, and one that really heated things up was, "If
your significant other had a fling on a business trip, and there were
no repercussions—pregnancy, stalking, ongoing relationship—
would you rather know or not know?" Here's what I said that night:
Yes, I'd want to know so that I could have the opportunity to address
the deficiencies in the relationship that caused her to cheat, and try
to fix them. But here's what I was thinking: Hell, yeah, I'd want to
know, so I could either dump her or have a get-even lay of my own.

But if I played that game today, with Marie as my cheating
significant other, I'd have a different answer. No. Don't tell me.
Keep your trap shut. Because if I ever found out she'd done that,
loved another guy that way, once I had that image blistering in
my brain, I'd be forced to break up with her. Or live with it. And
either way, I wouldn't be able to eat or sleep or breathe, which
means I'd probably croak, quick. So the best option would be
never to know. And if she has a twinge of guilt, that's fine—she
should—let her go to a priest or rabbi or Rosie and spill the whole
affair and get it all off her chest, cry a river of tears if need be, but
don't tell me. Let me play the oblivious fool till the day I die.

But I can't do that to her.

I get up from the bed. "I slept with Katharine."

The way I say it, apropos of nothing, I can tell she doesn't know who I'm talking about—Katharine *who?*—then she does, and then she's grasping at the other part—that I *slept* with her—and then she's trying to put the two together: that Mitch, her fiancé, slept with Katharine Longwell.

"The day we ran into Hannah and you found out who I really was. I flew to Chicago that night and we talked about my book and had dinner and slept together."

There's a mighty relief in saying it, finally getting it off my chest, and it's clear now that we could've never started a life together, not an honest one, without my telling her. But keep this in mind about getting something off your chest: once it leaves there, it goes somewhere else. In this case, that's Marie, and all she keeps hearing is, "I slept with Katharine, I slept with Katharine." I'm losing her fast.

"Marie, please, listen to me. I saw that look on your face in the mall, when you told me never to touch you again. I panicked. I did something stupid and cowardly and horrible, and I'm so sorry, and it's the worst thing I've ever done. But you need to know, I only did it because I thought we were over."

Silence. She doesn't move, doesn't blink, no tears, no words. She just sits there. It's haunting, really. And it's beginning to dawn on me that when she finally does come around, there's no way we'll be able to work through this tonight, or sleep in the same bed or room or hotel. One of us has to go. *I* need to go. But I'm not going to make the same mistake I did the first time; I'm going to say what I need to say.

"I did an awful thing, Marie. I know that. But I love you. And I want to spend the rest of my life with you."

She says just the sort of thing that you'd expect in a situation like this: nothing.

I slip into my clothes and don't bother to comb my hair or grab any toiletries, and I barely remember my wallet and don't even try to get my watch, because it's on the nightstand on her side, and the whole time I don't look her way, don't say a word, and best as I can tell she still hasn't moved. Only when I have my jacket on and I'm standing in front of the door do I hear something from her, which sounds like her clearing her throat, and I allow myself to turn her way.

"Why now?" she asks. She's still on the bed, still with her arms wrapped around her legs, and I can tell she wants to be strong and furious, but her voice is twisted-up and whispery. "Why did you tell me now?"

I think I know the answer. *Because I wanted to give you the power to crush me, because I've done something to crush you.* But I don't say that. I stare as long as I can bear it into those beautiful, terrible eyes.

"I thought you deserved to know."

And then I go.

I'm out on the street and it's after ten, and the voices that visited me the day after Thanksgiving to tell me it was over with Marie show up again, now in Dolby surround sound. And I don't suppose it'd be too hard in New York City to find something—or someone—to take my mind off everything for a while. But of course, that's what got me into trouble in the first place, so this time I hit the mute button, unplug the system, toss the whole thing into the sewer. I find another hotel, which costs a fortune. I zone out in front of TV and keep my cell phone on, in case she calls, but she doesn't. Nor does she call the next morning, but I don't panic. She didn't want to come anyway, even before I dropped the bomb on her, so I put on last night's clothes and head for the meeting, reminding myself that I did everything I possibly could last night to let her know how I feel. I'll handle this. We'll get through this. I won't do anything stupid. (That is, other than telling her I slept with Katharine in the first place.)

I get to Michael's right at noon, and I'm led past modern art and chrome chairs and numbered booths filled with people who look like they're someones to a larger, airy room with lots of windows and a garden out back. Katharine is already at the table, in a violet cashmere sweater with her hair pulled back, and she looks even better than last time, if possible. (Of course, I also saw her naked last time, so this clothed version is competing with *that* version and doing funny things to my head.) Brent's hair is longer, blonder, and he's swapped the brown leather blazer for black. Susannah reminds me of Judi Dench: short cropped gray hair, sparkly blue eyes, stylish pantsuit. They all look great. The man who doesn't look so great, at least compared to the trés chic trio, is Sheldon Leifer, publisher at Regency House. He's bald and has grizzled whiskers and a wrinkled forehead, and he's the kind of guy that if he were a dog, once he got a stick in his mouth, you'd never get it back. We shake hands and I take a seat next to Katharine.

"I hope you haven't been waiting long," I say.

Sheldon waves it off. "No problem, Mitch. We just walked in ourselves. We were about to order drinks. What can I get you?"

"A soda would be fine."

"Come on, kid. Your cousin's getting a book published. We're tossing around a few mazel tovs, celebrating. Now, what can I get you?"

"I guess I'll have a glass of wine."

"Good man." He turns to the others. "How about I order a bottle of the Martelet de Cherisey?"

Katharine, Susannah, and Brent nod. It's obvious Sheldon is

used to getting nods. He signals to the waiter, who practically trips over himself to get right over.

Katharine lays a hand on my shoulder and leans in. "And when will Bradley be joining us?" she says in a low voice.

I try to keep a pleasant face. "She wasn't feeling so well this morning."

"Which means she's running late?"

"Well . . . maybe worse."

"How much worse?"

I shake my head. "To be honest, I don't think she'll be able to make it."

"What do you mean she won't be able to make it?" It comes out a little like a hiss. "Mitch, it's the one thing I asked you."

"I'm sorry, Katharine. This was out of my control."

She gives me a hard stare, and Brent, who has obviously picked up on her tone and body language, gives me one too. Susannah frowns.

Sheldon glances over. "Katharine, dear, is there a problem?"

She adjusts one of her bracelets. "Um, well, perhaps. We might have an author who's ill this morning."

"But she's coming."

She readjusts the same bracelet. "Well, that's just it . . . she may not be able to make it."

Sheldon looks at me like I'm to blame, though he knows I'm not, though I am. But I'm not telling. "That's not good," he says in a way I find menacing.

"It's really no problem. Sir. I can do whatever needs doing. I've been handling it all along."

He gives one of those chuckles that lets you know he's the opposite of amused. "Hey, kid, that may all be well and good, but I need to meet with the author. *Capiche?* And since that ain't you, I'm starting to think that maybe we can all have a pleasant drink together, a good chat, but in the end we're just wasting our time."

I can tell that they're all upset with me. But what if she really were sick? Would that be my fault?

Sheldon gives Katharine a look. "I thought we had an arrangement here," he says, his voice steely.

Katharine swallows, and for the first time since I've known her, she's at a loss for words. It's her chance to throw me under the bus. "I'm sorry, Sheldon."

Everything is crashing down in front of my eyes: I've embarrassed Katharine in front of a high-profile publisher, Sheldon may bust my kneecaps, even Brent has turned against me. Susannah doesn't even know me and already hates me. The fallout from this will be enormous, and the sound of contracts being shredded pierces my brain.

"Hello. Sorry I'm late." We all turn to the voice. Marie.

I just sit there, mute as my fork, but Katharine practically leaps from her seat.

"Bradley!" she trills.

Marie doesn't nod, doesn't say yes, but she does manage a smile, which, in this situation, is all she needs to do.

Katharine gives her a quick hug, then introduces her to everyone. She takes the chair next to me, avoiding my gaze.

Sheldon gives her a look over the top of his glasses. "Sweetheart, you just saved your cousin here from getting the old heave-ho out to the sidewalk," he says, and they all laugh.

The wine has come out and everyone's smiling now, even Marie, though I'm not sure what's plastered on my face. It must be okay, whatever it is, since no one has pointed at me to say, "Oh my god, look at him!"

"First, my compliments on the book," says Katharine. She lays her hand on Marie's, and I can only imagine how this makes

Marie feel. "You did a wonderful job." Sheldon echoes the senti-ment, as do Susannah and Brent, all of their faces considerably thawed since Marie's arrival.

Marie bows her head. "Thank you. And thanks, all of you, for bringing this about. But as I'm sure Mitch explained, I'm not one for the spotlight. I just wanted to stop in and say hi and thank everyone, because I knew that was important to you, Mr. Leifer. But I really must be going."

Sheldon looks disappointed. "Stay. Chat. Order some food. I have this beautiful bottle of wine, I'll order a second."

"That's very nice. But if I could be on my way, please, I'd be very grateful."

"Then as you wish, my dear. I'll make this brief."

Sheldon picks up his wineglass—"A toast," he says—and we all follow suit, except Marie. She picks up her water goblet.

"Bad luck to toast with water, darling," Sheldon remarks.

"I'm sorry. This is the best I can do right now."

"Then good enough," he says. He holds his glass higher. "To Bradley. Welcome to the Regency family. May your time with us be healthy and prosperous."

"Here here," we all chime in.

Marie barely takes a swig of her water and puts it down. "And now, if you'll excuse me. I assume Mitch can handle everything from here." She stands up and pushes her chair in. "Again, thank you for all you've done."

She smiles again to the group and we all say goodbye, then she's off, weaving her way through the tables to the front door, and as she does so, I hear Sheldon say he plans to rush the book through production, six months tops, and absolutely no author photo for the jacket, to play up the mystery of it all, and Katha-rine agrees, then I realize they've asked my opinion.

"Great. Listen, I need to make sure she's okay."

I dart to the front door and outside, where I'm met by a frigid blast of January air and a million people. But Marie hasn't gotten far. She's on the corner, waving for a taxi.

"Marie, wait up!"

I push my way upstream through a wave of bodies to get to her.

"Can you believe it, Marie? We did it! *You* did it. You were fantastic in there. They loved you. You couldn't have been any better if you actually were Bradley."

I step forward to give her a hug, but she stiffens, pulls back. I freeze.

"Marie...?"

She takes a breath, which immediately disappears over her shoulder as a ribbon of vapor. "You didn't have to tell me, Mitch. You could've kept me in the dark about the whole thing, played it off like it never happened, and I never would've found out. You know that. But you did tell me, even though you knew I could walk in there today and spill my guts and ruin everything for you. You gave me that much. So that's why I came."

Her eyes are turning glassy.

"But I spent the whole night tossing and turning and crying, that image of you and Katharine...*together*, playing out in my head. But you know what made it worse? Wondering where you'd gone and what you were up to, and had you gone back to her, and were you doing it again, *right now*. Can you imagine how that made me feel, thinking my fiancé was out screwing someone else?"

Sick. Insane. Just the way it'd make me feel.

She gives me a bitter stare. "So did you?"

I deserve that.

"No, Mitch, don't just stand there. This isn't a fucking rhetorical question. I want you to look me in the eye and give me an answer. Did you sleep with Katharine last night?"

"Marie. No. God. I got a hotel and went to bed. That's it. That's the truth."

"That's such a comfort, coming from you. *Jason.*" She says it with a meanness I've never heard from her. "And you didn't even think about it, going off to a bar, club, some place to take your mind off us, do something stupid?"

I'm silent.

"Jesus, you *did.*"

"Maybe something crazy flashed through my head, I don't know. We all get crazy thoughts. The important thing is I didn't *do* anything."

"*This* time. But what about the next? Or the next? Can't you see, Mitch, that's what I'll always be wondering, what about the next time? What if things get dark enough or bleak enough and you think it's over, so you go off and do something again?"

You can see how angry and disgusted she is with herself for having these thoughts, for grilling me like this, for being backed into this corner in the first place, and I want to sweep her off the sidewalk, take her back to the hotel room, sit her down, and tell her this is all a horrible misunderstanding. But the Marie I know and love has checked out of her skin and I'm talking to someone else.

"Look at me. I'm a wreck. I'm a fucking paranoid wreck. Because I have this thought in my head now, the seed is there, and I can't get rid of it. I can't claw it out, even if I want to." Tears are streaming down her cheeks, and she tries to wipe them away with her sleeve but misses most of them. "I'm sorry, Mitch. I can't do it. I can't live a life always looking over my shoulder or holding my breath, wondering what you're up to when things go bad, and not trusting you, and feeling so awful about myself. I won't live my life that way."

A taxi pulls up to the curb.

"So what are you saying?" My throat clamps down, shutting off air, and I can't swallow.

She reaches into her pocket and pulls something out. Her ring. I didn't even notice it was off. She presses it into my hand.

"Goodbye, Mitch," she says, and slides into the darkness of the cab.

There've been a dozen or so movie versions of Dickens's *A Christmas Carol*, and I've seen most of them, including the classic with Alastair Sim. But there's a scene in the one with George C. Scott, from the mid-eighties, that gets me every time. Scrooge travels back in time with the Ghost of Christmas Past, and he's looking at a twenty-something version of himself meeting up with his fiancée, Belle. They're out by a frozen pond and haven't seen each other in a while, and she senses hesitancy in Scrooge's eyes about continuing their engagement. When she asks him what's wrong, he says that instead of getting married now, he wants to work for a while longer, amass his fortune, because then they'll be happier when they marry. She gives him a sad, sad look, and her eyes tear up, and she releases him from his engagement promise. As she walks away, the Old Scrooge gets a fiery look in his eye and you can see he wants to shout out, "Damn the money, boy! Go after her!" and the Young Scrooge feels it too, wants to chase her down. But he doesn't. He just lets her walk away.

As I watch Marie's cab pull away, I have the feeling that if I run out in the street and stop the cab, and make her get out and tell her that I love her; that if I pull her by the hand back into the restaurant, stand in front of Katharine and Brent and Sheldon, and confess what I've done; if I promise I will never do anything like this again, and beg her just to be patient, and work with me, and let me talk when I feel any strange or panicky urges, she'd listen, and she'd know how much I love her, and she'd take me back, and she'd wear my ring again. But I don't. Like Scrooge, I just stand and watch her go.

CHAPTER TWENTY

There's little fanfare to greet me when I get back to St. Louis. In fact, there's no fanfare. But why should there be? Only two people knew why I'd gone, and one of them has given me every indication she never wants to see me again. I can hardly expect the other to be waiting at the airport, ready to strike up the band, especially if Marie has gotten to him first and regaled him with all the details: "The Empire State Building was tall and the food was good, but Mitch fucked another woman, not in New York, but not so long ago, so I dumped him. Here's his flight information, in case you wanted it."

I collect my bags and catch a cab to the apartment, which is plenty cold since it's cold outside and I turned down the heat before I left. I take as hot a shower as I can stand without giving myself third-degree burns. Afterwards, I slip into my sweats and start unpacking. I save Marie's ring for last, which I pull out of the pocket of my jeans. What does one do with a used engagement ring? I suppose I could keep it, hope the next woman I meet, if

I ever meet another woman, will have exactly the same taste as Marie. In fact, I hope she's like Marie in *every* way, except for the fact that I won't have cheated on her, or whatever it is I did. But what're the odds of that? Besides, maybe that's not the brightest idea, kicking off a new life with someone with a ring that failed the previous owner.

I put it on the tip of my pinky and polish it against my shirt. It's a good-looking ring, and it looked great on her. The center stone was the perfect size for her finger, and the little diamonds that speckled all around the band gave it a sort of Goldilocks gleam: not too little, not too much, but just right. I hold it up to my nose, to see if it still has her scent on it, that cocoa-butter cream she's always slathering on. But it doesn't. In fact, you'd have a tough time finding any clue that it was ever on her finger at all.

When I finally get hold of Bradley, he's at Skyler's, and it's obvious Marie hasn't broken the news: he suggests the two of us come over and tell them how it went. In truth, this is exactly what I'd love to do, but seeing how there is no longer a two of us to come over, I suggest a different two of us — he and I — meet at Colchester's. Once we've settled in and ordered sandwiches and a round of beer, and I've told him what I think of New York — massive, frigid, fun — I tell him about the contract. And the amount.

"Get lost," he says, and wipes his mouth with the back of his shirt cuff. "And they also want you to bat cleanup for the Yankees."

So I pull out my copy of the contract, which I brought for exactly this reason, and slide it over to him. He reads it, then does a couple twitchy things with his brows and lips.

"That's *really* how much you got?"

"That's really how much I got. Pre-tax, of course. And before Susannah takes her cut."

"Still." He leans back in his chair, clearly in awe. "Son of a bitch."

"Yeah. Son of a bitch."

He's taking this part very well, which he should, since his best friend is more than halfway to being a millionaire, and he knows this means a lot of free beer and sandwiches and pool and many other things, for a long time, so I have a feeling it's all going to be okay. I decide to ride the good-time momentum. "Hey, not to change the subject or anything, but there's something I want to tell you." I pause. "Marie and I hit a rough patch while we were up there."

"Hmm? Lovers' quarrel?" He's still eyeing the contract, and all those zeros.

"Yep, that's exactly what it was. Lovers' quarrel. Maybe a bit worse. In the sense she gave me my ring back."

Now he snaps to. "Wait. What?"

"She gave me my ring back. We pretty much broke up."

His expression turns stormy quicker than I expected. "You broke up? What happened?"

"Actually, it's kind of a long story."

I give him a jokey smile to let him know the worst is over, and I'm doing okay, and that there are bits of humor to come, probably, though I don't know where, or when. What I'm looking for, really, is a way to paint the *whole* picture, give him all the shades, since I know he'll be talking to Marie, and I want him to see that this wasn't a one-issue breakup, that, sure, I slept with Katharine, which was wrong, but we both realized we weren't the best people for each other, or would have in time, since that's what she basically said when she told me she couldn't be with me, and that other problems were already knocking on the door, or just around the corner, or somewhere in town. Maybe.

"You did something stupid again, didn't you?" His tone is

cold and flinty, and I don't like the accusatory finger poking
through it.

"What do you mean, *again?*"

"Jesus, Mitch. Do you have amnesia? Don't you remember
Jason?"

"That wasn't stupid. That was just a lapse in judgment. A mis-
communication. We've been over this."

"It was fucking stupid. It was idiotic. And then I had to bail
you out."

"You didn't bail me out. I talked to her. I gave her the truth."

These, from the look on his face, are the most ridiculous words
a person has ever spoken. "You gave her the truth all right. After
I talked to her every day for a week and listened to her scream
and cry and told her you were my best friend and not some psy-
cho, and there had to be a reason why you did what you did,
so why don't you let him explain?" He glares at me like I'm a
snotty-nosed kid. "What, did you think it was your charm and
good looks and chocolate pies that got you over to her place that
night? Don't flatter yourself."

I've never seen him this pissed.

"So what was it?" he sneers. "Did you gamble away a few thousand? Pick up a prostitute? Tell her she was an imbecile because
she couldn't keep her Turgenev straight from her Tolstoy?"

"Why are you getting so hostile, man?"

"Because she's my sister. *Man.*"

Something in the way he says "man" triggers it, like what he's
really saying is, "You're not a man at all, but a good-for-nothing
screw-up, which is what you've always been, and I'm her brother,
and you had no business being in the same city as her, much less
engaged to her."

"Oh, I get it. The two of you are *so* close. I don't hear about her
for five months when she moves back from North Carolina. You

tell me to go to the studio where she dances, to listen to her and her retard friends. And now your heart breaks when you hear her cry. Give him a medal, for brother of the year."

"Fuck you," he says, shoving the table at me as he scrambles to get up. The beers spill all over the place. I get up too and we both stare each other down.

"I thought I owed you an explanation," I say. My breathing is ragged and shallow and my pulse is thrumming in my ears. "But apparently you already have all the answers. So I guess I don't owe you shit."

He takes a step back, then lunges forward and smashes his right fist into my face. What I see is a burst of light, then the ceiling, and I realize I'm on the ground. He's standing over me, towering and humongous from this angle.

"Now we're even," he says, and storms away.

I've never been in a fight, not unless you count childhood spats on the playground, which I don't, since that's more pulling on hair and shirt collars and rolling around in the dirt. The closest I ever got was about five years ago, when I witnessed a car accident, and the two guys got out and started pounding each other. A few of us saw where this one was headed, the Skipper thrashing Gilligan, so we jumped in and pulled the big guy off and pinned him down for a couple minutes, till he cooled off. Now, as I pick myself off the floor of Colchester's, I realize I still haven't been in a fight: a fight requires two, an exchange of punches, an Ali and a Frazier. I've just been flattened.

I assure everyone I'm okay, then go to the bathroom and splash cold water on my face. I open and close my jaw a few times, to make sure it works, and it does, barely. I stare into the mirror at the spot, gingerly poking at the skin to differentiate the parts that hurt from the parts that don't—my right cheek is already swelling up. Then I take a look at the larger picture. Me. As a whole. Where do I go from here? And I don't mean, do I go back to my table or home (though it is a legitimate question, since I've a feeling I need a bag of ice, and soon), but more, how do I view myself in light of all that's happened with Marie. I suppose I could just slink around town with my guilt and regret, wait for the next roundhouse-right sucker puncher to knock me on my ass ("Go ahead and sock him: he cheated on his woman"). But when does it end? I told Marie the truth when I didn't have to, I apologized and sincerely meant it—and she dumped me. I brought Bradley to Colchester's and sat him down, bought him beer and a sandwich, tried to break it to him gently—and he did his best to jack a few teeth down my throat. Fine. I get it. Message received. I'm an asshole. You don't want any part of me. Now if you'll both excuse me, I have a life to live. I splash a last bit of water on my face and towel it off. I feel better. I'm okay. I'm fine.

And I am. I have my health (except for the pain in my jaw), my brain (except for a slight concussion), and over half a million dollars coming my way. This is my chance to improve my life, make a difference, be kind and charitable, all those things we all say we'd do if we ever won the lottery, and though this isn't exactly winning the lottery, it's as close as I'll ever come. And while I'm not saying money is the answer to everything, or many things, it can, to paraphrase what I heard Oprah tell Cameron Diaz not too long ago, be a good thing.

CHAPTER TWENTY-ONE

When the check finally comes from Susannah—all six fig-
ures of it—and I've deposited it, and I've waited a few days, and
there's no knock on my door from the bank manager, police, or
FBI wanting to know whom I robbed, what I'm laundering, or do
I have any other counterfeit checks in circulation, the first thing
I do is buy my Malibu. The purchase price is in my lease agree-
ment, and I'm probably paying a few bucks more than if I'd gone
to a dealer and haggled, but so be it: I've grown fond of my little
Chevy.

I'm teaching again this semester, and this new batch of students
is a lot like the last one—hardworking, interested, chatty—
without a Molly. This makes things a little boring, and if you're
waiting for me to say something like, "Gee, I actually miss her and
all the excitement and drama she brought," keep holding your
breath; sometimes you just want to walk into a classroom and
have the kids do their work, and not feel like you're co-starring
in an episode of *Gossip Girl* or *The Hills*, or some other angsty

teen drama. Now's that time. And for the most part, over the next few weeks, the students oblige, which lets me teach in peace and work on my dissertation, since, by the grace of God, I was able to wheedle and coax and cajole — but mostly grovel — my way back into the good graces of my dissertation committee, after missing various appointments and deadlines over the last four months.

Scott invites me over for a Super Bowl party in early February. A few of his college buddies and lawyer friends are there, and we spend the afternoon eating nachos and pretzels and pizza, drinking beer and soda — all before the game even starts, thanks to a sixteen-hour pre-game show.

My father shows up just before kickoff, with Nathan.

"Did we miss anything?" Nathan asks anxiously.

I assure him he didn't, after which he settles in with a soda and handful of chips.

"He was getting a bit antsy," my father leans over to tell me. "We've been working at the course all day."

"I thought you were closed for the season."

"The course is. But I'm renovating inside the clubhouse. I've put if off all winter, but if I want to open up in early spring, now's the time to get it done."

"You're doing it yourself?"

"What I can. I have help from my course manager, Kip, and a couple of guys he's hired."

The game gets under way, with a near touchdown on the first run from scrimmage.

"I could help out," I say, a few plays later. "If you need it."

He slows down on the pretzels he's chewing, aware that this is something of a moment. "That'd be great."

And almost like nothing happened, we go back to watching the game.

*   *   *

I stop by the course the next day, after teaching. There's progress already: the old carpet is up and the walls have been measured for drywall. (My father thinks it'll be easier to put drywall over the paneling, then paint, rather than ripping the paneling off. I'm sure Bradley would know which way is best, but it'd be hard to get an answer out of him since we don't speak to each other anymore.) Kip and I and the crew finish around seven, having pried up the tack boards and installed new ones halfway around.

On my way home, because it's not that far out of the way, I swing by the studio. It's my first time going since Marie and I broke up. I don't go in. I just cruise past the lot, slowly, to see what I can see, and what I don't see is Marie's car. That doesn't necessarily mean anything: she probably just skipped out on tonight's lesson, or she's parked around back or beside an SUV, and I just can't see it.

But I go again on Thursday, and this time I pull into the lot and actually go up and down the aisles, and there's definitely no VW. Maybe she's gotten a new car. Maybe the lessons with Adonis aren't on Mondays and Thursdays anymore. Or maybe she just stopped going. That's the possibility I like least. I don't want to think she stopped doing something she loved doing, especially if it had anything to do with me. If that's the case, I'd like to tell her just to go back to the way she was before we met, happy going to dance class and out for drinks and karaoke and whatever it was she did. But it doesn't always work that way after a breakup, does it? Slipping back into your old life.

Back at my apartment, I'm feeling a little gloomy myself. I've always been on the loner side, with one or two great friends—like Bradley—but being with Marie changed me, made me more social, since we were always hopping around here or there, especially with our studio friends. I miss all that, Rosie and her *vavooms!*, Fran and her cats, even Gina and horny Dave. Now it's just...me. The apartment feels too big. I've been watching TV just to hear people talk. There are days when I don't even feel like writing. So on Saturday morning I get up, get dressed and eat, and head out to pick myself up a new friend.

Going to the pound can be brutal. You know dogs were meant to be with people, and none of them wants to be here, cramped up in one of those absurd cages, so you start feeling you might have to take all of them home, but you can't, of course, so you think maybe you should just work here, see that they all get taken care of; but you realize some of them wind up being put down, which you wouldn't allow, so you might be tempted to sneak in after hours and set them all free, which could land *you* in a different sort of pound. How about those thoughts for a Saturday morning?

But I have a plan. As I walk the line of cages, I'm not looking for the cute dog, the one with irresistible eyes or a playful demeanor or sturdy frame, because dogs like that have no problem finding a home. I want the dog that may not be around next week, and not because he's been adopted. I think I've found him.

He's lying in the back of his cage, not really facing me. I crouch down and he doesn't react. He's not what you'd call a pretty dog; his coat is dark and a little dull, and he looks like he has a bit of German shepherd in him. He's also too skinny. I give him a few "hey boys" and still nothing, just a little once-over with his eyes, and what his eyes are saying is "I'm tired." Not tired from a morning of chasing squirrels or fetching a tennis ball or Frisbee or digging in the yard, but tired of this, being in this cage, lying here, seeing all these people, watching the other dogs come and go.

I flag down an attendant and ask if I can take a dog outside. She says they prefer to keep them inside, in the visiting room. But when I show her which one, she says okay, as if realizing this is a special case. On the leash heading out, he doesn't try to pull and trails a little bit behind me, and I get the feeling he thinks he's on his way to the room where dogs go and don't come out. To his surprise, I think, we head toward the front doors and daylight, which brings a slight flutter to his tail.

I bring him to the patch of grass and trees on the side of the parking lot, and he immediately does what all dogs do: sniff. But I don't think he's sniffing it like other dogs, just for the hell of it, just to see who's been there; he's sniffing *grass* and *trees* and *dirt* and *fresh air*, all the things he doesn't have inside his cage. And as I watch him go about his business, and the tail gets a life and his ears perk up, and there's a bounce to his step, and he turns his nose to the breeze and tracks the flight of a yellow jacket and nips at it, and angles himself in front of me when he sees another dog, as if to protect me, I get the feeling that if I march him back into that place and let them take him back to his cage and the fluorescent lighting, and the noise and smell of the other dogs, and the people who just file by with barely a glance, he'll find a way to make his heart stop before the sun comes up tomorrow.

I have a dog.

We go to the pet shop and pick up a bed and food and collar and leash, and they also have one of those machines that makes a name tag. I always figured that when I got a dog, I'd name him after a character from Greek mythology or favorite artist or literary theorist, so that when I called his name — "Here, Derrida" — people would look at me and think, "Now *there's* a guy with taste." But watching him sit on the floor, like dogs are supposed to sit, I realize he *is* a dog, and that's what he wants to be. Why should I saddle him with some pretentious name that's more about feeding my ego than letting him be what he is? The name on his card at the pound said "Bo," which seems like a perfectly good name for a dog. So Bo it is.

When we get back to the apartment, I let him sniff around and make friendly with the place and let it sink in that this isn't a dream. I take him for a walk and serve him his first meal, which he scarfs down, and since I don't want to leave him by himself, not on his first day, we hang out together and watch some hockey. He isn't the most friendly chap, not yet anyway, and he likes to keep a bit of distance between us, so I respect that, let him lie on his bed in the living room, and when I tell him goodnight, he's still there. But before I fall asleep, I hear him pad into the bedroom and come to the side of my bed. I put my hand out and he licks it, then he settles at the foot of my bed.

Katharine calls the next day to bring me up to speed on everything. I'd expected her agent or publicist or Brent to take over *Catwalk Mama* update duties after we signed the deal in New York, but apparently she thinks Bradley's a darling and can't get enough of being *Catwalk Mama*'s midwife.

"Hear that sound, Mitch? That's the sound of people *loving* this book. Susannah's sent out a few promotional copies and gotten some quotes for the back cover. Listen to these." She shuffles some papers. "'A new kind of chick heroine is slipping into her stilettos: the sexy, sassy, soccer mama. This one scores, early and often.' That's from the woman who wrote *Mr. Right Now*. Here's another, from Sandra Greene: '*Catwalk Mama* is a p-u-r-r-f-e-c-t-l-y scrumptious read.' And she even got one from Lauren Weisberger."

"*The Devil Wears Prada* Lauren Weisberger? What'd she have to say?"

She tells me.

"Holy crap."

"I know. It's great. Regency House is also getting the front cover together. It's a plain Jane looking into a mirror, and the face staring back is a drop-dead gorgeous model. Do you want me to have them send you and Bradley a copy?"

"Do you like it?"

"I love it."

"Then that's good enough for me."

There's a pause, and I think I've said the wrong thing, that she's picked up I'm not interested. But then she laughs. "You know, it's a pleasure working on this with you. You're so easy."

Ah, yes, Katharine: I'm easy all right. Which is what got me in trouble in the first place.

She tells me I should have Bradley put together her author bio in the next couple of weeks, which is doable, then we chat about the movie deal she's got in the works for *The Cappuccino Club*, the new car she's bought (a Mini Cooper), and the fact that she's gone back to blond—again. Somehow it comes out that I've broken up with my girlfriend, and that tidbit hangs in the air for a moment.

"I'll be in Chicago next weekend," she says. "If you want to come up..."

There's no good reason why I shouldn't. She's single. I'm single. And it's not like she's looking for a commitment or promise ring or anything. Just a few days of adult-consenting playtime. But I get the feeling it'd be one of those cotton candy weekends— addictively, deliciously fun—and when it's all said and done, I'd feel sick. And guilty. And hungry for something else. So I tell her I'm helping my dad.

"Ah. *C'est la vie*, Mitch. Perhaps another time."

And, because she's Katharine Longwell, and probably has a dozen other guys on hold right now, she says it without missing a beat.

*   *   *

For Bradley's author bio, I could say all sorts of things about how she loves chocolate and shoes and shopping, that she has a collection of Marc Jacobs clutches and hopes to fit into a size eight one day. But Katharine told me to keep it short and simple, to play up the mystery angle, so I do. Besides, why should I embellish at this point? Bradley is enough of an embellishment, in her own skin. So here's what I come up with: "Bradley enjoys dancing and music, and lives in St. Louis with her dog Bo. This is Bradley's first novel." Short and simple and all true, except for the pronoun *her*. But even that bothers me, as does using Bo's real name, since, if I'm not comfortable enough to attach my name to the project, why should he? Thus I revise: "Bradley enjoys dancing and music, and lives in St. Louis with a dog named Belle. This is Bradley's first novel." Substitute Mitch for Bradley, Bo for Belle, and you've got nothing but the truth. Besides, it's not like I called the thing a memoir and made up stories about all the time I spent in jail, then got outdded on Oprah because she picked me as her book club selection and then got embarrassed when it turned out I'd made a lot of it up. It's a novel. It's fiction. I made *all* of it up. Including the author.

CHAPTER TWENTY-TWO

It stays cold for most of February — St. Louis celebrates President's Day with its annual barrage of furniture store sales and eight inches of snow — and even into March, but I keep going to the course, doing what I can. By the time March gives way to April, and warmer weather, the clubhouse is finished and we turn our attention from inside to the course itself.

Maintaining a golf course is more than just keeping the grass cut short and watering it. You need specialized grass — Kentucky Bent, around here — and all sorts of specialized information about it, such as how to cut it, when to cut it, in which direction to cut it, what kind of machine to use, and how to deal with spike marks and bugs and disease. It's like keeping a vineyard, only the end result isn't a glass of wine; it's an immaculate canvas of green that promises true bounces and honest rolls, so that when the day is done and the golfer has shot his round, he can blame his spotty performance on his clubs or his ball or his playing partner or the angle of the sun — sometimes, even himself — but never the course. Fortunately, our course manager Kip, with his twenty years' experience in the field, is a genius at doing it right.

I prefer to be outside, on the course, but I do hang around inside at times with my father, mostly to humor him. He likes to show me how the books work—payroll, insurance, equipment fees, beer and concessions, even the damn electric and water bills—and he's so earnest when he does it that I don't have the heart to tell him that it's not interesting to me. I'm not a numbers or money guy. And speaking of that, it's pretty clear this isn't a huge moneymaker. He does okay, but he's never going to be a gazillionaire off his par three course. Of course, that's not why he does it.

I still haven't figured out what kind of a dog Bo is, in terms of his breed, but at least I do know what he was born to do: live on a golf course. I bring him with me every time I go and he loves it. So much, in fact, that I feel bad bringing him back to the apartment. At the course, he has fresh air and geese to chase and warm grass to lie on, a best buddy in Shep, and golfers who scruff him under the chin; at the apartment he has hardwood floors, and me. But he seems happy enough just to have a home, and he treats me like I'm the greatest person on the face of the earth. Which, I have to admit, I like.

My mother and I get together the first weekend in June to celebrate the end of her school year and mine. When I get back to the apartment, there's a box for me on the doorstep. It's a box of books. *Catwalk Mama* books. I'm holding *my* book.

"I persuaded them to send the first batch your way, so you could get them right to Bradley," Katharine practically squeals when I get her on the phone. "The rest ship out next week, all over the country."

"To stores?"

"To stores, Mitch. That's where they sell them. And the publicity machine's already cranking into overdrive. They've had ads in *USA Today* and *People*. I've even shuffled the publicity rounds for my own material to coincide with the release, so I'll make sure *Catwalk Mama* gets plenty of attention. Which gives me a thought..." Even through the phone, I can hear her mind do something of a double take. "What about you, Mitch?"

"What about me *what*?"

"How about we team up, you make a few appearances with me."

Oh Christ. "I don't think that's such a good idea."

"I think it's a *great* idea. Think about the angle. You come on with me, explain how we met at the coffee shop, how you told me about your cousin. People will eat it up."

I panic for a moment, then several, before a lightbulb flips on in my brain. "But then they'll know it's my cousin," I point out triumphantly, relieved to find a flaw in her plan. "Her anonymity would be shot."

She barely slows down. "Then we won't say she's your cousin. We'll say she's a friend. An *acquaintance*. Which means Bradley's off the hook."

And I'm back on it, right through my jugular vein. "I just don't know..."

"Come on, Mitch. This is nuts. Don't make me beg." She says it with half a laugh, but there's more than a trace of exasperation in her voice. "Besides, this isn't about me. It's about Bradley and her book and the chance to change her life. Do it for her, why don't you."

Do it for her. *Why don't you.*

And just like that, the curtain falls and my eyes snap open and I get a glimpse into what's been fueling Katharine's fervor to get Bradley published these last few months: that, yeah, maybe she likes me and enjoys the hanky-panky and wouldn't mind more, but this has always been about Bradley and her book. Because she sees what she once was in Bradley and wants to make her dreams come true. My made-up cousin means that much to her. It almost chokes me up.

"Okay, how about we make a deal," Katharine continues. "I have *Regis and Kelly* at the end of the month. If *Catwalk Mama* is in the top five, you come on with me, just for a few minutes."

"In the top five what?"

"Bestsellers."

"*Times* bestsellers?"

"The one and only."

Jesus. "If *Catwalk Mama* is in the top five of the *New York Times'* bestsellers, then yes, I'll come on *Regis and Kelly* with you."

"Promise?"

"Promise."

"Good. See you in a few weeks."

After we hang up, I sit down with a beer and a copy of my book and page through it. After all those months of seeing it as scribbled notes in a notebook, and blue-bordered chunks of text in a Microsoft document called "catWmama," here it is: a hardback book, with crackly spine and fancy typeface and new paper smell. I run my hands over the glossy cover, read the quotes on the back jacket, trace my finger over both the American and Canadian prices. I show it to Bo and he sniffs it, and when I tell him that's my ISBN, the only book that will ever have those digits, he cocks his head and gives his tail a little thump on the floor, because I think he gets it. The funny thing is, I could get hit by a car tonight and die, and no one would ever know I'd written it, because Bo wouldn't tell; and when they came to clean out my apartment, they'd see the box of *Catwalk Mama* books by Bradley Gallagher and scratch their heads and say, "Why the hell does he have those?" Maybe I should write a note and tape it to the mirror in my bathroom, or leave it in my sock drawer, explaining everything. Of course, I could also just trust that Bradley and Marie would come out of the woodwork and clear things up, cement my posthumous legacy.

Then again, I should probably just write that note.

Scott wants to do Father's Day at his house, have our dad and his father-in-law over for a barbecue. That's fine with me, since he actually has a tradition with Dad for this day. I have no tradition, other than sometimes picking up the phone, sometimes dialing it, and sometimes speaking to him. But I insist that the day before, we head down to a Cardinals game, the three of us, along with Nathan and Jessica and Kyle.

It's one of those June St. Louis afternoons that's warm for the season (technically we're still in spring, but tell that to the humidity). Nathan and Kyle have brought gloves in hopes of snaring a foul ball, and Jessica has brought a stuffed Dalmatian named Raz, which offers no help in snaring a foul ball, but she didn't want to be empty-handed. We've also brought a cooler with sodas and goodies to munch on. The game flies by, and Nathan keeps score on the scorecard, trying to explain to Kyle how it's done, and Scott documents a little bit of everything with his digital camera.

During the seventh-inning stretch, after I've sung along with everyone else about buying peanuts and Cracker Jacks and rooting for the home team, I head to the concession stand. I've got thirty bucks burning a hole in my pocket, so I grab beers for the three adults. I'm not happy with the way they're situated in the little cardboard carrying tray, and I'm standing next to the counter trying to adjust them when I hear someone call out my name.

"Yo, Mitch."

I turn. It's Molly.

"Hey there," I say, and quickly lick spilled beer off my hand so I can shake hers, but she's a little quicker on the draw and gives me a hug. It's one of those press-her-body-in kind and I can feel her legs against mine.

"So, what's going on?" I ask when we've separated.

"Nothing much. Just watching the game, same as you, I imagine."

Truth be told, at that very moment I'm having difficulty remembering why it is I *am* here, because she's wearing a cottony summer dress—sophisticated, a little sheer—with flip-flops and a golden tan.

"Yep. Watching the game. You bet." I clear my throat. "Are you here with Pete?"

Her face turns slightly gloomy. "Nah. With some other friends. Pete and I broke up a few months ago."

"Oh, that's too bad. I'm sorry to hear it didn't work out."

"Yeah, thanks. We're still good friends, though. We talk a lot. Or debate. Or argue. Whatever it is we do."

She tells me about her semester, which was good, even though *Cosmo* decided to pass on the article after all, but no big deal, since she's going to spend the next year abroad, in London, studying theater.

"I think I found my niche," she says. "Flair for the dramatic and all."

"You'll be great." There's a glow about her, and it's not just the tan, and I have a feeling she won't be throwing herself off the side of Mount Everest anytime soon.

We talk about my dissertation—things humming along nicely on that front—then say our goodbyes. I gather up my tray of beers.

"Hey, Mitch," she calls over, still hanging around. "Are you on campus this summer?"

I shrug. "Sometimes. I'm not teaching, but I make it out there every now and then."

"Same office?"

"Yep."

"Then maybe I could stop by sometime and we could head over to the café for lunch."

Two guys around my age are standing off to the side, ogling her, and apparently following enough of the conversation to realize she's basically asking me out. That would explain why they both have that dropped-jaw, gimme-a-break, I-did-not-just-hear-that look plastered to their faces. Suddenly that Joe Jackson song "Is She Really Going Out with Him?" is running through my head.

"Yeah. Sure. We could do that."

"Great," she says, and gives me a smile that will last me all day.

The rest of the game breezes by. Neither Nathan nor Kyle snags a foul ball and the Cards come up short, but it's tough for any of us to be very disappointed, since we've all had such a great time. Outside the stadium, we snap one last set of pictures in front of the statue of Stan Musial. Scott wants to get my dad and me and him striking the same pose we did when we were kids and Dad brought us here—bat in hands, poised for the swing, the way Stan is—so Nathan snaps that one. There's brief talk of heading out for dinner, but we're all still stuffed from the game, especially my father, whose stomach is bothering him from a hotdog that went down the wrong way, and plus he's a little tired, so we nix those plans. Besides, we'll be spending tomorrow together.

Back at the apartment, I take Bo for a walk, grab a late dinner at Colchester's, then the two of us get cozy on the sofa and watch TV. But I keep thinking about Molly, how good she looked and healthy she seemed, trying to convince myself that I didn't just say yes to lunch with her to impress those guys at the game, that we could actually have some sort of relationship outside the classroom, though not *that* type of relationship, because eighteen is still eighteen, for chrissakes; and all of it's still so much on my mind that when the phone rings at 2:48 and wakes me up, my groggy-minded knee-jerk reaction is that it's her, calling to say she doesn't want to wait until summer to have lunch, she wants to make plans now, since she has some questions about London or Shakespeare or the theater, and she knows I'd be a font of information. But it's not Molly at all. It's Leah. She's at the hospital and sobbing. My father is dead.

When I was a kid, my dad had a habit of taking a nap when he got home from work, and I had a habit of sneaking in to watch him sleep. He'd be flopped on his back, longways on the bed, one arm draped over his eyes, the other across his stomach. Sometimes he left his watch on, and I'd try to get close enough to read the numbers; other times I'd bring in one of my baseball cards and tickle the hair on his arms, till he tried to brush the sensation away. When I felt most daring, I'd try to balance a marble on his chest and see how long it'd stay, which usually wasn't very long, since he'd shift or stir or let out a grizzled snore or just take one of those deep-sleep breaths, and the marble went tumbling off.

I'm thinking of that marble as I stand with Scott and Leah at the hospital and we stare at my father's body. He looks exactly the same as he did a few hours ago, same wrinkles and age spots and hair, even a patch of sunburned skin on the tip of his nose, and I keep expecting a little movement, a breath, something to indicate that he's alive, that he's just taking a nap, that he's managed to hold his breath for a long time, and at any moment his eyelids will flutter, or his lips will part, or his throat will swallow, or his fingers will twitch, or his leg will shake out. But none of it happens, and it's not going to happen, not even if we stay here till dawn. And it's all starting to sink in that if I placed that marble on his chest now, it would stay there till the end of time.

I'm out at the golf course just before seven, waiting for Kip. I give him the news and he can't believe it, and he just keeps shaking his head and crying and asking if there's anything he can do. I tell him he can call the others, break the news to them, and let them know the course will be closed for a few days. I consider putting up a sign on the front door of the clubhouse—"Course closed till further notice"—and leaving, but the people who know my dad deserve better, so I stick around and tell them in person.

Over the next two days, I stay in touch with Leah and offer to help her or Nathan or Jessica in any way I can, but she already has a whole army of family and friends providing meals and comfort, and it's not like we're the closest people anyway, so I stay in the background. Plus, my dad already took care of all the funeral arrangements after the first heart attack.

On Wednesday we meet at the cemetery for the service. It's another hot day, so there's a tent up, but it's not big enough by far, and people spill out the back and around on both sides. The immediate family sits in the front row, and I'm next to Scott, on the end. Several people get up and say a few words about my father, including Scott, and it's nice to hear that people thought so highly of him—and loved him, I'd have to say—though I don't get up and speak, because what would I say: that I thought the world of him for the first ten years, hated him for the next eighteen, and started to like him again these past few months. No one needs to hear that, and I don't want to pretend it was any other way. He and I knew what it was, and where we were, and how far we'd gotten, and that's what matters.

After the eulogies and prayers from the rabbi, we all throw a shovelful of dirt on the casket. It's a long line of people, and I see a lot of familiar faces from the course, a few from the Hanukkah party, and one I haven't seen in a while, near the back: Bradley. Instinctively, I scan the crowd for Marie, but she's not there. People come over and offer sympathy and hugs, and by the time Bradley has thrown his bit of dirt on my father, I'm standing under a tree, trying to keep cool.

"I'm sorry about your dad," he says, shaking my hand.

I nod. "Thanks for coming."

In my mind, there are a thousand different ways this conversation could go. But in reality, there's only one way it can, in this place, under these circumstances.

"It was another heart attack."

He makes a grim face. "How's everyone doing?"

"Leah's a mess, inside. But she's a strong woman. She's hanging in there as best as she can. And Nathan and Jessica, they know what it means, obviously, that their dad's dead, but they can't really grasp it yet. She's only nine. Scott's taking it hard."

He studies my face. "And what about you?"

The question catches me off guard, and my thoughts shoot in a dozen directions. "Honestly, I don't know. I feel sad. I'm sorry he's gone. I feel bad for Leah and the kids. But I also feel frustrated. Pissed, actually. Can I say that? I guess I'm just angry we wasted all this time, that there was something good between us all along and we didn't do anything about it. Or not enough. We could've been at this point ten years ago. And there were things I hadn't said, and probably would have, in time." I pause. "But it was good at the end, and that's better than nothing, I guess."

I regret it as soon as I say it, that last part, because it's a stupid and empty expression, and not even true. Sometimes you are better off with *nothing*, because the something you get is so small, and so good, that the taste of it lasts only a second, but the missing of it and longing for it and living without it will haunt you the rest of your life. I change the subject.

"How have you been?" I ask.

"Good. Working outside a lot."

"And Skyler?"

"She's great."

I rub the side of my jaw. "And Marie?"

He considers this carefully. "Marie's . . . okay. She's been busy." He's sufficiently vague and evasive, which I take as a sign that she told him not to say anything. "She wanted me to give you this." He hands me a card. "She thought about coming, but figured it'd probably be better if she didn't."

It's a beige envelope with no name on the front, which isn't so odd, I guess, since she probably only gave Bradley one envelope and he knows who gets it. Unless she couldn't even bring herself to write my name.

The crowd is beginning to disperse and head for their cars. One of Nathan's friends slips his tie over his head, the grieving over for him. For Nathan it's just starting.

"We're going over to Leah's house to sit shivah," I say. "You're welcome to come."

He gives his head a soft shake. "I appreciate that, Mitch. But I don't think so."

No, not since he knows it's for family and close friends, and Bradley and I are neither these days.

I take my keys out of my pocket and loop my finger through the ring. "I should get going," I say.

He looks off to the distance, then kicks at a rocky clump. "I hate the way things are between us, you know."

"Yeah, me too."

"Anything we can do about that?"

"Your being here is a start, I think. And when all this is

over, I'll give you a call. Maybe we could go for drinks. Or shoot baskets."

He turns to me, and for a moment I see Bradley, and Bradley sees me. "I'd like that."

We shake hands again and he leaves. As I watch him make his way down the path to the parking lot, the sun beating down on his back, I allow myself to think that maybe there's one aspect of my life that's headed in the right direction.

There's food galore at Leah's, and the house is swarming with people, since it's too hot to be outside. The little kids are running around, because for them it's just a party, sort of like Hanukkah without the dreidels or candles. Leah seems to be holding up well, buoyed by all the hugs she's getting, and Nathan and Jessica seem too distracted by friends and cousins to be showing much emotion. I manage to read the card from Marie, and it's generic Hallmark, sorry about your dad, thinking of you in your time of loss, etc., but just what it needs to be. But I can't help thinking that this is the woman who would've been standing with me right now, and I'd be fetching her a drink or a slice of pie or a second helping of kugel, and she'd be asking me how I'm holding up. Instead I have a three dollar card.

I don't stay till the end, because it's clear Leah's parents and siblings have that honor, so after I swing by my apartment to take care of Bo, I head over to my mom's. Scott is there with Melinda and Kyle, and we sit out by the pool for a while, reminiscing. Then Scott and his family leave, so it's down to my mom and me and the two of us talking, then she goes inside. It's just the pool and the night and me.

My father used to sit here on summertime evenings and listen to the ballgames on AM radio. Sometimes I listened with him, sometimes I didn't, but after the game was over, he'd find a station and listen to jazz. I didn't know it was jazz then, only that it wasn't the type of music I liked, which was rock or pop or whatever they were playing on MTV. It was just Dad music, and when I went to bed and he was still out there, I'd open my bedroom window, even when the AC was on, just so I could hear the murmur of the piano or saxophone or bass as I drifted off to sleep on those summer nights.

It's been nearly two decades since any of that happened, and to be honest, I hadn't given it much thought, till tonight. Sitting here in the spot where he used to sit, I strain to hear some echo of what once was, hoping that maybe the trees or grass or stones collected a fragment of those tunes, even a few notes, and will play them back for me. But of course, they didn't, they can't, they won't. And even if my mom and Scott and I assumed the places and clothes we had in 1984 or '86 or '88, and we all played Yahtzee or Monopoly or Scrabble, the games we used to play, and made popcorn—even if we all agreed to do it for just one more night, for old time's sake, it wouldn't make a difference. I can never go back into that room and open my window and hear my father's music and know he's out here on the patio, and I'm safely tucked into bed. He's gone. He's *gone*. And for the first time since Leah called with the news, I cry.

There are no surprises when my father's will is read, no strange requests that his remains be shot out of a cannon or fed to the sharks or buried on the eighteenth green (which is good, since any of it would require digging him up and going through it all over again, and no one wants to do that). Everything is divvied up the way you'd expect it; in other words, it all goes to Leah and the kids, with something set aside for Kyle. The only part of it that takes me by surprise, but apparently no one else because they already knew, is that he wants the golf course to be sold.

"But why?" I ask my brother, as we sit on his back deck drinking a beer.

"Dad made it work because he knew how to pinch pennies and scrimp and run a bare-bones operation. In the wrong hands, it would go bust, and he didn't want to leave Leah strapped with that."

"So this makes more sense, financially — to sell it?"

"Yep. His life insurance policy pays off the remaining debt, plus leaves a little extra. Then Leah can sell the course, which is pure profit. Dad even left us a list of guys who'd already expressed an interest in the land."

"That's an odd way to put it, 'the land.'"

"Unfortunately, the course is more valuable as land for developers than it is as a golf course. Dad knew it, too."

"So you mean some guy will buy it and put up a row of condos or villas or something?"

He gives his head a sober nod. "That's exactly what it means."

This comes to me like a punch in the gut. Knowing how hard he'd worked to keep it going, the pride he took from it. It was a labor of love. And what about Kip? But my father must have known this was the way it would go. Still . . .

"So give me a ballpark figure," I say. "What kind of money are we talking about for 'the land'?"

He gives me a ballpark figure.

"What if I knew someone who could give Leah just about that and keep the course in the family?"

"I'd say, give me the number."

"Brother, you already have it, probably on speed dial."

He looks at me like I'm crazy. "What the hell are you talking about?"

That's when I introduce him to my sugar lady *Catwalk Mama*.

CHAPTER TWENTY-THREE

I'm out on the course playing eighteen with a guy named Joe Magditch. Joe's a T-shirt vendor, and I need T-shirts for the charity tournament I'm planning for August. Joe also loves to golf, so we have a friendly wager in play: if I win, I get free T-shirts from Joe; if he wins, he gets free golf for the rest of the year. We're on the sixteenth hole and I have a two-shot lead, but he has a short putt to cut the lead to one. That's when my cell phone—which I can't believe I forgot to turn off—rings. It's Katharine.

"Hey, stranger. I thought I'd hear from you by now."

"Oh? And why's that?"

"Like you don't know." She pauses to let me fill in the blank, which I don't. So she does. "To coordinate our plans for New York."

I step off the green and away from Joe's evil eye. "I don't follow, Katharine. Why would I be going to New York?"

"Because you said you would. *Hello.* The bet."

The only bet that comes to mind is the one I have with Joe.

But I don't think any of the conditions we discussed had me going to New York with Katharine, and how would she know, anyway?

"*Regis and Kelly*, Mitch. I'm on next Tuesday. And you said you'd go on with me if the book—"

"*If the book made it into the top five*," I cut her off. Suddenly my heart starts pounding in my throat. With everything going on with my father, I haven't been paying attention to any of that. "Are you telling me we made it into the top five?"

"You might say that. We just squeaked in...at number *one*."

Oh sweet Jesus. What the fuck have I done?

I've never been on TV. The closest I came was my junior year of high school when I was out for a jog in Forest Park and a local news crew was interviewing people about how they were coping with the sweltering heat and I gave them my secret strategy: ignore it. But when the story aired, all I saw was a bunch of shirtless guys with six-pack abs talking about drinking lots of water and sticking to the shade. I felt slighted. This morning, however, sitting in my dressing room, I'd love to see any one of those bare-chested underwear models again, so I could trot him out there onto the *Regis and Kelly* stage and everyone would forget about me.

I don't need much time to get ready. A woman comes in to do my makeup and hair. She does what she can with it, even though I can tell it's too long, and it winds up looking a bit slick for my tastes. I wear the blazer Katharine got me in Chicago, with the same shirt, but this time I wear jeans. I head down to Katharine's dressing room, which is huge and luxurious, and she's getting the final touches on her makeup. Her hair is Heather Locklear–blond now, even though the face is still Demi Moore. It's a good look.

"Nervous?" she asks. She's sitting in her chair in a robe.

"A little."

"Try not to think about what's happening when you're out

there. Ignore the camera. Pretend Regis and Kelly are two old friends. We're all just having a conversation. It's like we're sitting in the coffee shop, or back at my place."

I'm better off thinking we're at the coffee shop. If I think of her place, I might think of her bedroom, and what the two of us did in her bedroom, which could be distracting.

A production assistant named Megan pops in and briefs us that Katharine will be out there for two segments: the first is all Katharine, for her to talk about what's going on in her life; then, after the commercial, I'll be out there to talk about the book.

"What do I say?" I ask Megan. Megan turns to Katharine. Katharine turns to me.

"Whatever you want," she says with a smile. "Obviously you want to keep Bradley's identity secret. But otherwise, talk about her favorite books, any hobbies she has, if she ever dreamed of being a model herself. Anything that would help people get a sense of her. And talk about the way we met. That's a good one."

The stylist rubs in a little powder on Katharine's cheeks to give them a bronze hue.

"You look great, Katharine."

"Why thank you, Mitch. You don't look so bad yourself."

Megan asks me if I'd like to meet the musical guest, Tony Bennett, and of course I'd like to meet Tony Bennett. Who wouldn't? But I pass, since I figure the less this whole thing feels like an event—and meeting one of the most famous American singers of all time would tend to do that—the better. I'll stick with Katharine's notion that I'm just here to chat with a couple old friends. The problem is, though I've had friends named Kelly, I've never had a friend named Regis. Tim or Ed, yes. Can I call him Ed?

I camp out in the green room and the show starts. Regis and Kelly come out and do their bit. Regis talks about how he was at a party at Al Roker's house and he was disappointed that Spike Lee wasn't there, since Spike Lee always stares at him, and he wanted to ask Spike why he always stares at him, and is it because Spike wants him to be in one of his movies. Kelly thinks Spike wants to do the Regis story, starring Regis, and he wants to get a good look at him from all angles, and she says she wants Elisha Cuthbert to play her in the movie, and Regis asks her why she thinks she'd be in the movie at all. Then Regis tells us that this is the warmest year on record for the Netherlands: an average of eleven degrees Celsius, and let's give a hand to the Dutch. Then they spin the wheel and ask a trivia question about Matt Damon, and a woman named Gerry wins a trip to Barbados, and the lucky member of the studio audience in seat 152 gets three pieces of luggage. Also, just before the commercial, they single out William and Gladys Davenport, here to celebrate their sixty-fifth wedding anniversary, with children and grandchildren and great-grandchildren. She stands up, and he takes a bit longer, because he's using a cane, and it's not even clear when he *is* standing up, since his spine looks to have rolled itself into something of a C after eighty-five-plus years. They get a nice round of applause.

After the break, Katharine comes out in her Dolce & Gabbana dress, graceful, elegant, sexy, and when she perches on her stool it's hard not to notice her legs, or chest, or face. She talks about *The Cappuccino Club* being made into a movie, and what it's like to work on the screenplay version of your own book, and how it feels be on *People*'s best-dressed list year after year, and who she's been linked with; and it's funny to see her tossing out names of celebrities like they're her friends, when they are her friends. What's even stranger is to think that in a few minutes, I'll be leaving this room where I am, watching them on TV, and I'll be out there sitting next to them, *on* TV. It'd be like watching an epi-sode of *ER* and seeing Dr. Kovac work on a guy, then they go to the commercial, and when they come back, you're standing in the room now, too, handing him a syringe loaded with ten cc's of epinephrine, stat. Anyway, now they're getting around to *Catwalk Mama*, because Regis is talking about Katharine being not only a great writer herself, but also a finder of great writers. He holds up a copy of my book.

"Coming up, you'll meet the man who just might be able to shed some light on the surprise smash book of the season."

Megan walks me out on stage, gets a mic hooked to my blazer, and makes sure it's working. I shake hands with Regis and give Kelly a quick hug. He's a funny guy, that Regis. He takes one look at me and barks at Gelman in that Regis sort of way, Will he *ever* schedule a guest who's shorter than him? I get myself propped on my stool and take a breath. Kelly tells me she likes my blazer, so I tell her Katharine picked it out, and the shirt, then the two of them start talking clothes, and Regis gives me a wink, and it almost feels like I'm back in the studio, minus a few "vavooms." I just might make this. I just might be fine. We return to live.

"Okay, we're back with Katharine Longwell, celebrated bestselling author who you all know, and we're joined by Mitch Samuel. Mitch is an acquaintance of the author of *Catwalk Mama*, and here to perhaps shed some light on our mystery writer. But first, Mitch, let's talk about you. Where are you from?"

"St. Louis."

"Ah, Gateway to the West. The Cardinals. Italian restaurants on the Hill. Great city. And what do you do there?"

"I teach at the university." I try not to look at Katharine, since this is news to her, too. "I'm also working on my PhD."

"On what, may I ask?"

"Chaucer. *The Canterbury Tales.*"

"Oh, *The Canterbury Tales*. You know, Mitch, that's Kelly's favorite book. She loves those Canterbury Tales. Talks about them all the time." The audience starts to laugh. "Go on, quiz her. Ask her anything about them."

Kelly makes a face. "At least I wasn't around when they were written, like Rege was."

The audience loves that one.

"Now, changing the subject, if I may..." Kelly says, holding up a copy of *Catwalk Mama*. "I love this book. We all do. My girlfriends and I have a theory about the cover. Since there's no photo of the author, we've decided that the cover photo is actually a photo of the author. A sort of with makeup, without makeup shot. And, *and*, rumor has it it's also someone you're related to. Am I right?"

I turn to Katharine.

"Come on, Mitch. No help from Katharine. Can we get a close-up here, with the cover? Do a split screen with Mitch." Apparently they do a split screen. "Huh, see the resemblance? Especially the woman in the mirror, glamour girl. Audience, what do you think?"

They applaud.

"No, honest, that's not her," I say.

Kelly tries to soothe me. "Nothing to be ashamed of, Mitch. She's an attractive woman. I wouldn't mind having those lips, that body. Fess up."

Regis perks up on his stool. "Who are you, Eliot Ness? You got the kid under FBI interrogation? Give him some room to breathe. He'll say what he wants to say." Regis makes a gesture of giving me the floor. "But tell us this much, Mitch. Did she go to Notre Dame?"

I know why he's saying it. Anyone who knows anything about Regis knows why he's saying it. He's a Notre Dame alum and he loves Notre Dame and he loves to talk about it whenever he can, especially during college football season. But it's obvi-ous that William of Gladys and William doesn't know that, or didn't hear what was said, because while everyone else is smiling or laughing, he looks lost, bewildered, swimming in confusion, which, for some reason, bothers me a lot, seeing that old man with such a helpless look on his face. But Gladys is on top of it, sensing he's floundering over there (I guess after sixty-five years with someone, you get to sensing things like that), and she leans over and cups her hand over his ear, and whatever she says, it works, because his face eases itself and warms. And then, in what I can only assume is a gesture of gratitude for reeling him in when he was out there alone, he reaches over to her, with a whole lot of stiffness and creakiness, and takes her hand in his and pats it with the other, which makes her smile even more.

And that's when I want to cry.

There's a poem by the Irishman W. B. Yeats in which he addresses the woman he loves and assures her that when she is old and gray and full of sleep and nodding by the fire and has just about reached the end of her days, she'll be able to look back over her life and realize that he loved *her*—and her *soul*—and not anything physical or superficial or fleeting about her. Now, this was written by a twenty-seven-year-old Yeats to a twenty-seven-year-old Maud Gonne, and it's easy to say, yeah, sure, you'll love someone till the end of time, when she gets wrinkled and her hair is gray and she has lumps and tumors and blemishes and age spots and skin that isn't so elastic anymore, when you're both only twenty-seven and her hair is still thick and strong and dark and she has all her teeth and her skin is radiant and her hips are fine and nothing is sagging yet, and you get the feeling he just might be saying all that stuff about loving her soul just to get her in the sack.

But William's gesture is not that of an amorous young man trying to woo his love. It's the gesture of a man who *is* old and gray and full of sleep, to his wife who is also old and gray and full of sleep, that says, looking back on everything, if I had it to do all over again, I would do exactly the same thing and be with you; and the proof is not a three-stanza poem that rhymes *abba*, it's in our children and grandchildren and great-grandchildren, and in the way you tie my shoes when I can't tie them, and the way I open the door for you, as best as I can, and the way you explain jokes to me when I don't quite hear them. We've traveled this road together, just about to its end, and there's no one I would've rather traveled it with than you. And then I think of Marie, and that this is how it was supposed to be for the two of us, not in a week or anytime soon, but someday, with all our kids and grand-kids and wrinkles and bald spots and creaky bones, and I blew it. And now I'm sitting here in front of all these people, Gladys and William among them, lying, and what the fuck am I doing, and who am I, and when did my life turn into this...

I'm aware that everyone is waiting for me to speak. I wet my lips. "No, she didn't go to Notre Dame. In fact, she didn't go to any uni-versity. And that's because...there's no such person as Bradley."

Kelly looks at her book, like there must be, because here's her book. "No such person as Bradley? But..."

"Well, there is. But he's a guy. But he didn't write the book, even though he thought it was a funny idea. I did."

Kelly looks like she might fall off her stool. Katharine doesn't look like she's breathing. Regis appears to be the only one who's kept his wits about him, who sees this isn't necessarily a disaster.

"Ah, Katharine. Clever girl. You got us all. Championing a book by a mystery author, finally revealing the author to be this strapping young guy."

"Katharine didn't know about it either," I interject. "She thought my cousin wrote it. My female cousin. I lied to her too."

Maybe you've been someplace where you could hear a pin drop—the symphony, church, a moment of silence at a sporting event—and you know how quiet that is. That place would sound like a rock concert compared to this. You couldn't even drop your gaze in here without it sounding like a clap of thunder.

"I, uh, guess I should just try to explain this, best as I can." I clear my throat, and the sound startles me. "My name really is Mitch, and I really am working on my PhD. I'm also a writer. I wrote a novel, a serious novel, that got rejected by everyone. So I walked into a bookstore where Katharine was making an appearance, and I saw a display of her books, and it made me crazy, since here I am writing *real* literature and she's writing chick-lit, and guess who's in print? So I, um, picked up a copy. The next morning I went to the coffee shop to read part of it, see how terrible it was, which it wasn't at all, but I couldn't see that yet, and of all people, Katharine shows up and sees me and asks what I think. I wanted to tell her what I thought, right to her face, but for some reason, I made up this story that I had a cousin named Bradley who was also a writer and wanted to be like her. Katharine said she'd be willing to look at anything Bradley wrote. That's when I came up with a plan: if Katharine could do it, why not me? So I started to write it."

I allow my eyes to flash Katharine's way, only for half a second. But it's enough time to see that someone sitting on the stool I'm sitting on might be strangled before the next commercial break.

"The problem was, I didn't know how to write about women who were obsessed with shoes and calorie counting and fitting into a size six and all the bargains at Bloomingdale's. So I went to a place where there were women who did. A dance studio. But it wasn't what I expected. The people were funny and warm and generous. I felt better about myself when I was around them, and better about life, and a lot of things made sense. Like being thoughtful, and happy, and enjoying life. They became some of my best friends. One in particular. A hairstylist. Actually, I fell in love with her."

There's a gasp from someone in the audience.

"Anyway, the writing got better, and I sent what I'd written to

Katharine, and she loved it. And suddenly I was doing exactly what I wanted: writing a book that would make people smile, spending time with my friends, loving my girlfriend, who became my fiancée. I was the best version of myself that I've ever been. But it was too good to be true. I did something stupid once, she forgave me. I did something stupid again, and she let me go. But at least I still had my book. Or Bradley did. I could still cling to that. So that's why I kept up the ruse, because I didn't want to lose that, too."

I can see that William is following what I'm saying without any help from Gladys. I'm glad: I want him to know the truth, too.

"There's no good excuse for what I did. I know that. So to all of you, to anyone who may have bought the book or liked the book thinking it was written by someone else, I'm sorry for cheating you. And I apologize to Katharine. How could I have ever even thought of deceiving you this way? You're a beautiful, intelligent, amazing woman, and I'm humbled to have gotten to know you. And finally, I want to apologize to a woman named Marie. I know I was meant to be with her, spend a lifetime collecting memories and experiences for the scrapbook of our life. But I wrecked that. I love you and I always will, Marie, and I'm sorry with all my heart."

In the movie version of this scene, here's what happens next: the crowd sits in stunned silence for what seems like forever — dazed, confused, breathless — then one brave soul stands up and starts to clap (the Lone Clapper, let's call him), and the Lone Clapper claps softly at first, timidly, but then he starts to get into the clap, really feel it, then a Second and Third Clapper join him, and they get on their feet, too, till the rest of the audience sees this trio of clappers and is stirred by them, and a feeling of relief and release begins to sweep over everyone, and pretty soon they're all on their feet, cheering, pumping their fists, wiping tears from their eyes, hooting and hollering and screaming, like an episode of *Oprah's Favorite Things*, and William and

Gladys are crying, and Katharine gives me a "you silly kid" shake of her head, and Kelly hugs her copy of the book, and Regis gets me in a playful headlock and tousles my hair, and there's such a feeling of merriment and celebration and good cheer in the air that it's starting to look like the end of *It's a Wonderful Life* where everyone is pouring into the Baileys' living room and telling George how much they love him and leaving money and pocket watches, even Mr. Gower and the guy who "busta the jukebox" and the black woman who was saving all her money for a divorce if ever she got a husband and Violet, who's decided she's not going to go after all, then Gelman hushes the entire studio—"Quiet everyone. *Quiet!*"—and announces a phone call just came through and it's not Sam Wainwright cabling money—it's Marie!—and she saw the show and wants me back, and there's a priest in the audience and he can marry us over the phone.

Unfortunately, this isn't *It's a Wonderful Life*. It's my life. So even though the audience *does* sit in stunned silence when I finish, it stalls right there. No Lone Clapper, no cheering, no dancing. William and Gladys do not cry. Katharine does not give me a teasing look. Kelly does not hug the book. There is no good-natured headlock from Regis. Gelman does not hush the audience (why bother: they're already hushed). No Mr. Gower or Violet or even Uncle Billy. Just unbearable, unbroken, unending silence.

Finally Regis stirs. "Okay, then. The book is *Catwalk Mama*. Thank you Katharine Longwell, and, er, Mitch, and we'll be right back after this."

I'm aware that someone is speaking to me, and it could be coming from off camera, or right next to me, but I don't turn, don't say a word, don't make eye contact with anyone. I yank off my mic, slip off my stool, and head for the nearest exit.

* * *

Katharine and I had made plans to spend the rest of the day in the city, hitting Battery Park and Tribeca and the Village, maybe toast our *Catwalk Mama* with a dinner at a place called Evviva. I revise those plans, slightly. I go to the airport and get a return ticket to St. Louis. I'd like to get a flight that's leaving in ten minutes, but the best they can do is 2:20, which means I have a few hours to kill. I buy a Yankees cap and a pair of sunglasses, just in case anyone has seen the show and might recognize me as the guy who was talking crazy on *Regis*. Paranoid, maybe, since there are thirty million faces in the airport, and all of them more interesting than mine, but I'm not taking any chances. I buy a *People* and bury myself in that, and there's no mention of the story — yet. Eventually I give Katharine a call.

Of course she picks up, and of course she's been waiting to hear from me. She informs me that I was right to assume our plans for the afternoon were scrapped: it would've been a paparazzi feeding frenzy, the two of us strolling glibly around the city, like nothing was wrong, stoking the idea that it was all a contrived publicity stunt. And she actually agrees that I'm not being paranoid with my hat and glasses, since there is a ton of buzz about what happened. Oh, and she's pissed.

"Do you realize what you did, Mitch? You made Susannah and me look like goddamned fools. Like we don't even know what's going on right under our noses. And we don't. I don't even know who the hell wrote the book I'm out there hawking. Do you have any idea how humiliating that is?"

"I'm sorry, Katharine."

"You're damned right you're sorry. And you'll be even sorrier when Sheldon gets hold of you. He chewed my ass out up and down. And I had to take it. Because I'm the one who vouched for you and this project. And now it's all blown up in my face, and his face, and Susannah's face, and we look like chumps. He's got a good mind to drop that contract with you, Mitch. He could sue you, for misrepresentation, falsifying information, whatever he wants, get all his money back and then some, probably all the money you'll ever make in your life, and your kids' money, and their kids' money. How's that sound to you? Scare you a little?"

"Yeah. A whole lot."

"Good." She pauses, then gives something that sounds like a laugh. "He won't, of course. You just made him triple the money he could've ever hoped to make off this. Going on national TV, duping the queen of chick-lit, apologizing to her, pouring your heart out to your ex-fiancée. They won't be able to keep that thing on the shelves. But that's not the point. The point is, you deceived a lot of people. You can't just go around lying to people like that, Mitch."

"Believe me. I get it." I think it's clear from my tone she knows I do, and in matters that have nothing to do with *Catwalk Mama*.

For a long time we don't say anything. Then she lets out a sigh. It's almost like the tide has changed and we're in friendlier waters now.

"I know it's a tough market, Mitch. I understand your frustration, being closed off to a world you want to be part of. I can see why you did it. And I'll be honest with you: if I'd known from the start a guy had written it, I don't know if I would've been as interested. How's that for irony? When I thought Bradley was a woman, I loved it. A fellow sister writing about fashion and dating and relationships and fretting over all the things we fret over, and it sounded so funny, so sharp and self-deprecating. Now that I know a man wrote it, I'm not sure how I feel. A guy writing a book like this is a harder sell. Susannah and I would've had to work our asses off, and I'm not sure we would've been willing to do that."

"I don't blame you. I wouldn't work my ass off for me."

She doesn't say anything for a while, and I wonder if she's regretting that she did any of this and why didn't she come to that conclusion a long time ago.

"Mitch, I'd love to be able to hold all this against you. It's hard, when you say things like that."

I'm tempted to tell her I know a woman who can help her out with that.

"And in New York. Bradley. That was Marie?"

"Yeah. It made her sick to do it."

"I can see why."

She tells me this will probably play out in public for a while, that the tabloids and *Inside Editions* will be all over it. I should just give the truth about everything, because that's what she plans to do, and that way our stories are straight and we look like we have nothing to hide, that it was what it was. She also lets me know that she may need me for some appearances and signings, now that Bradley's identity is out in the open. I tell her that's fine.

"One more thing, Mitch." She lowers her voice like she wants to keep whatever this is in private. "During your interview, you said you did something stupid to Marie that caused her to let you go. Did it have anything to do with your last visit to Chicago?"

I'm silent.

"I'm sorry, Mitch."

"You didn't do anything. It was my choice. I did it."

"Still, I'm sorry for the way it turned out."

Yeah, so am I. "Thanks."

She tells me to try to stay loose, that this will all work out, and she'll be in touch with me in the next few days.

"Oh, and about your book..." She pauses, like she needs to make sure that she's *absolutely* certain she wants to say what she's about to say, given everything that's happened. "It *is* a great story. Bradley or not. Just so you know."

And that, if you can believe it, is one of the nicest things anyone has ever said to me.

I make one more call before I turn my phone off for good. This
one to set up a reunion when I get back to St. Louis.

The sun's been down for about half an hour now, and the course
is empty. It's one of those clear nights, no moon, no clouds, and
we'll be able to see a million stars before too long. We're sitting
on the fringe on the eighteenth green, in the warm grass. He has
a beer, I have a beer, and neither one of us has our shoes on.

"So how's it going, running a course?" he asks.

"Good, so far. Something new to learn every day. Such as, did
you know grass reproduces itself sexually and asexually?"

He looks back at his hand, supporting him in the grass, like
maybe he's got his fingers in something they don't need to be
in. "No. That's one thing I can honestly say I didn't know. But
thanks."

"Kip told me. The guy knows everything about this place."

Some geese are floating out on the water, Shep and Bo keeping a careful eye on them to make sure that's where they stay, in
the water. It's the deal they've worked out: keep your feathered
asses in the pond, and off the greens and fairways, and we'll let
you be. Because even they know that while golfers love getting
birdies and eagles on the course, they do not love getting a goose.
Or stepping in what a goose leaves behind.

"So what's Kelly like?" Bradley asks.

"Cute. Very very cute. And tiny."

"And Regis?"

"Funny. Very very funny. And tiny."

"I wish I would've seen it. I mean all of it, live. Not just the
clips I caught on the news."

"Don't worry. You saw the best parts. Or the worst. Take your pick."

He scratches the sole of his right foot with the toes of his left.

"People been calling, I guess?"

"Nonstop. I don't even answer anymore. There's nothing more to tell them. Check your TiVo or YouTube. I pretty much said everything I wanted to."

Down by the shed, a kid named Aidan is splashing off the last of the carts for the evening. He stops to talk to Brandi, the counter girl in the pro shop, who just got off. Aidan has a thing for Brandi, Brandi has a thing for Aidan, but they're sixteen, so they haven't quite gotten around to letting each other know, though everyone else does. It's sweet. My guess is they'll figure it out soon, probably by the end of the month.

"So what's the plan from here?" Bradley asks.

I shrug. "For the time being, run the course. Katharine may need me for some appearances, god help us all. I'll finish my dissertation in the fall. No teaching, though. And that's pretty much it."

"And what about your writing? Plans for another book?"

I shake my head. "No, not for a while. Eventually I'll open a notebook, get started on something. But what, I don't know. Maybe a mystery. Historical fiction. Something about vampires."

"But not chick-lit?"

"Nah, I don't think so. I feel like I'm tapped out with that. Like if I did another, I'd be cheating on my *Catwalk Mama*."

"Go out on top, then. Like Ted Williams. Hit a home run and retire."

"Right. Though without the being-cryogenically-frozen-after-I-die part."

"I don't blame you there."

A rabbit slips out from behind a shrub near the sixteenth tee, just across from us. Shep sees it first and tears off, Bo on his heels. I don't think they're much interested in the rabbit itself — they see them all the time and don't bother with them — but it gives them an excuse to get up and stretch their legs, since they have far more energy than Bradley or I.

Bradley takes a long pull on his beer.

"I talked to Marie before I came out here," he says. He gives me a close look, but his eyes aren't hard or flinty anymore. They're the eyes of my best friend. "She saw the whole thing this morning, Mitch. Every word of it. She liked what she heard." He reaches into his pocket. "She wanted me to give you this."

He hands me a piece of paper with some numbers on it.

"What is it?"

"Her work hours this week." He tries to keep a lid on his smile, but it's not working. "She said your hair looked a little long, and she'd like to help you out. If you'll take her out for dinner."

"*Oh? Is that the deal, then?*" I'm trying to be funny, cool, composed, but inside I'm eight and it's Christmas morning and I just hit the jackpot with Santa.

"Me, I don't know hair," Bradley says. "It looks fine to me. But she's the expert. All I know is the best man gets included in a lot of photos, and I don't want your sloppy hair messing up any of the wedding shots. Got it?"

"Yeah," I say, tipping my bottle of beer his way, "I got it."

Over by the shed, Brandi has her sleeves rolled up and is helping Aidan with the last cart. They're both a little wet, but I think it's because they've been tossing the sponge at each other, and laughing. Which means I was wrong: maybe it won't take till the end of the month for them to figure out how much they like each other. And who knows: maybe good things will be happening for the rest of us a lot sooner than I could've expected.

ABOUT THE AUTHOR

I didn't want to write this book. I was working on another project, not having much luck with agents, but I wanted to keep my head there. In *literature*. My wife said I should change gears and write something fun and upbeat, like chick-lit. Nope. Sorry. Not my genre. Chick-lit is written by...*chicks*. But we writers are always looking for plot ideas (warning: be careful what you say around a writer; it could turn into a book), and my wife's comments got the wheels churning. How about a guy who has no business writing a chick-lit novel deciding to write a chick-lit novel? Hmm. Why doesn't he want to write it? What would drive him to do it? And what would the outcome be? I couldn't believe my luck (and my wife's brilliance) and decided to give the novel a shot. Boy, am I glad.

I'm a big fan of pop culture and sports and literature and love, and writing a book like this let me bring all those elements together. (My first story, written in the fifth grade, had none: just a monster whose weakness was salt (!), and lots of dead bodies.)

I had a great time spending the past few months with Marie and Rosie and Katharine and Molly, getting to know their worlds, paging through glam magazines, watching movies like *The Devil Wears Prada* and *Notting Hill* (after which I, uh, watched every movie with Al Pacino to, you know, balance things out). Spending time with Mitch wasn't so bad either, when he wasn't being a snob. But I think he worked it out in the end. In fact, I'm envious: he got to meet Regis Philbin, and spends all day on a golf course. We should all be so lucky.

Till the day I can say the same, I live in St. Louis with my best friend Robin, who's also my wife. You can check out what I'm up to at danbegley.com. Or let me know what you're up to by e-mailing me at dan@danbegley.com. Thanks for reading!

Dan

Five most outrageous instances of men impersonating women in literature, film, and song

5 Edward Rochester: *Jane Eyre*

Mr. Rochester throws a party at Thornfield Hall. He wants to know what the ladies—especially Jane—think of him, so he does what any sensible man would do: straps on a black bonnet, poses as a fortune-teller, and chats them up. This fools everyone, including Jane. If Rochester were a real fortune-teller, this is what he would tell her: "You will fall in love with a married man who keeps his pyromaniac wife locked in the attic. Run. Now." Oddly enough, this tradition of the host crashing his own party as a cross-dressed clairvoyant to find out who has the hots for him is no longer in vogue.

4 (tie) Michael Dorsey, Daniel Hillard: *Tootsie, Mrs. Doubtfire*

Dustin Hoffman plays an actor who wants to work; Robin Williams is a divorced dad who wants to spend time with his kids: hello Dorothy Michaels and Euphegenia Doubtfire. *Tootsie* is probably the better movie, but that scene in *Mrs. Doubtfire* where chunks of Robin Williams's lemon meringue facial mask keep plopping into Mrs. Sellner's tea makes me laugh till my head hurts. Every time. Even when I know what's coming.

3 Norman Bates: *Psycho*

He seems like a nice guy: soft-spoken, polite, boyish in a way. Till he puts on a wig, grabs a knife, and visits you in the shower. *Mamma mia!*

2 Joe and Jerry: *Some Like It Hot*

Tony Curtis and Jack Lemmon get dragged into drag in this classic from Billy Wilder. After witnessing the St. Valentine's Day Massacre, bass-playing Joe and saxophonist Jerry slip into hiding—and high heels—as Josephine and Daphne, members of an all-girl band. They get pinched and ogled and fix each other's torn-off breasts. Watching Curtis as a faux Cary Grant millionaire seduce ukulele-playing Marilyn Monroe is hilarious; watching Jack Lemmon's Daphne gush about his/her fiancé Osgood Fielding III is even better.

1 Steven Tyler: lead singer, Aerosmith

The tights. The scarves. The hair. The eye makeup. Those *lips*. Dude *definitely* looks like a lady.